The Professor's Daughter

Piers Paul Read was born in 1941, brought up in Yorkshire and educated at Ampleforth and Cambridge. He spent two years in Germany, one in America and travelled extensively in the Far East and South America.

His other novels are *Polonaise*, *Game in Heaven with Tussy Marx*, *The Junkers*, *Monk Dawson* and *The Upstart*. He is also the author of *Alive: The Story of the Andes Survivors* and *The Train Robbers*.

Piers Paul Read lives in Yorkshire with his wife and two children.

Piers Paul Reid

The Professor's Daughter

Pan Books London and Sydney

First published in Great Britain 1971 by The Alison Press/
Martin Secker & Warburg Limited
This edition published 1979 by Pan Books Ltd
Cavaye Place, London SW10 9PG
© Piers Paul Read 1971
ISBN 0 330 25602 5
Printed in Great Britain by
C. Nicholls & Company Ltd
The Philips Park Press, Manchester

It is believed by some that modern society will be always changing its aspect; for myself, I fear that it will ultimately be too invariably fixed in the same institutions, the same prejudices, the same manners, so that mankind will be stopped and circumscribed; that the mind will swing backwards and forwards forever without begetting fresh ideas; that man will waste his strength in bootless and solitary trifling, and, though in continual motion, that humanity will cease to advance.

Alexis de Tocqueville – *Democracy in America*

Introduction

1

In the autumn of 1967 a girl was to be seen following an older man across Boston Common. It was late afternoon. The air was cold and damp. The sky was grey, the grass dark green and the tree-trunks black. The girl wore a brown coat and a yellow woollen jersey which showed beneath the coat at her neck. Her legs were long and were covered with russet stockings which matched the colour of the leaves at her feet.

The face of this girl was fixed and still. Her eyes were wide open, their glance direct on the shoulders of the man in front of her. Her nose was narrow, and red in the cold: the line of her jaw was taut – the skin close to the bone. Only in her mouth was there a shapelessness inconsistent with the clarity of her other features.

The appearance of the man she followed was in most ways a contrast to hers. His features too were well spaced and balanced, but moulded in flesh, not formed by the bone. From a distance these uniform features might have been to his advantage, though from any proximity he would have seemed unattractive, for his nose was fat and his lips were thick and the skin on his cheeks was clogged and pitted. He was a heavy man and the clothes he wore – a jacket with padded shoulders – made him seem heavier still. His trousers were tight and badly pressed. When a movement of his head allowed his fat neck to separate from the collar of his shirt, there could be seen the scum that had passed from the one to the other: and the bright tie he wore was darkened at its knot by the filth of the fingers that had tied it.

This man, moreover, was twice the age of the girl. The line of his greased black hair retreated over the horizon on his flat scalp, yet the girl – this thin child with serious, staring eyes – came as close as ten steps behind him and kept pace so doggedly that he sensed her related presence and stopped. She stopped behind him. He turned and looked at her. Their eyes met. His were cold and defensive – but their expression changed as soon as he saw the expression in hers. He waited. She approached, faltered and then joined him and they continued side by side across the Common towards Charles Street.

The girl, as she walked, drew in her breath – the first half of a broken sigh – and glanced up at the man.

'OK,' he said, 'but I haven't got much time.'

She released the air from her lungs. 'No,' she replied. The wisps of vapour faded into the air of the evening.

'Have you got a place,' the man asked, 'or shall we go to a hotel?'

'No,' she said, 'no. We can go to my apartment.'

Her voice was soft, its accent almost English. The words from the man's mouth were stubby and nasal – the tone of the Boston docks.

'Hey,' said the man. 'You're not underage or anything, are you?'

'No,' she said. 'I'm . . . I'm nineteen.'

'You never know,' he said.

They came off the Common onto Arlington Street and walked down towards the Charles River. On the north side of Beacon Street the girl opened the door to what had once been the family home of rich Bostonians but was now divided into flats. Her own was made up of the attics at the top. The man, who was heavy, lost his breath in climbing the stairs: he stood in the small hall-way to recover it for what they had come there to do.

The business between them took little more than ten minutes. The man was abrupt, lowering his trousers as he would to defecate and kicking off his shoes. The girl had time only to remove those clothes that had to be removed before he moved onto her and shoved the rest up into her face.

When it was over the girl beneath the man started to cry. Her inhalations became sobs.

'Please . . . would you mind . . . getting off,' she said.

'Sure,' he said, raising himself. 'I've got to be getting on anyway.' He moved his feet onto the floor, pulled up his trousers and then started to untie the knotted laces of his shoes. The girl, quietly crying, climbed off the bed and went to the dressing-table in the corner of the room. She stood still in front of it.

'Look, would you please stop crying,' said the man. 'I mean to say, you wanted it, you got it. So what is there to cry about?'

The girl said nothing. Her sobbing seemed to stop. 'I'm so hot,' she said, and went to the window.

'Sure you're hot,' said the man, buttoning up his trousers.

'What do you think you've been doing for the last quarter of an hour ...'

She opened the window – a sashcord window – from the bottom.

'... jumping and squeaking like a pack of rubber balls?' The man went on: 'You college girls, you make me nervous.'

She sat on the ledge, swung her legs over and dropped.

The man was straightening his tie. 'Oh Christ,' he said, 'Oh Christ, oh sweet Jesus.' He went to the window. There below was the Charles River and Memorial Driveway. He looked along the small lane that ran beside the building: he could not see her body. Then his eyes came nearer to the wall and he saw her form sprawled on the fire-escape two storey's down.

'Jesus Christ,' he said.

He pulled his head back into the bedroom, looked around, saw his jacket, picked it up and put it on. He then left the apartment, went down the stairs and out of the building. He walked as far as Commonwealth Avenue before he came to a call-box. There he dialled the number of the City Police.

'Look,' he said into the telephone, 'this is none of my business, but there's the body of a girl lying on the fire-escape of twenty-three Beacon Street.' He then disconnected the line.

2

The police broke into the apartment on the second floor and, from the window, they were able to retrieve the unconscious body of the girl. An ambulance was called and arrived some minutes later to take it in charge.

The police – a sergeant and a patrolman – then went up to the next floor of the house. 'She sure dropped further than that,' said the sergeant. They climbed to the top. 'This is more like it,' he said. There was no sound from inside, so he drew out a set of pass-keys and let himself in. The patrolman entered behind him.

The hall was small: a grey coat hung on a peg. They went into the living room which was tidy – furnished and decorated in plain, subdued colours, with books on the shelves and pictures on the walls.

'It's the wrong side,' said the patrolman.

'I know, I know,' said the sergeant.

They went back into the hall and then into the bedroom.

'Well, look at this,' said the sergeant.

The window was open: the bedcover was crumpled and half off the bed.

'It looks like a struggle,' said the patrolman.

'On the bed?' said the sergeant.

He went towards the window but before he reached it he saw, and stooped to retrieve, the russet stockings on the floor.

'Hey, it looks like some dirty business,' said the patrolman.

The sergeant said nothing. He looked at the stockings, the bed, the open window.

"What do you think, sarge?'

'We'd better call the station.'

The detective who arrived was young and exact. He glanced at the same objects – the bedcover and the discarded stockings – and then crossed to the window. He looked down at the fire-escape, then into the room again and then across at the two uniformed policemen.

'Who was she?' he asked.

The sergeant shrugged. 'There's no name on the door.'

The detective nodded. He went back through the hall to the sitting room and sat down at the desk. He started to go through the few papers, like a bank clerk counting dollar bills, and eventually drew out a letter signed 'Dad'. He sucked at his gums and nodded to himself as he read the name printed on the paper.

3

The detective (Peterson) drove across the Charles River from Boston to Cambridge. It was now nearly dark – towards seven in the evening. He joined Massachusetts Avenue and passed through Harvard Square – his face passive but for the occasional sucking at his gums. The radio in his car carried messages that were not for him.

Half-way down Brattle Street he stopped, got out and stood straight. He walked about twenty yards up the street and then stood silently for a moment outside a large house on the corner, set back from the street in a garden. The rooms on the ground floor were lighted. The detective walked up to the front door, hesitated and then rang the bell.

A man, aged between forty-five and fifty, opened the door. He looked at the detective through the screen door left up from the summer.

'Peterson,' said the detective, 'Boston Police Department.'

The owner of the house pulled back the screen door.

'Do you have a daughter called Louisa?' the detective asked,

'Yes.'

'Living at twenty-three Beacon Street?'

'Yes, that's right.'

'I'm afraid she's had an accident, professor. . . .'

'Won't you come in?'

Peterson stepped forward and was immediately in an atmosphere of light and elegance – a long hall-way with pale yellow walls, a wide staircase with a white balustrade.

'Would you mind coming into my study?' said the professor. 'I'd rather hear about this before we tell my wife.'

'Certainly, sir,' said Peterson, removing his hat.

They crossed the hall and passed into a small room whose walls were lined with books. On one side of this room there was an antique, leather-topped desk and on the other two upholstered armchairs placed at an angle to the fire-place. Professor Rutledge sat back in one of these chairs and the detective, Peterson, perched on the other, his hands holding his hat, his elbows resting on his knees.

'She fell from the window of her bedroom onto the fire-escape ... two storeys down. She's in Mass General right now.'

"How did it happen, do you know?'

'Well, sir, we couldn't question her, you see, because she was unconscious, but there is some evidence that someone else might have been involved. We were tipped off, you see. That's how we knew she was lying there. Then her bedroom was in a . . . state of disarray.'

'Yes,' said the older man, nodding his head.

'Of course we don't know what any of that means – not yet.'

'No.'

There was a moment of silence.

'Perhaps,' said the detective, 'perhaps you'd like to call the hospital?'

'Yes,' said the professor, in a subdued, dull voice. 'Yes, of course.' He stood and crossed to the desk. He picked up the telephone and then fumbled with the directory.

'Seven two six two thousand,' said Peterson.

'Oh . . . oh, yes,' said Henry Rutledge. He dialled the number and when he was through he asked after his daughter. He listened, thanked the speaker and then replaced the receiver.

'She's conscious,' he told Peterson. 'It's not serious. Concussion, and she's broken a rib . . . that's all.'

The detective nodded. 'She's a very lucky girl,' he said.

'Yes,' Henry Rutledge sat down again. He pressed the tips of the fingers of one hand against those of the other. 'How could it have happened?'

'I'm afraid we'll have to ask her that,' said the policeman.

'Yes; yes, of course.'

'Perhaps you'd care to come over to the hospital with me?'

'Yes. That'd be very kind.'

They both stood.

'What about your wife, professor?'

'I'll tell her . . . if you'll just wait.'

The detective stood by the fire-place and watched the tall, slim academic leave the room. He looked around at the books – Hobbes, Aristotle, Marx. His eyes stopped: Karl Marx – *Capital*. V. I. Lenin – *The State and Revolution*. J. V. Stalin – *The Foundations of Leninism*.

He heard a woman's voice – somewhat harsh – from across the hall. 'Oh Christ . . . Is she hurt? Well I'm not surprised. No, you go . . . I can't . . . I can't *move*.' Slurred, hiccupped words.

The professor returned. His hair, which was turning grey, was neither long nor short but as well cut as his clothes. The lines on his face were evident but distinctive – as suited to his eminent bearing as his clean shirt and polished shoes. 'Shall we go now?' he said.

They drove back through Harvard Square. 'If there's anyone else,' said the detective, 'we'll find him.'

The professor nodded. They were both silent.

'Look . . . if there's some kind of record on your daughter, sir, perhaps we ought to know about it.'

'No,' said the professor, shaking his head. 'She was married earlier this year . . . and they broke up. That must have upset her.'

'She's kind of young for that.'

'Yes, she married young. It didn't last.'

'So she might have just jumped?'

'Yes, but ... I don't know. You'd have to ask the psychiatrist, Dr. Fisher.'

4

'There was evidence,' said the doctor, 'that your daughter had been engaged in sexual intercourse very shortly – in fact immediately – prior to the fall.'

The professor said nothing. He looked straight down the corridor in which the three of them walked abreast.

'This has nothing to do with her injuries,' said the doctor, 'but we had to examine her and it was – well, quite evident.'

'It fits,' said the detective.

'You had better call Dr. Fisher,' said the professor.

They came to the room. Peterson left them, to call the psychiatrist. The parent and the doctor went in to the girl. She lay on her back. She wore a white smock laced up to her throat. Her hair was combed. Her eyes were closed. A nurse sat across the room from the bed.

'Only a minute,' the doctor whispered. 'She needs rest.'

Henry Rutledge nodded. He went nearer to the bed and sat on the chair beside it, leaning over towards his daughter. He said nothing while her eyes remained closed, but then she opened them and he said her name. She turned her head, saw her father and without any expression returned to face the ceiling.

'Poor Louisa,' said Henry Rutledge. 'I am sorry. My poor little girl.'

Her face remained quite still.

'Can you tell me what happened, Lou? The police want to know. Did you fall?'

She did not answer.

'Was there a man? Was someone there? Please tell me, darling, and I'll tell the police. . . .'

She turned her head towards the wall and closed her eyes.

5

Dr. Fisher was at a party but Peterson reached him there. He said he would come. His hostess saw him putting on his coat and begged him not to go so soon: he smiled and shrugged. 'One of my patients just threw herself out of a window,' he said, 'so you see. . . .' He smiled again – she was a rich and pretty woman – and promised to come back.

When he reached the hospital, Professor Rutledge sat alone in the lobby. They shook hands.

'She won't talk to me,' said the parent. 'I'm sorry, I should have waited.'

'No, no,' said Dr. Fisher, 'You were right to try.'

He was middle-aged but dapper, this psychiatrist, his suit as well cut as the father's, his shirt as crisp and clean. Together they walked down the bare, ill-lit corridor.

'What happened?' asked Dr. Fisher.

'We can't make out. Someone called the police and said she was on the fire-escape under her apartment. They found her. She'd fallen two storeys. She might have fallen all the way.'

'Yes. Strange, though . . . I wouldn't have thought she would do that.'

They reached the door.

'You'd better let me see her alone,' said the psychiatrist.

'Yes . . . yes, of course.'

Henry Rutledge waited in the corridor. Dr. Fisher went through the door, stood for a moment, as if hesitating, and then gestured to the nurse to leave. He approached the bed. Louisa, his patient, lay as before on her back, her eyes closed, her head half turned to the wall.

'Louisa,' he said softly, 'Louisa?'

She opened her eyes and looked up at him.

'Oh . . . Dr. Fisher.'

'How are you feeling?' His voice was soft and deliberately solicitous.

'Well . . .' she began, '. . . you know.'

'Yes. You had a bit of a fall.' He sat down by the bed.

'Has Dad gone?'

'He's waiting.'

She rolled her head. 'I'm sorry for him . . . I *am* . . . but I wish he'd go away.'

'He will, Louisa, he will. But he's worried.'

'Yes, well, I'm all right now.' Her voice became hard.

'Was it . . . what was it like?'

She sighed.

'Why, Louisa? I mean . . . I thought you were over it all?'

'Yes. I'm sorry. It just came . . . suddenly . . . you know.'

Dr. Fisher looked at his watch. 'Look, Louisa. You've got

to sleep now, but I'll call in tomorrow if you'd like me to ...
and we can talk about it.'

'Yes.'

'You sleep now.'

'Yes.'

The psychiatrist stood up. 'There wasn't ... there wasn't
anyone with you, was there? I think the police want to know
that.'

She closed her eyes. 'No ... not really,' she said.

6 3

Henry Rutledge found his wife where he had left her. She
was waiting in their living room, her glass filled to the same
level with bourbon and ginger.

Well, how's the little brat?' she asked.

He did not answer her. 'Is Laurie in bed?' he asked.

'She's in bed ... yes.'

He crossed to pour himself a drink, then turned and looked
at his wife. She was upright, even when she was drunk, and
glamour clung to her however lowered and abusive she became. Her hair was blonde and set to seem tousled: the skin
on her face was soft from cream and her tall, thin figure was
covered by a silk blouse and long skirt. She was six years
younger than her husband.

'Well, Harry,' she said. 'How is she? How's your little darling?'

'She's all right. A broken rib. That's all.'

'So we'll see her around for a while longer.'

'She wouldn't talk to me. Fisher came.'

'What did he have to say for himself?'

'He called it a relapse.'

Lilian laughed. 'That's good. What else could he call it?
Hardly a cure, anyway.' She held up her glass, which was
now empty again. Henry crossed to fetch it: he took it to the
sideboard, filled it, and returned it – all without concentrating on the movements.

'The police think there was someone else involved ... some
boy.'

'Someone threw her out? Who'd throw her out when she'd
jump?'

Henry set his face. 'She'd ... she'd been in bed with some-one just before.'

'You don't say so?'

'Please, Lilian. ...' The professor walked across the room to the wall, stopped in front of their Bonnard – a nude – and turned his glass round and round in his hand.

'For God's sake, Harry, let's not pretend. ...'

'She may ... she may have one or two beaux,' he said in a higher and louder tone of voice, turning now to face his wife. 'We just don't know.'

'No,' said Lilian, ' we don't know.'

'If she does, I dare say she sleeps with them. She's been married, after all.'

Lilian had noted a change in her husband's tone of voice: she said nothing.

'But she doesn't just ... I mean to say, she isn't promiscu-ous,' said Henry.

Again, Lilian said nothing.

'You just have to look at her,' Henry went on. 'You can always tell. She had a bad time from that husband and that may have ... it must have upset her. Well, it's difficult. I don't have to be a psychiatrist to know that it would be difficult.'

'I'm going to bed,' said Lilian, dragging her body out of the chair onto her feet.

'Yes,' said Henry.

'Where's she going to go from the hospital?'

'I don't know. Home's supposed to be bad for her ... at least Fisher says it is.'

'Home's bad for everyone.'

Henry looked at his wife. 'Yes,' he said, 'Yes, it seems to be.'

7

The morning after his daughter's attempt at suicide, Pro-fessor Rutledge walked to his rooms at Harvard, his head bent, watching the fallen brown and yellow leaves moisten his well-polished shoes. It took him less than a quarter of an hour to pass out of the quiet, residential district where he lived into the area of shops and bars around Harvard Square and through it into Harvard Yard.

The seven students in the seminar were waiting for him. They had been chosen from a long list of applicants – a midwesterner, two girls from Radcliffe, a Negro, a Jew, a Jesuit and a Mexican-American – the group's composition thus reflecting, to some degree, the mixed elements in American society, a coincidence coinciding with Professor Rutledge's liberal principles.

They began at once a discussion on Adam Smith, following the lecture he had given the day before. Henry Rutledge seemed to have little to say himself: his students spoke, as they were supposed to do, but they became disappointed when they noticed their professor's distraction and their comments became interspersed with silences until one of the girls, Kate Williams, made extravagant claims for the influence on Smith of Quesnay which the Jesuit, Alan Gray, enthusiastically rejected.

'And what,' asked Professor Rutledge, who had not been listening to the discussion on the physiocrats, 'and what do any of you think of Smith's moral philosophy?'

There was a silence.

'I should have thought, sir,' said Daniel Glinkman, 'that Smith is of more interest as a political economist than as a moral philosopher.'

'Yes. Yes, of course, but one must know about *The Theory of Moral Sentiments*. Have any of you read it?'

'Yes,' said Alan Gray, 'I read it.'

'And what would you describe as its fundamental doctrine?'

'Well, isn't it that our moral sentiments arise from sympathy?'

'Exactly – "that principle of our nature which leads us to enter into the situation of other men and to partake with them in the passions which those situations have a tendency to excite".'

'Yes,' said Alan. 'I don't think it goes very far. . . .'

'Go on,' said the professor.

'Well, it's inconsistent with any concept of the supremacy of conscience, or of any ethical absolute. A society of totally sympathetic men would be morally paralysed.'

'Yes,' said the professor. 'All the same, a man with no capacity for sympathy would make a poor kind of saint.'

The class laughed, taking this as a pleasantry at the expense of the priest: but the professor's celebrated smile had faded into an expression of perplexity.

8

Henry Rutledge returned home for lunch It had been prepared by Lilian; and Laura, his second daughter, fifteen years old, was there. She was fairer than her sister, but equally slim and pretty. She wore an Indian shawl over her jeans, and sat slouched in an armchair in the living room staring into space until she was called to the table by her parents.

'I cancelled the Clarkes for tonight,' Lilian said to her husband.

'Why? Because of Louisa?'

'Elaine's so damned know-it-all about mixed-up kids. It's not as if hers are any better than ours.'

'No. All right. I don't think I could face them.'

Laura came into the kitchen and the three of them sat down at the table. There was soup and hamburgers which they made themselves into sandwiches with onions, lettuce and mayonnaise.

'Does Laura know – do you know, Laura?' asked Henry.

The girl turned her wide eyes towards her father.

'She knows,' said Lilian.

'About Lou?' asked Laura.

'Yes.'

'Yes. I know.'

'Can you think of why she might want to do it?' asked the father.

Laura shrugged.

'I mean – did she tell you anything? About boys, or something like that?'

Laura shrugged again. 'We don't talk about that sort of thing. Anyway, I haven't seen her in weeks.'

'You can't ... you can't imagine why she might want to do it – I mean, now that she's over Jason?'

Laura dunked her hamburger into the soup, then took a bite. 'I can *imagine* ... yes.'

'Well, why?' Henry spoke irritably, as if vexed in advance by what his daughter might say.

'You wouldn't understand.'

'Try me.'

'Well ... you all think life's lot of fun, but ... I don't know ... I mean, I don't know if it is.'

'Do you think Lou might have thought it wasn't?'

'Just then, when she jumped, I guess she thought it wasn't.'

'But why? What sort of things in *her* life made *her* feel that it wasn't worth living?'

'Well, I was thinking – in school this morning – why did you call me Laura?'

Henry Rutledge looked at his wife and she, someone uneasily, looked at her daughter.

'We just thought it was a pretty name,' she said.

'Yeah.' Laura was silent.

'Why do you ask? Don't you like it?' Henry asked.

'I like it well enough: but then you called Louisa Louisa, and Mother's name is Lilian, isn't it?' Laura kept her eyes on her hamburger.

'So what?' asked Lilian.

'Well, we were learning about ... I forgot what it's called now ... but a lot of words beginning with the same letter.'

'Alliteration,' said Henry.

'That's it. And I just thought – Lilian, Louisa and Laura. And I wanted to ask you if that's why you called me Laura. Because of the L.'

'For Christ's sake, Laura,' said Lilian. 'What is all this? It's a nice name.'

'I know. I just wanted to know, that's all – about the Ls.'

'Yes,' said Henry slowly, 'Yes, it was – partly – because of the Ls.'

'I thought it was,' said Laura.

'Do you mind?'

'It made me kind of depressed. . . .'

'Why?'

'I don't know ... like being a word in a sentence written by someone else. I guess Lou may have felt like that.'

9 ✓

Henry and Lilian were particular about coffee. They bought it in the bean from an Italian delicatessen in Boston; they also had a selection of elaborate machines, collected over the years since their marriage, being unable to decide once and for all which method of infusion was best. At this particular time, they both favoured a filter system using a glass container, and the professor of Political Theory stood over the filter-paper pouring small amounts of boiling water onto the coffee from time to time.

The door-bell rang; Laura was sent to the door. She came back into the kitchen. 'It's a man,' she said to her father. 'He wants to see you.'

'What man?' asked Henry.

Laura shrugged and collapsed into a kitchen chair.

Henry went out into the hall and recognized, through the screen door, the detective who had come the night before.

'I'm sorry to trouble you, professor,' said Peterson, 'but there have been some developments that you ought to hear about.'

'Come in,' said Henry Rutledge. He took the detective into his study again and they sat on the same two chairs. Peterson's eyes looked uneasily from left to right: then he grinned. 'We got him,' he said.

'Who?'

'The man.'

'What man?'

'The man with your daughter. Could be a case of rape.'

'How – how did you get him?'

'Prints. Prints on the bedstead. We had them on file. A stolen car job he did in the 'fifties.'

'But ... is it proof?'

'He's confessed. We picked him up in Belmont and he kind of confessed. He said he was there, anyway. He tried to say she asked him in – but my guess is that he followed her home and stuck a knife in her back. Something like that.'

'But ... but did he pushed her out of the window?'

The grin changed to a frown: Peterson lost his air of optimism. 'Well, that's a tricky one because, between you and me, he's not the kind to do that. I mean, he's not a Strangler type. He's just a slob. And he's the one who tipped us off, you see. He says she just jumped.'

'He may be right,' said Henry Rutledge. 'I mean ... after that....'

'Yes ... maybe.' The detective gripped his thumb with his teeth. 'But then it's kind of funny that he called at all.'

'What kind of man is he?'

'He works in a bar downtown. His name's Bruno Spinetti, forty years old, married, two kids.'

Henry Rutledge was pale. 'You'll have to get Louisa's testimony?'

'That's right.'

'Lilian came into the study carrying a tray with the coffee and three cups. She smiled at Peterson. 'How do you do,' she said. 'I'm Louisa's mother.'

The detective stood. 'How do you do, Mrs. Rutledge. We sure are sorry about this.'

They sat again, Lilian at her husband's desk. She poured out coffee for all of them.

'It seems to be rape,' Henry said to her.

She nodded but said nothing.

'They found the prints of the man. He's confessed.'

'Well, ma'am,' said Peterson, 'to put it accurately ... he's confessed to being with her when she jumped.'

'Ah,' said Lilian.

'But he must have forced his way into her apartment,' said Henry. 'He's middle-aged, married.'

'Yes,' she said.

Her husband leaned forward in his chair. 'His name is Bruno Spinetti,' he said with distaste.

'I was going to ask you,' said the detective, 'if you'd like to come along to the hospital and be there while I question your daughter.'

Lilian and Henry looked at one another. 'It's only fair to tell you, officer,' the mother said, 'that we haven't been on very good terms with our daughter recently. . . .'

'Uh-huh.' Peterson nodded gently.

Lilian smiled at him. 'The generation gap, you know.'

'Yes, ma'am. A lot of parents have trouble with their kids these days.'

'We blame ourselves, entirely, of course,' she went on, with well-modulated touches of irony and complicity in her voice, 'but it does mean that you'd be more likely to get the truth out of her without us.'

'Yes,' said Henry. 'Yes, you might.'

'If we were there,' said Lilian, 'she'd probably say she raped the man.'

The detective laughed. 'I know,' he said, 'I know. There they go. They leave home, want to live on their own – then they get into this kind of trouble.'

Dr Fisher telephoned at four in the afternoon. 'The hospital wants to release Louisa this evening,' he said. 'She's got her ribs strapped up – but otherwise she's all right.'

'Thank God,' said the professor.

'There is just the question of where she should go,' said the psychiatrist. 'Now, we've been talking it over, and we thought that perhaps she should come home to you.'

'Yes,' said Henry, 'of course. If you think so.'

'Well, I don't think she should just go on her own again.'

'No, of course not.'

'And I don't think staying with us would be a particularly good idea this time, either. Between you and me, professor, Anna and I have been having a little trouble. . . .'

'I'm sorry.'

'No, no – it's nothing big. But it mightn't be quite the right atmosphere for Louisa. No. There's McLean's, of course, but I was talking to Lou about it in terms of her psyche and we agreed that perhaps the inability to adjust to you and Lilian – her parents – was at the core of her depression.'

'Yes.'

'And that it might be a good idea to go straight in there and tackle the problem at the root.'

'Yes, of course.'

'Do you think Lilian would go along with that?'

'She'll go along. Yes. I think so.'

'I'll bring her round, then.'

'We could fetch her.'

'No, professor. If you'll forgive me for saying so, I think it'd be better if I did that.'

Henry went through to his wife in the kitchen. 'Fisher thinks she ought to come back here,' he said.

'Does he,' said Lilian, stretching to place a joint of beef in the infra-red oven.

'We must try,' said Henry.

Lilian turned and looked at him. For a moment it seemed as if she might burst into tears: but when Henry noticed this, his eyes shifted from her face down onto the table.

'No – oh, I'll try,' Lilian said. She crossed the kitchen to fetch ice for a cocktail.

Louisa came out of Dr. Fisher's black limousine with a rug around her shoulders. She entered the house without looking at her parents, the psychiatrist attending her like an impresario with his prima donna. Her face was pale, and she carried herself erect, being tightly bandaged around the ribs.

The house was warm, so she dropped the blanket onto a chair in the hall. Beneath it she wore a plain grey dress. Dr. Fisher followed her into the living room and Henry Rutledge offered him a drink. Then he offered one to Louisa but she shook her head. While they drank, she sat in an armchair chewing her knuckles.

'I think,' said Dr. Fisher, 'I think we ought to be quite open about this ...' – he made a gesture to denote openness with his two moderate arms – 'and call a spade a spade. Now, it's not going to be easy for any of you, but I know you all want to make it work, and I think you can.'

The two parents nodded. The girl sat still.

'I'll be off, now,' said Dr. Fisher, glancing at his watch, 'but Louisa's coming to see me tomorrow and ... and, well, we'll see how it's going.'

He rose, smiled at Louisa, and then left the room with Henry who saw him to the door.

Lilian looked at her daughter when they were alone and drank her bourbon and ginger. 'The ... er ... cop was round ... about the man,' she said.

Louisa looked up at her and then nodded. 'Yes,' she said. 'He came by the hospital.'

'What did you tell him?'

'To let him go.'

'Yes, that's what I thought, but your father. ...'

Henry came back into the room. He smiled at Louisa.

'Dad,' she said, 'I'm sorry ... at the hospital yesterday. I wasn't mad, or anything ... I just felt so terrible about it. ...'

'I know, Lou. You don't have to be sorry.' He crossed to pour himself another drink. 'Did that detective come and see you?' he asked. 'They've got the man who did it to you.'

There was a silence. Louisa swallowed. Her face then set in an expression of resolution. 'I told them they had to let him go,' she said.

'But ... why?'

With evident effort, but deliberately, the daughter looked up at her father. 'Because he didn't rape me, Dad.'

Lilian looked down at her glass. Henry took a drink from his and sat down. 'No? Well, that's relief, really,' he said, speaking quickly, 'because it would have been a terrible thing to have happened to you. I just thought that ... well, he didn't sound like the kind of man who'd be a friend of yours ... Luigi something ... Spinetti, wasn't it?' his voice trailed off.

'I don't know,' said Louisa, quietly but deliberately, 'I don't know what his name was. I just met him ... yesterday ... on the Common.'

'He ...' her father began.

'No,' said Louisa. 'No. *I* picked him up and took him home. It was me. I did it.'

Part One

1

Henry Rutledge was born on 18 March, 1920, in New York City. There was for him at that time the certain prospect of success and good fortune, for his family was one in which many élites converged: of birth, wealth, culture, lineament, influence and intelligence. Through his father he was the direct descendant of an Englishman – a younger son who had come to America before the Revolution to make his fortune. He had made it and stayed there; and later spoke and fought for American independence because, like all Englishmen, he knew the money-value of political freedom. He had imparted these values to his sons, and they and theirs secured and increased his initial fortune while continuing as a life-style the special blend of self-righteous theory and self-interested practice that the Anglo-Saxons have given to the world.

The tradition was intact when Henry was born and he grew up in that East Coast aristocracy that is all the more exclusive for being denied by the accepted notions of American democracy: and nothing that happened to him in his early life led him to revalue the class or the country to which he found he belonged. Even the economic depression which came to America when he was nine years old did not disturb his childhood: the Rutledge stocks were safe in minerals, real estate and oil.

He went to school at Exeter, then to college at Yale. His experiences in both these institutions only confirmed the fitness of his way of life. When the war started in Europe his older brother Randolph left to join the Royal Canadian Air Force while Henry stayed on to graduate.

In 1941 his own country, the United States, entered the war and Henry went to fight for it. He was in Europe as the Allied Armies drove the Germans back to the Elbe, uncovering as they did so the evidence of crime and cruelty never imagined and so never feared. In the course of his work for Military Intelligence Henry saw and absorbed the magnitude of this wrongdoing and it spoiled his trust in human nature but not his faith in America.

He returned home to discover that his brother Randolph had been killed in the Pacific. He was told the news by his parents in the living room of their house on the Hudson River; then his mother went to the window to arrange flowers in a vase and Henry went with his father into the garden.

'If I had to lose a son,' said the older man, 'I'm glad it wasn't you. Randolph was a nice boy but he'd never have done much with himself.'

They went down the hill, away from the house, towards the river. Henry said nothing because if he spoke he would cry: the unique love of his brother now led to a unique sorrow.

'I'd get into the law, if I were you,' his father said to him. 'It's the best way into politics, and that's what you want, isn't it?'

Henry focused his eyes, through his tears, onto the bark of a tree. 'Yes,' he said, 'it is.'

'It's the only life that's worth while. It gets a man out of his skin. I made a mess of any career I might have had by being the only Roosevelt Republican anyone's ever heard of, but you've got a clean start. You can even be a Democrat, if you want to.'

'I'd like to study some more,' said Henry, 'I'd like to go back to Europe for a year – to Oxford.'

'What in God's name do you want to study?' his father asked him.

'Politics,' said Henry. 'Politics and history. I want ... I want to know what to do if I ever get elected to anything.'

The old man shrugged. 'You can't do what you like. You've been fighting, so I guess you've earned a year kicking your heels, but sooner or later you'll have to get back to America and make a name for yourself. We've money – you know that – but it takes more than money these days.'

2

The experience of chaos and slaughter in Europe had convinced Henry Routledge that history must never be so mismanaged again, nor politics at home or abroad be left to self-interested adventurers. At first this was an opinion, not an ambition, but his father's assumption of a political career for his son had precipitated the personal decision: and the fact that his brother had died, and not he, reinforced his confidence in his own fitness to serve America and the world.

He did, however, want to know more, to understand more,

which was why he had made up his mind to return to a university: and he chose Oxford because he was curious about the English – about their manners and values. In the autumn of 1945 he went back across the Atlantic and spent a year at Balliol College.

Henry expected much from Oxford – the intellectual home of his ancestors – but he received nothing more than a cold room in the college. His fellow graduates he found immature and dull, their political vision limited to the patching up of their empire and the drab reform of its mother-country, whose dugs were dry. His only friend – and this friendship he later considered the chief benefit of the year abroad – was another American and another millionaire, Bill Laughlin.

'What do you make of this place?' Laughlin asked him when they first met, standing with his hands in his pockets and his back to the small gas-fire in Henry's rooms.

Henry shrugged. 'Disappointing. . . .'

'I'll say so.' He gave a broad smile: his eyes were large and blue, his hair thick and black. 'I mean to say, you either get the snobs – who are friendly, and invite you to their damn great country houses where you freeze to death ... have you been through all that yet?'

'Yes,' said Henry, smiling and sitting back in his armchair, 'once.'

'Did you get the giggling daughter bit? Smiling and agreeing and saying they *hope* you don't mind sleeping in the room next to theirs?'

Henry laughed and nodded and agreed.

'The British upper-crust really must be desperate,' Bill went on, 'because I may be rich and American, but I'm an *Irish*-American. . . .'

'They're very broad-minded these days,' said Henry.

'They've even got a socialist government.'

'They're certainly more broad-minded than the socialists,' said Bill. 'That's the other side of the coin. Do you know the sort I mean? Your Balliol Bolsheviks? The ones who look at you and grunt – each grunt to signify a volley from the firing-squad!' Bill staggered, as if shot. 'Down we all fall, American capitalists, British land-owners, Humpty Dumpty and all.'

In their eight months at Oxford, these two Americans were thrown together by their antipathy towards the other students and, by the time they returned to America, they were close friends. There was more to their friendship, however, than jokes at the expense of the English, and the conversations in their staterooms as they recrossed the Atlantic were often quite serious, for Bill was as committed as Henry to a political future. Together they had made up their minds to be Democrats. Neither of them thought much of Truman: both felt an envious nostalgia for the early days of the New Deal, and in the same spirit were fervently optimistic about America – touched, almost, with a sense of destiny.

They began to see the disruption of the recent war less as a result of anything in particular, and more as the God-sent pre-condition for a universal acceptance of American values and principles of government. Fascism, Imperialism and Communism were now, after all, discredited, and both these young men felt that they themselves must make the one remaining option, Americanism, an example to the world – not just of prosperity but of decency, efficiency and justice.

Of the two, Bill Laughlin had the more practical ambitions and had already made contacts in the New York Democratic organization. Henry intended to complete his doctoral thesis at Columbia before entering active politics. When they reached New York, both proceeded to fulfil their intentions – Bill working for the party, while Henry studied in the Low Library and wrote position papers for the Democrats which were sometimes read and sometimes not.

3

On the afternoon of his twenty-seventh birthday Henry left his place in the Low Library earlier than usual and came out onto Broadway at 116th Street. It was not yet spring – still a totally cold day with ice visible on the Hudson and a wind blowing over it onto the West Side.

Henry was, at this time thin and youthful in appearance – a man who did not bother much with his clothes, but when he did happen to buy them did so from Brooks Brothers or some other good store downtown. He was tall and had a long neck which was stretched by his chin as he jutted it forward into the wind and looked for a cab. He wore no hat, and his hair was soft so it blew around his head, but that did not seem to bother him.

An hour later he entered his aunt's apartment on Park

Avenue and, almost immediately, was introduced to Lilian.

'What do you do?' he asked her.

'I'm a senior at Sarah Lawrence.' She smiled and turned down her mouth.

'Is it that bad?'

'Well, you know, all very social.'

'Don't you like that?'

'Yes,' she said, shrugging, 'now and then. But I don't like it all the time. There are moments when I feel that life should be taken more seriously.'

'How?'

Lilian smiled. 'That's rather a serious question for a cocktail party.'

'I know. But I'm interested.'

'Well,' she said, 'I'd like to know what I'm doing in life, not just blindly live it out doing things because they're done – like going out with boys and getting them to like you, just because you're meant to do that kind of thing.'

Henry listened to her – to her soft, frank voice – but his attention parted from what she was saying and began to apply itself at last to her beautiful manner and appearance. It was not just that she was twenty-one – a girl with her aura of girl-ishness – but also that the proportions of humour, gravity and intelligence in her personality, as expressed in her face, were as pleasing as symmetry in music or architecture. Her body was slight and around five foot nine inches tall; her legs and arms were thin and straight. She had light brown hair down to her shoulders, and eyes that were of an ordinary blue but so alert to feeling – his and her own – that their expression changed as often as the size of their irises, sensitive to the changing light.

'So you don't go out with boys?' Henry asked, smiling at her.

She looked confused. 'Well, I don't *not* go out with them,' she said. 'It depends on whether I want to. I wouldn't do it just for the sake of a date.'

'Would you like to come out with me when this is over?'

She looked up at him. 'If you aren't laughing at me,' she said.

'I am a little,' he said, 'but not really. In fact, I agree with you.'

'The war,' she said, over her soup, 'it must have meant more to you than it did to me, since you fought in it. . . .'

'Hardly,' he said. 'I worked in Army Intelligence.'

'I just read about it, and saw the newsreels ... but you must have seen it all much closer, and then studied it. What do you make of it all?'

She asked him earnestly, and her expression compelled him to be serious, though he felt light-hearted and would rather have teased her.

'I guess it shouldn't happen again,' he said.

'How can we prevent that?' she asked. 'It seems to me to be enough of a challenge not to make a mess of one's own individual life – not to end up divorced or drunk or suicidal. But that's only the beginning, isn't it? Because then there's the life of the society in which we live, and international relations. . . .'

'You can't always do so very much.'

'But you've got to try, haven't you?'

'Certainly.'

'How, though? I mean, are you trying?'

'Well, I'm sort of in politics . . .'

'Are you? Are you really?' She leant forward, forgetting her soup. 'You're a Democrat, aren't you? You've got to be a Democrat?'

'Yes, I am.'

'What do you do?'

'I go to meetings – sometimes – and I research for a friend of mine who's really very serious about it all.'

'Who's that?'

'Bill Laughlin.'

'Oh, yes. I've heard of him. He sounds good.'

'I write most of his speeches,' said Henry, smiling.

'That's great,' said Lilian. 'It's doing something, isn't it, because you've got to have power. You can't just bitch on the side-lines.'

'What do you do?'

'About . . . about the world?'

'Yes.'

'Nothing. That's the trouble. I study hard because I want to be informed, but I always thought I'd wait until I graduated before *doing* anything. I finish in June, though, and I've no idea of what I'll do then.'

They both ate *filet mignon*. 'I guess it's kind of hard for girls,' said Henry, 'because they're supposed to be equal and all that but when you come down to it the odds on you becoming President are small'

'You've said it. That's the dilemma.'

'The most powerful women in history,' said Henry, 'have been the mistresses of kings.'

'Perhaps that's what I'll do,' said Lilian.

'It's not so easy.'

'Thank you,' she said, in mock offence.

'But if I were king,' he said, 'I'd let you run the whole show.'

'Thank you,' she said, sincerely.

'In return. . . .' he said.

She blushed.

He ate ice-cream and she ate fruit. 'If there's any excuse for being rich,' said Lilian, 'and you are and I am, relatively, it's to free you to help other people instead of having to look out for yourself.'

'I quite agree.'

'What's so sickening about the last hundred years or so is that the rich just haven't been responsible: they've always been out for themselves, getting richer and richer regardless. . . .'

'I really don't think it'll be the same with our generation,' said Henry.

He took her back in a cab to her parents' apartment on East 63rd Street. Both were silent: it was not that either felt that there was nothing more to be said – only that the emotions Henry, at any rate, wished to express were not easily put into words.

'Well,' she said, having stepped out of the cab, 'thanks for the dinner.'

'Can I call you?'

'I'm going back to Sarah Lawrence tomorrow. . . .'

'Can't I call you there?'

'Yes,' she said, and she gave him a number which he wrote down on a matchbox.

He walked with her across the pavement to the apartment building. The porter recognized Lilian and opened the door. She turned and smiled and they said good night from a distance of ten feet.

He telephoned the following day and asked her out that night. She said that she had to go back to Connecticut and Henry felt that this was a brush-off. 'Some other time,' he said. There was a silence over the telephone: he could hear noises in the background – others entering and leaving the room from which she was speaking. He imagined the girls standing there, giggling perhaps, and Lilian looking sour and bored.

Then she said: 'You wouldn't like to come out to Cos Cob, would you?'

Instantly his mood changed from melancholy to exhilaration. 'I would,' he said.

'Well, come for lunch on Sunday.'

4

Her father was a partner in the firm of lawyers for which Bill Laughlin worked at the time. 'You know Bill, don't you?' the older man asked Henry.

'Yes, sir,' said Henry. 'We were over at Oxford for a year.'

'Well,' said Mr. Sterne, an almost sad expression coming onto his face, 'I dare say he'll go a long way.'

'He certainly wants to get things done,' said Henry.

'And you're political too, aren't you?'

'Well, sort of, but I don't see that I'll ever be as active as Bill.'

His host nodded. He was a superficially handsome man, but his face was colourless and his eyes and words were slow. 'Politics is a lousy business,' he said. 'I don't believe that a nice man can do well.'

'Really, Dad,' said Lilian, irritably, 'that's just too defeatist.'

Her father shrugged. He looked out of the window of the dining room across the lawn to the sound. 'Maybe,' he said.

'If the decent, intelligent people didn't treat politics like a stinking fish,' said Lilian strictly, 'it just might not be as lousy as you say it is.'

Alfred Sterne turned to his daughter. He looked amused by the severity of her tone. 'I'm glad you feel like that at your age,' he said, 'but you just see if that fish doesn't still stink when you're mine.'

Henry could see that Lilian was ill at ease with her parents. Her father was depressed and her mother removed from the three of them. The daughter seemed impatient and cross while she remained in the house but then after lunch they went down to the shore together and she became more pleasant and calm. Their conversation was not as free and quick as it had been when they first met, but as they walked Henry became more aware of her physical attractiveness than he had been before. She wore a heavy Irish sweater and the shape of of her bosom and shoulder through this rough wool made him want to hold her, and her frail, white shins made him uneasy. He said nothing for some time – just absorbing these strong, physical feelings – but then she turned and smiled shyly at him, as if these feelings had been expressed, and he felt brave enough to take her hand and hold it.

'Your parents are really nice,' he said.

'Do you think so?' she asked.

'Yes. Don't you?'

'Yes,' she said; then she added: 'They will annoy me sometimes.'

'Yes. . . .'

'They're so weak.'

He knew what she meant: he shared that feeling – the contempt of energetic youth for the enfeebled old who disguise their debility as moderation – though he did not, apparently, feel it as strongly as she did, for he had never used so cold or dismissive a word as 'weak' for his own mother and father. Nor did he notice her vehemence, for his mind was on his hands clasped to hers. His face was soft with an expression of love, and on hers there was a fixed, small smile.

The train back to New York stopped at Bronxville, where Lilian should have got off. 'I should,' she said, but he held onto her hand, suggesting that she come back and have some dinner in New York. Lilian could not bring herself to break his grip and so they went on to Manhattan and climbed out of the train at Grand Central Station.

'Are you hungry?' he asked.

'Not really,' she said.

'We could make a sandwich at my place.

'Yes.'

She entered his apartment with great care – her movements as solicitous in exploring his home as her eyes had been in studying his face. It was, in fact, a dreary place, its furniture not his own and the decoration untouched for ten years. There were books on the shelves and an empty coffee cup by the armchair – these were the only signs that he lived there.

Henry took hold of her hand and kissed her. He had

planned and planned how he would do it – in the past two days and on the train journey – but now he forgot his plans and lost consciousness of what he was doing. They moved towards the sofa with their mouths still held together as they sat on it, their hands slipping on the clothes on their backs, so much did they show passion in the strength of their embrace.

Eventually he began to unloose the buttons of her blouse without thinking in particular whether he should: but then he felt her body which had been so fluid, stiffen – and this brought to him some awareness of what he was doing.

'I'm sorry,' he said. 'I meant to . . . only if you wanted.'

Lilian straightened herself on the sofa. 'Not now,' she said, 'not yet.'

He caressed her courteously from then on. Some minutes later they separated, poured themselves drinks and then started to talk again – words pouring out of them in the form of disclosures and recollections – so that when he finally took her back to her apartment he knew much more about her: and they both knew, since they had both declared it, that they loved each other.

They met again next night and again they went to his apartment and again they kissed and fell, kissing, onto the sofa: but this time, when the moment came, she had changed her mind. She gritted her teeth and said: 'I think . . . yes . . . I will.'

5

From this she became pregnant. On Henry's part what they had done had been so much an expression of love – so little calculated – that he had not considered what its consequences might be. Lilian had perhaps just hoped for the best: she was depressed, almost panicked, when her state became plain.

'You don't have to marry me,' she said.

'But Lilian, we only hadn't talked about it because we knew we would.'

'Yes,' she said, her face severe, 'I guess we did.'

Henry smiled at her and kissed her face. 'You did want to marry me, didn't you?'

She looked at him. 'I thought we'd wait a while,' she said, 'and see what happened.'

'But you love me, don't you?'

'Yes,' her tone still hesitant.

'What?'

'I sometimes feel I don't quite know you.'

'My darling. . . .'

'Perhaps I just love what I think you are.'

'What's that?'

'Someone who's strong.'

He smiled again. 'I'll be strong, you'll see. We'll marry now, then you graduate, then we'll set up house, have the child, and then we're off. . . .'

She seemed largely convinced, but the next day when they met again her doubts had returned.

'I think I should try and get rid of it,' she said.

'But why, Lili, why?'

'I don't like things happening I didn't intend.'

'Did you intend to fall in love with me?'

'I guess not.' She smiled and shrugged and then seemed to look into herself to find further explanations for her doubts. 'I just don't feel particularly maternal,' she said.

'It'll come. . . .'

'And it might have been nice to have had some time on our own.'

'We'll get someone to look after it. . . .'

Lilian had little time to make up her mind, but by the end of that week she had done so. They were married a month later. The parents on both sides may have suspected the reason for this precipitate wedding but no allusion was made to it. Judge Sterne gave his daughter fifty thousand dollars as a wedding present and Eliot Rutledge settled three and a half million on his son.

The young husband and wife went to Arizona for their honeymoon but they returned to New York after that, to a new apartment on the East Side. Henry completed his doctoral thesis and Lilian finished at Sarah Lawrence. They spent July and August upstate with Henry's parents. Bill Laughlin came up for one weekend and other friends at other times. They were both happy: Lilian, who had been sick in the first weeks of her pregnancy, now carried the child casually, hiding the bulge with her height, taking green iron tablets each morning as the only concession to her state.

In October the academic year began again. Henry went to Columbia to lecture on the origins of the First World War and to do further research – now on Wendell Phillips. Lilian had lunch with her girl friends and then waited in the apartment for her husband's return. She listened to gramophone records and read the books she had put aside at Sarah Lawrence as irrelevant to the courses she was taking. They entertained or were entertained on most evenings of the week and kept up with plays and movies in New York. The child was born two days before Christmas – a girl whom they called Louisa.

6

When Bill Laughlin ran in the Democratic primaries in New York, he was opposed by a union organizer called Max Rosendorf, who had the support of Tammany Hall. Laughlin's organization had money enough and a body of idealistic volunteers – friends and contemporaries from Harvard – who believed in their candidate's special qualities. It did seem, however, that Rosendorf's record would give him the votes so, while his other friends went out on the streets, Bill turned to Henry Rutledge.

Henry, with a certain sense of excitement, laid aside his academic work and retired to the libraries to read back issues of *The New York Times* in the hope that Rosendorf had done or said something that could be used against him. All he could find, however, was a small item dating back to 1940 when Rosendorf had organized a strike in the Lemprière Machine-Tool Company in New Jersey. There had been, it seemed, a good case for a strike: at any rate, there was no suggestion in *The Times* that it was not a genuine dispute, yet it took place in that period between the Nazi-Soviet pact and the German invasion of Russia, when the American Communist Party had done its best to sabotage the manufacture of arms for Britain. Lemprière's had not themselves made arms, but had supplied the metal lathes for almost all the arms-manufacturing companies on the Eastern seaboard. Henry noted this down, for what it was worth, and handed it on to Bill Laughlin.

It was used to good effect. America was now at war, in Korea, against communism. Would Rosendorf, it was asked, support such strikes now? Had Rosendorf known then that the strike he organized fell in with the Communists' plan? Might he not again cooperate with their strategy?

At first Rosendorf ignored this aspect of Laughlins campaign, but then his allies became embarrassed and he had to deny that he was a Communist which was enough to suggest that he might have been one. When it came to the vote, he was defeated. Laughlin was nominated and, in November of 1952, elected to the House of Representatives.

Henry and Lilian went down to the victory celebrations and pushed forward to the platform where Bill stood, over-excited at his success, with Jean Amberly, the girl he later married. He saw his friends on the floor below and beckoned to them, then took them both by the hand as they came up onto the rostrum.

He leaned forward and spoke into the microphone: 'I'd like you all to meet Harry and Lili Rutledge here. Harry's going to be writing some speeches for us, aren't you, Harry?'

Henry smiled and Bill gave Lilian a kiss on the cheek and everyone applauded.

7

In the years that followed Henry did write speeches for Bill Laughlin and the Congressman acquired a reputation for perception and intelligence in large measure from his friend's phrases. The two men complemented each other well, for as Bill became more involved in practical politics and less free for, or inclined to, reflection, Henry gained interest in his scholarly work and grew increasingly averse to crowds and rhetoric. Yet he retained his commitment and hoped never to become Wendell Phillips' 'figure on a silver coin, ever looking backwards'. So while he was happiest alone in his study or the library, it satisfied his conscience to spend a day every now and then in conference with Bill Laughlin and his advisers, providing them with apt quotations, historical precedents and long-term prognostications.

At the same time, his own academic career developed with the same speed and success as the political career of his friend. He went to Princeton in 1952 where his second child, another girl, was born. Here he completed and published two works on political thought – the monograph on Wendell Phillips called *Theory and Agitation* and a more extensive study, *The German Tradition in American Political Thought*. This last was a giant endeavour which had involved him for five years in the investigation of complex cross-currents of intellectual influences which in themselves are difficult to identify: but the scholarship was sound and the anti-Hegelian bent most acceptable, so the book won for him not only definitive recognition as a theorist but also fame as a man. He began to be thought of as a one-man committee on un-American ideas, one of the few anti-Communists competent to fight the corrupt ideology at its inception. This was certainly reading an attitude into his work that was not there (a mistake made, perhaps, because of his known association with Congressman Laughlin): re-read in the 1960s, *The German Tradition in American Political Thought* seems no more than a thorough un-mixing of the pragmatic English from the dogmatic Continental philosophies of state. But Henry did not discourage this political interpretation of his work, and with lectures and articles he greased his reputation, and his fame increased until, in 1960, he was appointed the Addison Professor of Political Theory at Harvard University.

By then he had been married for more than ten years and changes, of course, had taken place. He had grown older, his wife had aged and Louisa and Laura had grown from babies into children. The couple – Harry and Lil – had become the family, the Rutledges, with parents, daughters, furniture, clothes and crockery, a growing collection of pictures and books, as well as blankets, bath-towels and Persian cats. Henry himself remained thin: he was lucky enough to consume, with no exertion, all the calories from the food he ate. His face was still youthful but had taken on an expression of suave gravity which went well with his lecturing style – the East Coast voice, wry humour and off-hand profundity. His appearance made him popular with the students, and with the one or two young women he went to see when passing through New York.

Handsome, charming, intelligent and rich, he was an asset to any campus, and Lilian was equally well-cast in her rôle as wife of such a meteor. She was beautiful, and had kept her figure after two children with only the small sacrifices of toast, potatoes and sugar in her coffee. She was, self-evidently, a competent wife and mother: the house in Princeton had been well-run and filled at proper intervals with other wives and the colleagues of her husband. If any criticism might have been made of her, it would have been that she dressed too well which reminded the other academics that the campus was just one aspect of Henry and Lilian's life – that for the Rutledges there was also Washington and New York. Another flaw, in the eyes of some of their colleagues (and it went with them from Princeton to Harvard), was the Porsche motor-car owned and driven by Henry Rutledge – a possession which revealed to some an inconsistency with the anti-Hegelian bent of his magnum opus.

And then there were rumours in Princeton that Harry Rutledge had been seen in the Porsche with Cecily Drummond, the wife of a Fellow at the Institute of Advanced Studies, rather more often than might be thought discreet: and the rumours found substance in the minds of the suspicious in the sad looks of this dark, rosy-cheeked, English girl in the weeks after the Rutledges' departure to Cambridge.

But there is always campus gossip and most of the husbands – those under analysis, at any rate – would admit that they were just jealous of Harry; that Arthur Drummond was a grey bore, who never left the lab; that there was little point in being a meteor if one could not raise a few sparks in the sky.

8

In November 1960 John Kennedy was elected President of the United States and this public event was for the Rutledges, as for many other Americans like them, a private joy – not just because they were Democrats and had voted for him, but because he was one of them, an embodiment of that confidence in themselves that had been with them since their youth.

There was a certain disappointment, of course, among their circle, that it was John Kennedy rather than Bill Laughlin; that Schlesinger was the President's special adviser, rather than Henry Rutledge; but Bill himself was confident that, sooner or later, he would be drawn into the administration and so gain executive experience in readiness for the next decade.

There were consolations for Henry, too. The position he filled at Harvard would not have been there if its previous incumbent had not been called to Washington; and, since it was unlikely that he himself would be needed there for another ten years, he bought for the family a large house on Brattle Street in Cambridge.

It was also that he felt as near to power as makes no difference. John Kennedy was so much the ideal of every American liberal – and the Rutledges were such – that they lived out those first hundred days and the days that followed – the exciting, dazzling days of the Vienna summit, the Bay of Pigs, the missile crisis – as if they themselves were in the White House. The President's mistakes were their mistakes; his agony, their agony; his triumph, theirs. 'Let the word go forth from this time and place, to friend and foe alike, that the torch has been passed to a new generation of Americans – born in this century, tempered by war, disciplined by a hard and bitter peace, proud of our ancient heritage . . .' – that was them.

It is not difficult to imagine, then, the despair they felt when this President was shot dead. Like all his fellow-countrymen, Henry could remember long afterwards the circumstances of first hearing this news: he was in New York, returning from a conference in Baltimore. He had half-arranged to dine with a former classmate of Lilian's now divorced, called Beverly.

'Haven't you heard?' she said when he called her. 'The President has been assassinated.'

And then, though Beverly was sobbing, Henry made his excuses, rang Lilian, who knew, and told her in the same dead tone as hers that he could be back on the next flight.

She met him at Logan Airport. 'Even Laura cried,' she said.

He took her hand and held it, and they went home.

They spent the evening with friends, in silence, watching the television, not because any news could affect them but because it distracted their minds from despair.

At eleven that night Bill Laughlin telephoned from his villa on the Virgin Islands, where he happened to be at the time.

'It's terrible, yes, it's terrible,' he said, 'but we've got to face up to what it means in political terms.'

'Yes,' said Henry. 'Johnson won't last.'

'The country won't stand for a Texan in the White House,' said Bill, 'and Bobby's made too many enemies.' The Congressman was thinking aloud over the long-distance telephone wires. 'There's Hubert, of course, but he'd be such a painful contrast. Dammit, Harry, this could just be our break.'

'It could,' said Henry – almost automatically.

'Look, Harry,' said Bill Laughlin. 'Could you and Lili get down here tomorrow? We're kind of stuck since Jeanie's busted her hip. I'll call Bud and Stratton and get them to come too.'

'I guess I could cancel my lecture,' said Henry. 'Yes, we could come down.'

'You do that, then. It'll be better all round – away from the Press.'

When he had finished talking to Laughlin, Henry went back from his study to Lilian in the living room. 'Bill wants us to go down to St. Croix,' he said to her.

'When?'

'Tomorrow.'

A look of excitement replaced the despair in her expression. 'OK', she said. 'But there's the children. . . .'

'Oh, they can come and stay with us,' said Anna Pritzler, wife of the Professor of Spanish, and she became a little excited as she took on this modest rôle in the making of history.

9

They had been to stay with the Laughlins on St. Croix before – flying from Boston to St. Juan and on from there. Henry never liked these vacations in the tropics – partly through distaste for the lush climate, partly because he felt less and less at ease with Bill and Jean and their friends. The differences in the two men's personalities that had once seemed complementary had now deepened to become contradictory – but just as he was unable to admit to Lilian or to himself a preference for frost over sunshine, so he kept quiet about his real opinion of Laughlin, the man's cant and inflexibility. He did not want to leave the team, for while he was happiest with books and students, it was his involvement in practical politics that made him more than an academic and fulfilled his ambition to be of use to America. In conference, therefore, he held back his conflicting ideas, knowing that it was fruitless to engage in radical arguments with Bill and his other advisers.

On this occasion they were among eight others – the whole inner circle of the Laughlin team. All were more or less shaken by the assassination – all more or less excited by what this might mean for their candidate and their careers. When they first foregathered, there were token lamentations – but the urgency of ambition soon overcame the lagging grief and that very evening the men among them went into conference in the house while their wives played bridge on the terrace overlooking the sea. Bill, slim and sunburnt, drank rum and Coke as he talked to them of the political opportunity that had presented itself – and the more he drank, the more of an opportunity it became. 'If it wasn't for our damned Constitution,' he said, grinning at his irreverence, 'we could move in now. No one wants Lyndon, no one.'

'We've got him until next year, Bill,' said Stratton James, the constitutional lawyer.

'We've got him in the White House,' said Bill, 'and we'll have him at the convention – but if he doesn't get it there on the first ballot, he won't get the nomination at all.'

'The Kennedy people won't vote for him,' said Bud Birnbaum from the New York organization.

'The convention will slip three ways,' said Bill. 'Lyndon, Hubert and Bobby. They'll get stuck there and, in the end, they'll look for a fourth candidate and that fourth candidate has just got to be me. . . .'

And so on, into the night. Henry said little because he did not have much to say. In his opinion, everything depended on the next months and Johnson's conduct in office. No strategy could be planned before then: only fantasies invented and indulged. He did not say this to his friends. He saw that Laughlin was in the grip of his dream – that his blood was up and would stay up until it burst out of him or, in time, subsided.

They went to bed at last in one of the guest-rooms of the villa. 'Poor Jean,' said Lilian. 'Her hip's all in plaster. She has to pee into a jar.'

They continued their discussions the next morning while the wives went swimming or lay on the beach. Bill was over-excited, as he had been the night before – his fantasy less endearing without alcohol. He seemed frustrated because he could not have what he wanted then and there, and further irritated by the absurdity of his impatience. Henry was aware that his silence exacerbated this mood, and yet he could not think of any contribution.

'What do you say, Harry? asked Bill in annoyance as the bell rang for lunch.

'We'll see,' said Henry – an answer which hardly satisfied the politician.

After lunch there was, as usual, a siesta. The policy group planned to meet again in the evening and its members were expected to take the opportunity of the afternoon break to sleep or swim. Henry went to the beach, leaving Lilian to rest in their room. He walked down the long flight of steps in his trunks and a shirt, smiling at Jean – bony and fragile in her plaster – as he passed her in the garden. He went for a hundred yards or so along the water's edge, then spread out his towel and lay on the sand. The sun was not too hot: he told himself that it was good for him and stayed on his stomach, dozing in the heat. Then, after half an hour, he went to swim but he was no sooner in the sea than he stepped on an empty can whose rusty edge cut into his foot. The wound was small, but he was afraid of infection; he therefore limped back down the beach, past Jean, asleep, and up the steps to the house – silent in the heat. He went to his room and opened the door to see his wife's bare body moving under that of their host.

Not knowing if they had seen him or not, he went back to the beach and sat on a rock, the pain in his foot conceding to the image of Lilian's suddenly unfamiliar groin and breasts seen by his eye at the door. He repeated to himself the reasons why he should not mind – his lips forming the words, but the larynx producing no sound. 'Do as you would be done by,' he mouthed over and over again, smiling, even, in a sad attempt at cynicism: but the barrage formed in his conscious mind would not hold. Memories of their love from the first, the delightful and happy moments of confidence and joy, burst through like salt water onto seeded soil. Is it possible, he thought, that I mind this ... this banality, more than the death of the President? 'The President, the President,' he repeated: then 'do as you would be done by' – but no words could stop the spread of baffling, incomprehensible sorrow.

He returned to the house at five. Lilian sat reading on the terrace. She looked up at him and smiled: he could tell, from the fear and uncertainty behind that smile, that she knew he had seen her in adultery. He said nothing but went to their room: he disinfected and bound his foot and then read until dinner.

There was conversation while they ate but Bill Laughlin seemed embarrassed: he glanced at his friend as inconspicuously as a politician can, hoping that all of them would follow the direction of his jaw, leaving his eyes free to inspect Henry's expression. Stratton and Bud and their wives were also ill at ease. None of the men asked Henry why he had missed the evening conference. Lilian was silent. Henry kept his eyes on his plate. Only Jean talked loudly – the flat, incessant drawl of words without much meaning.

The Rutledges left the next morning. They said nothing to each other on the flight to San Juan, but in the jet, as it circled away from Puerto Rico, Lilian said she was sorry, looking at her hands.

'No,' said Henry quietly – and he made a self-deprecating gesture. 'I mean ... if you ... you're free ... but I don't understand ... why *him*?'

Lilian looked up with surprise. 'Why?' she repeated – but the repetition was a question in itself, asking why he should need to ask.

10

The country and the Rutledges recovered from the murder of their President, for so many other aspects of their life remained unchanged. The third winter in Massachusetts was much like the first and second – a blackening of the colours of the autumn, a frost freezing the air, drying the pavements of Brattle Street, killing the leaves of the plants left out in the garden. Then there was snow, a heavy fall involving them all in urban heroics to get the car out of the garage and the children to school. Henry himself – being an American millionaire – shovelled the snow from the driveway and the path up to the house. Louisa and Laura put on their black rubber boots and bright coloured scarves and after school went to the Charles River to see if there was sledging or if the water had frozen over.

Then there was Christmas, with reminders that Kennedy was indeed dead, but also the singing of Christmas carols in the streets with the Cohens, who came from Europe and liked to do that sort of thing. There were trips to the Peabody Museum for Laura with her friend Sass and Sass's mother, Mrs. Obolenski; and dates and movies and ice-cream sodas for Louisa; and dinner-parties five nights a week for Henry and Lilian. After Christmas Lilian and the two girls met up with Bill and Jeanie Laughlin and their boys for a week's skiing in Vermont, as they had done for the last five or six years – though this year Henry stayed behind in Cambridge to write his book.

Part Two

1

One afternoon in the spring of 1964 Louisa, then sixteen, returned from the cinema in Boston in the midst of a group of her friends. Among the five of them, she walked first and in the centre. The other girls and the younger brother of one of them stumbled to keep up with her, attempting to face in towards her as they walked. She was talking about the film they had just been to see – giving her opinion now since none of the others would give theirs until she, Louisa, had told them what to make of it. She did not bother to look at her companions as she spoke to them, since they all looked at her, but she gesticulated with her slim hands to make her point and spoke clearly so that they all could hear.

She was taller than the other girls and much prettier, with fair hair to her shoulders. On her face there was a slight expression of youthful condescension, and when the boy, the younger brother, opened his mouth to venture an opinion, this expression deepened into one of decided contempt. He was, after all, only twelve – and fat and dressed in tartan Bermuda shorts – whereas Louisa wore a blue frock with a lace collar and her delicate legs were covered with white stockings.

The other girls dressed more like the boy. One wore sneakers and jeans; another, a crumpled skirt and an anorak; the third a dress that could have been handed down from an older sister. But all this was proper enough, since their fathers were all much less than Louisa's who was, after all, a full professor with tenure and a millionaire, and a friend of Senator Laughlin who might one day be President of the United States. Thus it was only right that Louisa should step on the bus first, and should lean on the aluminium post as the bus jerked across Harvard Bridge while Sherry, Fanny, Miriam and Saul all swayed and jumped to keep their balance.

When they reached Harvard Square they got off the bus and Miriam dropped behind to dismiss her brother. He was too severe an embarrassment to her, making crass remarks he meant to be funny which brought not a touch of a smile to Louisa's lips. Besides that, he was fat and ugly – which reminded Miriam that she was plump and plain. She was apparently resigned to this obesity, however, since she followed the other girls into a drugstore on the Square and ordered herself a giant-sized strawberry milkshake.

Louisa had bought a banana split and was eating it carelessly – yet nothing she ate, and no amount of it, seemed to affect her slim body, perched there on a stool. While Miriam guzzled and the other two spooned in the sweet and cold mixture with differing degrees of grossness, Louisa just stuck out her delicate tongue and licked with an elegant, almost European, style.

'Where's Saul?' she asked Miriam.

'He went home.'

'Didn't he want a milkshake?'

'I guess he did but ... hell I only said I'd take him to the movie.'

'You should have bought him a milkshake. I mean, he was with us.'

Miriam turned red and almost cried. The other two girls – Sherry and Fanny – looked up at Louisa with renewed respect. Then Sherry, who wore the handed-down dress, began to inflate herself, as if wind gave courage, and then spoke to Louisa in almost trembling tones. 'Say,' she said, 'say, Louisa, are you going to camp this year?'

Louisa blushed. 'I don't think so, no,' she said.

'Oh,' said Sherry, and she slumped on her stool as all the breath left her lungs.

'I guess I will,' said Fanny: but that seemed to be no consolation for Sherry. 'I don't know if I will, if Lou's not coming,' she said.

Miriam kept quiet.

'The thing is,' said Louisa, glancing modestly at her empty glass and twirling the spoon at the small residue of ice-cream it could not reach, 'I might have to go to Europe with Daddy.'

'Oh, yes,' said Fanny.

Sherry simply nodded.

'Yes, well,' said Miriam. 'Who'd want to go to camp if they could go to Europe instead.'

'I'd like to go to Europe,' said Sherry. 'I guess I will sometime.'

'I'm only going,' said Louisa, 'because Dad has to go to a conference in Paris and Mother doesn't want to go.'

'She doesn't want to go?' asked Sherry. 'To Paris?'

'No. Well, she's been there a lot, and she doesn't like the French. She says they're rude to Americans.'

'I guess it's different,' said Sherry, 'if she's been there ... a lot, that is. I mean, my Mom used to go with my Dad to New York, but she doesn't do that much these days.'

Louisa gave a smile of token interest, picked up her purse and then slipped off her stool. The other girls picked their bags and magazines up off the counter and trooped out behind Louisa into Harvard Square. There they split up. The three lesser little girls went down Mount Auburn Street, while Louisa crossed by the news-stand in the middle of the Square to enter Harvard Yard.

She passed through the gates of the University, acknowledging the deferential smile of a campus guard and nodding to one of her father's students who said; 'Hi, Louisa,' as she passed. She reached Eliot Building and, without knocking, walked into an office. The secretary in the ante-chamber looked up and she too smiled. 'He's waiting for you,' she said, and Louisa passed straight through to the inner chamber of the Professor of Political Theory.

The professor stood as she came in. Though a man and aged, at this point, forty-four, he was unmistakably her father, with such similar features and bearing. He too smiled at Louisa – another link in the chain of smiles with which her life was bound – but this link was certainly the strongest, since there was no deference in it nor any of the older man's reserved expression for this child. It was a smile of recognition and complicity, and it was returned.

Like her, he was tall, so he stooped to kiss his daughter, his delight in her soft face as evident in their embrace as hers in his rasping cheek.

'How was it?' he asked.

'Pretty bad,' she said. 'I mean, if you think of the book.'

'Good books usually make bad movies,' he said, closing his pigskin briefcase, 'and bad books very often make good ones.'

'I prefer the good books,' said Louisa, which might not have been strictly true. but prompted her father to put his arm round her shoulder as they left the office.

'Quite right,' he said – and then, after they had both said good night to the secretary with most particular politeness – he went on: 'You get more out of books in the long run. I find I can re-read *Anna Karenina* a dozen times, but there isn't a movie I'd like to see more than twice.'

'And novels,' said Louisa, as she passed through the gates again into Harvard Square, 'Novels are deeper, aren't they, because they go straight from one imagination to the other. You don't have actors and costumes getting in the way.'

'Well, that's what I think,' said the professor, and this was, indeed, his own opinion, spoken with his daughter's lips.

They walked arm in arm along the bottom of the Common and then turned down Mason Street. It was late spring and warm, perhaps too warm for such proximity, but they always walked arm in arm like this when Louisa fetched her father from his office, and the added heat of their bodies was small discomfort for the pleasure it gave to them both.

'Who were you with?' asked Professor Rutledge.

'Oh, Sherry and Fanny and Miriam. You know. And Miriam had to take Saul.'

'Who's Saul?'

'Her brother. The little one.'

'I saw their father the other day. He seemed very nice.'

'Well, she's all right. I mean she's pretty disgusting, but she's funny – at least, sometimes she is.'

'Why's she so disgusting?'

'Well, she's so fat.'

'You'll be fat one day,' said the professor, smiling and tickling his daughter where his hand held her on the ribs.

'I will not,' said Louisa, laughing and squirming.

'You will if you go on eating all those splits and milkshakes and sodas.'

'Me? Milkshakes?'

'I can see it on your lips,' he said. 'As sure as hell you were eating ice-cream while I was waiting for you.'

Louisa licked her lips. 'I said I'd come at six.'

The professor looked at his watch. 'Yes, well, OK,' he said. 'At least you weren't as late as you sometimes are'

Louisa smiled up at her father. 'Gentlemen are supposed to wait,' she said.

'Not for their daughters.'

'Mother isn't fat,' said Louisa.

'She doesn't eat ice-creams.'

'No,' said Louisa, glancing furtively at her father, 'but she drinks gin which has at least as many calories as ice-cream, and so do you, and you aren't fat.'

'All right, all right,' said the professor, pushing his daughter ahead of him as they came up to the gate of their yellow clapboard house, set back from the street in a large garden. 'You go and mix that cocktail, since you've had your ice-cream.'

And, laughing, Louisa ran up the steps and crashed through the screen door. She threw her bag at the table in the hall, not caring that it missed its target and landed on he floor. She went into the living room and made for the bottles and glasses in one corner.

'Pick it up,' said her mother, who was standing with her back to Louisa, facing Lautrec's depiction of a Parisian whore that hung above the fire-place.

'What?' said Louisa.

'Your bag.'

'It's on the table.'

'It's not.'

'I'm making Daddy his drink.'

'Pick it up.'

Louisa wobbled her leg – a suppressed stamp of rage – and went back to the hall, brushed past her father, picked up the bag and flung it onto the table.

'Where's that drink?' asked the professor.

Louisa turned, her face scowling and black: but her father held his smile which drew Louisa out of her tantrum. She went back into the living room and continued what she had started, throwing ice into a glass jug, paring the lemon, measuring gin and then adding, with a wince that mimicked her father, that touch of vermouth that was always too much.

Lilian Rutledge turned to face her husband and daughter. She too was tall and slim and fair, but in quite a different way from Louisa, having a better shaped body – more rounded, less angular. While the two others stooped, she was upright. Her age was around thirty-eight and, in a haphazard way, she was making the best of this last moment of feminine bloom.

She already had a drink in her hand: and she had changed for the evening into a skirt and blouse. She smiled at Henry with her lips turned down as he crossed the room towards her. He opened his mouth to ask her something, but his eyes fell away from hers and he shut it again.

'How was your day?' Lilian asked.

Henry shrugged. 'Nothing special.'

'And yours?' Lilian asked Louisa.

'Not too bad. I saw that movie in Boston.'

'Any good?'

'Crap.'

'I told you it would be.'

'I know, but I'd said to Sherry and the others that I'd go.'

'She preferred the book,' said Henry.

Lilian smiled at her husband: Louisa, intercepting the smile, looked at her hands, frowned, then turned to her father. 'Can I have some tonic? '

'Sure.

'Go and get some more if it's the last bottle,' said Lilian as her daughter returned to the bottles.

'Where's Laura?' asked Henry.

'She's round at the Brooks'.'

'Do we have to fetch her?'

'They said they'd run her back. She's eating over there.'

'Have we anything on?'

'No. For once not.'

'Thank God.' The professor drained his first glass of gin and vermouth.

2

The room where these three – father, mother and daughter – now sat together, reaching out now and then to bring their glasses to their mouths, was elegantly furnished and freshly decorated, but it was the pictures on the walls which suggested that the professor was rich as well as famous. Besides the Lautrec drawing there was an oil painting by Rothko, a small Tobey, a study of a rose by Renoir and a water colour by Camille Pissarro. At the back of the living room was the prize of their collection – the Bonnard, a portrait of a woman in a tub. It was as a back-cloth for this picture that a light beige had been chosen for the colour of the walls: it matched the Rothko less exactly.

On either side of the fire-place there were low, fitted bookcases, containing not the ordinary spines of the professor's professional volumes but the gold-embossed vellum and faded leather of the bibliophile. On top of these bookcases, and on various pieces of furniture around the room, there were several objects of beauty, interest and value: the outer casing, for instance, of a mummified child which came from Egypt of the fifth millennium; an inlaid scimitar such as Saladin might have used; and an engraved clock of gold-plated silver, about eighteen inches high, made in Paris in the reign of Louis XV.

Lilian's desk was of the same period as the clock: it was now open, showing her papers in some disorder. On its top there were two silver-framed photographs, one of Henry when younger – a conventional portrait of an eager young man – and the other of the whole family, taken three years before, when Laura was nine and Louisa a tomboy of thirteen. They looked happy in the photograph – happier than they looked now; but they were aware then that the shutter was about to open for a moment to record their image, whereas now, there was no camera around.

After quarter of an hour or twenty minutes, Lilian went into the kitchen to see to their supper: Louisa went up to her bedroom and Henry crossed the hall to his study.

This room was half the size of the living room and had a more scholarly atmosphere – if only because the books were not vellum-bound and the desk was piled with papers in heavy order, not elegant disarray. All the same, there was a pretty mantelpiece, two button-leather armchairs and a small painting by Braque on the one wall that was not lined with books, and this wall was painted a particular shade of brown which enhanced the mellow greens and yellow of the works of art.

Henry Rutledge sat down to read, taking advantage of the half-hour before dinner to look through a book on his subject that had recently been published. He glanced up to the shelves for a moment before he began, to look at his own copies of his own works – *Theory and Agitation,* and *The German Tradition in American Political Thought,* a book no student in Harvard or any other university could afford to read as cursorily as Professor Rutledge meant to read the book in his hand (but then few professors of Political Theory, with tenure, were as conscientious as Henry Rutledge in keeping up with the developments in their field). His eyes left the shelves, hovered for a moment on the small pile of typescript which lay on his leather-topped desk – the book he was writing – and then returned to the book he was holding. After a few minutes of reading, he took the first sip of his third martini.

In Louisa's room, where she now sat quickly checking on the book of the film she had just seen, there was a signed lithograph by Chagall which she thought of just as the woman and the bird that had watched her during the variety of childish sicknesses she had suffered in that room – just as Laura, now aged twelve, still thought of the Léger on the stairs as the cage of a sinister beast because an eye peered out from behind the cubist construction. Laura had come to terms with it now – at least, with its malignancy – and was not yet aware (as Louisa had recently discovered) that her monster was worth thirty or forty thousand dollars: or, if she knew that, was not particularly conscious of what it meant, so well had she been brought up, so little spoilt – for the Rutledges were certainly rich, even by American standards, but they had been rich on both sides for some time and they had developed, through the generations, a puritanical philosophy of what should, or should not, be done with money. Louisa and Laura had never had anything that the other children they mixed with did not have: and if those things they did possess – notably the clothes they wore – were of a better quality and a finer style, then that again was not something of which they were particularly aware.

By half-past seven Lilian had cooked the supper for the family. Louisa came down to the kitchen at the last minute to offer her help: her mother smiled sarcastically and told her to fetch her father. As the child went down the hall, Lilian picked a piece of meat out of the stew to taste it – to make sure it was the very best fillet and not just ordinary steak.

Henry came in. He had changed from his jacket into a cashmere cardigan and he sat down at the kitchen table, his face puckered by a particular preoccupation.

'We must decide about the summer,' he said, as Lilian handed him his food.

'Do you want milk or beer or what?' she asked.

'Oh ... some beer.' Henry himself stood up but Louisa darted before him to the fridge and brought out a bottle of imported lager. She handed it to her father with an intent look under her lashes. Henry sat down again and opened the bottle of beer.

'I really don't want to go,' said Lilian. 'We did all that kind of thing ten years ago, and I liked it, but I just don't want to do it again.'

'We never saw Ethiopia,' said Henry.

'No, but we did Egypt and Serengeti and so on. And it'll be as hot as hell in July.'

'Not Ethiopia. It's high – on a plateau.'

'Well, you go,' said Lilian. 'You go and take Lou and I'll go with Laura to the Vineyard. She's too young for all that archaeology, anyway. It'd be wasted on her.'

Lilian was now eating – automatically, removed from her food. She avoided her husband's eyes and he avoided hers: but Louisa looked at them both, her straight, staring eyes flitting from one to the other, her breath half held in her lungs.

'And I really think you ought to come to that congress' said Henry.

'Ought, hell,' said Lilian, drinking from the cocktail she had brought to the table. 'There's no reason at all for me to go, and not much for you so far as I can see. It's just a jamboree for dollar-happy European scholars to celebrate the great sell-out.'

'I like to see some of those people.'

'Well, you shouldn't. They just flatter you because you're on the top of their pile of shit ... and a friend of Bill's. Cultural Freedom, indeed!'

'It's an excuse to go to Paris.'

'I need more than an excuse to do that. I need a compelling reason.'

Henry was silent.

'*We* could go,' said Louisa, looking at her father and speaking with a timid tremor in her voice.

Henry smiled at his daughter.

'All I say,' said Lilian, 'is that we've a nice house by the sea on Martha's Vineyard and, come summer, there'll be a group of our nicer friends up from Washington and New York....'

'Yes,' said Henry, 'Yes, I know. I just thought we might pass all that up for once. For a month, at any rate.'

Lilian shrugged, and began to talk about something else, and the others joined her but all three faces remained brooding. After supper Henry returned to his study and Lilian went to read and smoke cigarettes in the living room.

Louisa followed her father into his study with the excuse that she wanted a book on Jefferson for school. She sat on one of the armchairs while Henry searched his shelves for something that might suit her. She leaned back, her head resting on the back, and she dangled her white-stockinged calves and rhythmically brushed her lower lip against her upper teeth.

'Daddy,' she said at last, 'we *could* go, couldn't we? Just us, I mean.'

The professor turned and looked at her over his half-rimmed spectacles. 'Would you like it, with just me?'

'I'd *love* it – to see Paris and the Emperor's lions in Addis Ababa.'

'You might get bored . . . without Laura and Lilian.'

'I wouldn't, I promise.' She sat up and leaned forward. 'I promise.'

The second promise, taken with the look in her eyes, was more an assurance that she would not bore him. Henry smiled and turned back to the shelves. 'What about the conference?' he asked. 'There'll just be a lot of old professors.'

'Well, you're not old.'

'They'll mostly be older than I am.'

'You never know. There might be some bright young man who'll take me to the Folies Bergères.'

'They don't date girls of your age in Europe.'

'Well, I'll say I'm older. . . .'

Henry turned again. 'They won't believe you.'

Louisa looked down at her insignificant bosom. 'Well, then I'll stay in the hotel and watch television . . . *J'aime Lucy* and *Monsieur le Batman.*'

Henry laughed. 'They don't even have televison in French hotels.'

'Then I'll pass the time with the bell-hop. What I mean is, you won't have to worry about me. I won't be a drag.'

'No, no. I'm sure you wouldn't be.' Henry turned and handed Louisa a volume on Jefferson. 'Just as long as you wouldn't be bored. It's only five days, anyway, and then we could go on to Athens and Cairo and Addis.'

Louisa half rose in her chair. 'Dad . . . that would be great. It would. It really would. I mean, I'd *learn*, wouldn't I? It wouldn't be like going to Florida or something.'

'I think you might. There are supposed to be some wonderful churches. You see, it's a whole civilization there which is Christian, and not yet Western. From the time of the Queen of Sheba they developed quite separately from the Europeans. . . . I think it'd do us both good to see that.'

'Oh *yes*,' said Louisa, jumping up and embracing her father. 'Say we'll go, say we'll go!'

Henry smiled. 'OK,' he said.

'Yippee,' shouted Louisa. She rushed out of the study and crossed to tell her mother in the living room. Henry sat down at his desk: a momentary expression of doubt passed over his face. Then he returned to his book.

The father and daughter arrived in Paris by air and went straight from Orly to their hotel in the Rue des Saints Pères. It was a small establishment, but luxurious; the foyer smelt of cigars and expensive scent. The porter wore a well-cut uniform of blue serge with cross-keys in brass on the lapels: he knew, from their passports, the relationship between these two Americans; he noticed, however, the concealed smirks of those in the foyer who did not but saw only a handsome older man check in with a pretty girl.

It was eleven at night, but neither Henry nor Louisa were tired since their bodies were accustomed to the time of day in Cambridge which was five or six hours earlier: so they left the hotel and walked up to the Boulevard Saint Germain and then along towards the Seine, both smelling the air, letting the fragments of confused nostalgia tickle their minds as the different scents evoked different moments previously experienced abroad. Louisa was excited: she seemed to want to run or fling out her arms, for she trotted forward and then turned back as if finding it hard to hold herself in check. Her father's memories, on the other hand, made him more thoughtful. He smiled, slightly, at what was passing through his head.

'I was ten, wasn't I, when I was here last?' asked Louisa.

'Yes,' said Henry, 'I should say so.'

'And Laura got sick. I remember.' She returned to her memory of that holiday: then she asked again – 'Was that the last time Mother came?'

'No. We were here two years ago.'

'She always came with you, didn't she?'

'Usually.'

They crossed the boulevard and sat at a table of the Café Flore. It was now past midnight, but the evening was warm and the tables on the street were mostly occupied. Henry ordered a Pernod for himself, and Louisa asked for *citron pressé*. His accent in French did not conceal his American origin, yet his knowledge of the language was quite good enough to impose a certain authority on the brusque waiter.

Louisa took a sip of her drink and then sat back in her chair in the relaxed manner of American girls – her eyes wide at the mixture of unusual sensations – the foreign city, the time change, the café on the boulevard at midnight. The passers-by were so young and casual; or old and fashionably dressed; or destitute; or ordinary in such a French way. She turned her head to look at her father and she smiled because he was well-dressed and at ease.

'When did you first come to Paris, Daddy?' she asked.

'I guess the first time was when I was about your age.'

'Did you come a lot after that?'

'Not until the war.'

'Were you here then?'

'I came here on furlough once. Yes.'

'It must have been marvellous . . . I can just imagine it.'

'What was it like?' Henry smiled at his daughter.

'All those slinky French girls and restaurants with accordions playing. . . .'

Henry laughed. 'That's Hollywood history.'

'What was it like, then?'

'No food. A lot of people without homes. . . .'

Louisa nodded. 'Yes.'

'You saw women with their heads shaved '

'Why?'

'Because they went out with German soldiers.'

'Really? Did they do that?'

'A lot of shooting of collaborators. . . .'

'Did *you* do that?'

Henry smiled. 'No. I was safe in the US Army.'

Louisa gave a punch in the air. 'The good old ninety-third.'

'That's it.'

'Was it terrible?'

'No. Just dull.'

'But all that fighting?'

'I didn't do much of it.'

Louisa's face suddenly became serious. She looked at her father to confirm that now, as indeed always, she could ask what she liked. 'Did you . . . I mean, did *you* ever actually kill anyone?'"

Henry smiled. 'Not with my bare hands.'

Louisa was still serious. 'No, but did you at all?'

Henry now looked grave. 'I may have been responsible for a few deaths.'

Louisa said nothing for a moment. She studied her glass on the table. 'But they were Nazis?' she said.

'Yes; German soldiers.'

When they got back to the hotel, Louisa was tired: it might still be early evening in Massachusetts but the journey across the Atlantic had exhausted her mind, if not her body, and she was ready to sleep.

She had a room of her own next to her father's. He kissed her good night in the corridor and, while she took a bath, he sat in a chair to read yet another book on his subject. He looked at the first sentence, then raised his head for a moment to consider his daughter next door – cursorily of her growing body now poaching in the hot water; more carefully of how young she must still be if she played so hard at being grown-up. Henry intended never to lie to her – nor to distract her from the truth with euphemisms – yet now, at sixteen, she had resumed the child's incessant questioning. When she was seven the questions had been tedious but direct: now she was exploring another world of intangibles, the adult world, and there were questions she might ask which he might not like to answer. He knew she was onto something, like a detective who suspects a crime without knowing what the malfeasance may be.

And Henry, of course, felt guilt – or, if guilt is too strong a word, a vague unease as if there might well be a crime and he the criminal. His conscious mind moved onto the various areas of his life – arranged geographically – and when it alighted on Martha's Vineyard (that summer resort for the rich and intellectual) he felt the twinge he had feared and the unease became acute. Yet he was not there: if any wrongdoing was being perpetrated on the beaches, or in the cottages above them, it was not his crime.

4

Louisa awoke in the morning in her strange, soft bed. For a moment her nerves and muscles tightened with uncertainty: then she remembered why she was there and moved her limbs in the bed – relaxing, stretching, settling and dozing again. But the excitement overcame languor. She wondered about breakfast, remembering croissants and hot chocolate – pondering whether hot chocolate might not seem childish now.

The handle of the door turned, but she had locked it. 'Louisa,' her father said, 'are you awake?'

She sat up and jumped out of bed – her lengthening legs

tightening the skirts of her nightdress like a stretched skin. She was at the door in a moment: she opened it and then jumped back into her bed and was lying in it in time to present her father with a beaming smile.

'Aha!' he said, sensing her exhilaration. 'Ready for a day in Paris?'

'You bet,' she said, sitting up and drawing up her knees for her father to sit down.

'And what about breakfast? Do you want it up here, or will you come down with me?'

She thought about that. 'I'll come down,' she said, jumping out of bed again.

Henry glimpsing the line of her stomach where the light shone through the night-dress, stood up and turned towards the door. 'I'll wait downstairs,' he said.

'No, wait,' said Louisa. 'Tell me what to wear.' She opened the wardrobe and pointed to the four or five dresses hanging there.

'I don't know,' said Henry. 'Anything, really.'

'But is it a *grand* day or just a kind of sight-seeing day?'

'We're having lunch in a restaurant with Professor Bonnefois.'

'Grand, I call that.'

'Maybe.'

'OK. I'll wear this.' She reached up and picked out a green-and-black checked dress.

'That'll do fine.'

She now stood waiting for Henry to leave. 'I'll be down,' she said.

Henry left her and went down in the lift to the restaurant on the ground floor. The waiter there smiled and asked if Louisa would not like her breakfast in her room.

'No,' said Henry, 'Down here.'

'*Alors, deux cafés complets.*'

'*Ah non. Je crois que ma fille prend du chocolat.*'

5

Professor Bonnefois was as good-looking as Henry Rutledge and as successful and, like him, was middle-aged. Although he was much disliked by a large number of French political scientists, left and right, for his Atlanticist views, he was nevertheless in a position of sufficient influence to arrange a congress of American and West European academics, not only in Paris, but at a time when the Gaullist government to which he was subject was revising its attitude towards the North Atlantic Treaty.

He and his wife both spoke good English and it was in this language that Yves Bonnefois began to pay direct and extravagant compliments to Louisa. 'But where has your father been hiding you?' he asked.

'I guess I was at camp last time he came,' said Louisa.

'But that is most unfair,' said the Frenchman, giving Henry a look of mock reproval.

'Louisa's only sixteen,' said Henry.

'Only? But that's quite old enough if you're as pretty and as grown-up as she is.'

'*Laisse* . . .' said Madame Bonnefois under her breath. She was herself beautiful, well-dressed and young, so if it was not jealousy which prompted her to umpire her husband's flirtation, then it was the uncomfortable expression on Henry's face.

Louisa herself was delighted. 'Daddy said French boys don't date girls of my age,' she said.

'I can think of a dozen who would be quite delighted to . . . date you,' said Bonnefois, glancing at Henry with a smirk.

'But they don't normally, do they?' Henry asked, ignoring the smirk.

'No,' said Charlotte Bonnefois.

'Not normally, no,' her husband agreed, 'but then Louisa is not normal. She is *ab*normally beautiful.'

'Well, we'll bring her back in a year or two,' said Henry.

'If there's anything you'd like to see on this trip,' Bonnefois said to Louisa, 'you just tell me.'

'Well, I would like to go to the Folies Bergères,' said Louisa.

'No,' said Henry abruptly. 'You're too young.'

'Too young?' said Bonnefois. 'You're never too young. Too *old*, perhaps.'

He laughed: so did his wife, reluctantly. Henry smiled, and then they left the subject of Louisa and talked of the congress.

'The government placed every kind of obstacle in our way.' said Bonnefois. 'They're becoming more antagonistic towards you Americans, who are supposed to be our allies, than they are towards the Soviets, who are supposed to be our enemies.'

'It sometimes seems like that,' said Henry.

'But your government plays it so well ... I mean to say, your President is so patient, whereas our old man ... he has not even good manners.'

'Well, our late President's wife is very francophile,' said Henry, smiling. 'Her maiden name's Bouvier.'

'But the others?' asked Bonnefois. 'Opinion in government circles? Senator Laughlin, for example?'

On hearing the name Laughlin, Louisa looked up from her snails.

'No – well,' said Henry, 'he is the kind of American who gets a little upset.'

'Exactly,' said Bonnefois, sitting back in his chair.

'Bennie Laughlin says the French are ungrateful,' said Louisa, 'and that it's damned cheek for them to turn against the Americans because we saved them from the Germans.'

'Bennie's their son,' said Henry.

'Like son, like father, I imagine,' said Bonnefois, beaming at his inversion of a foreign idiom.

'But he doesn't like the English either,' said Louisa, 'so I guess he's pretty dumb.'

'Why doesn't he like the English?' asked Charlotte Bonnefois.

'Oh, because of what they did to the Irish with the Black-and-Tans and things like that. But he only says it to annoy me because his grandfather was Irish while my great-great-grandfather was English...'

'A great-great-grandfather?' asked the kindly Frenchwoman, making up for her husband's over-estimation with an under-estimation of Louisa's maturity.

'That's right,' said Louisa. 'He came across from England and fought under George Washington and one of his cousins, named Daniel Rutledge, signed the Declaration of Independence – which is why Bennie is so stupid to hate the English, because the English *founded* America.'

'And what about Louisiana?' asked Yves Bonnefois. 'And New Orleans?'

'Yes – well, I guess the French did too.'

'And the Spanish and the Dutch,' said Henry.

'Yes,' said Louisa, 'but it was the Americans who had come from England who led the Revolution and made the Constitution, wasn't it?'

'Yes,' said Henry.

'Certainly,' said Bonnefois, 'certainly it was the English and the brave Mr. Rutledge.'

'He was named Daniel,' said Louisa, 'and Daddy's uncle was named Daniel too.'

After lunch they went to the afternoon session of the congress, which was being held in the Salle Descartes. A German professor in the social sciences was reading a paper on democratic values in industrial relations. There were few people present to listen to his lecture, and the large part of these were easily distracted by the entry of Professor Bonnefois with Henry Rutledge, the celebrated scholar from Harvard, the friend of Senator Laughlin, the acquaintance of the late President Kennedy. They turned and watched as the star of the show and the impresario seated themselves in the back row, flanked by a beautiful wife and a pretty daughter. The German speaker faltered, frowned and then continued his talk. Yves Bonnefois leant forward in his chair and placed his chin on the thumbs of his clasped hands, his elbows resting on his knees. He maintained this pose of concentration for ten minutes: he then whispered into Henry Rutledge's ear and rose to leave again. The heads of the eminent audience turned to watch him go: the German raised the volume of his voice – and the audience resumed their attention, since Professor Rutledge was still there and seemed to show interest in what was being said.

When the lecture finished, Henry Rutledge modestly left the hall, but half a dozen Europeans – acquaintances from former congresses – leapt after him, to congratulate him on this or that article he had written for this or that journal and to ask him, immodestly, whether he had seen theirs. Henry smiled and answered and mumbled, edging all the time towards the door. Charlotte Bonnefois held a corner of his sleeve with her two fingers, dragging him – symbolically – from the *mêlée* of the enlightened. Only Louisa was happy, graciously conversing with those who could not reach her father, answering their deferential questions and absorbing, with delight, their flattery. But then Bonnefois returned to the foyer and firmly saved Henry and the two women from the group of lesser delegates: they were guided out of the door and into a taxi.

'I am afraid they all try to get at you,' said Bonnefois, sitting next to the driver but twisting round to face the others.

'It doesn't matter,' said Henry. 'That's the point of the congress – to meet one's colleagues.'

'Yes, but those were all the less interesting ones. We'll have to arrange a few private groups – with Erzenberg, for instance, and Hindley. There's also that Swede – Halberström. Do you know him? He'll be there for your lecture tomorrow.'

That evening Henry took Louisa to the Comédie Française – *Le Bourgeois Gentilhomme*. She understood little of it, but there was dancing on the stage to Lully's music and she was able to look interested throughout. Henry rewarded her with a special hug and smile.

They ate breakfast together the next morning. This time Louisa countermanded the order for hot chocolate and drank coffee like her father. After that she went to wait in the lobby for Charlotte Bonnefois, who was going to take her shopping, while Henry returned to his room to go over his lecture.

Louisa became slightly sulky with Madame Bonnefois as they walked through the Galeries Lafayette because the older woman was particularly measured with her: there were no compliments, only a few impersonal questions.

'Your mother is at the seaside, isn't she?'

'Yes, she and Laura went to the Vineyard. They didn't want to come here.'

'And you'll go there afterwards?'

'Well, we're going to Africa first. Daddy says he's never been to Ethiopia and he wants to go there.'

'Why, that's marvellous for you, isn't it?'

'I guess it is.'

'You're a lucky girl.'

'Yes.'

They looked through a rack of dresses. Henry had given Louisa a hundred dollars to buy some clothes and the chic Charlotte Bonnefois was to advise her, only she seemed uninterested in dressing the girl. 'That's rather nice, isn't it?' she said, of half a dozen frocks; or, when Louisa saw a cardigan she liked: 'You should get cashmere in London. It's a waste to buy it here.'

When Louisa did finally decide upon a simple, mauve dress, Charlotte shrugged her shoulders and spoke quickly and sharply to the shop-assistant to complete the sale.

'And your mother?' she asked Louisa. 'Does she have friends on Martha's Vineyard?'

'Oh, yes,' said Louisa. 'She has lots.'

'What sort of friends? From Harvard?'

'Well, some, I guess – but they're mostly from Washington and New York. People like the Laughlins.. . .'

'Is Senator Laughlin her best friend?'

'Well, I'd say so, yes. I mean, Dad and Jean get on all right, but they don't have much to say to each other. But Bill and Mother really hit it off.'

Charlotte nodded. 'Do you want some *linge*? '

'Some what?'

She gesticulated. 'Some underclothes?'

'Oh, well, I don't know. I mean, I've got some, but I guess I could so with some more.'

'*Montrez-nous des jolies chemises et des choses comme ça,*' Madame Bonnefois said to the girl at the counter: and there were produced some fine petticoats and other more intimate underclothes in silk and lace.

Louisa was captivated by them. She stood touching the materials with a single finger. 'They are lovely, aren't they?' she said to Charlotte.

'Choose which ones you like.'

Louisa sifted through the elegant, embroidered clothes. 'It seems silly to wear such pretty things under your dress since no one will ever see them.'

'They will soon enough,' said Charlotte Bonnefois with a short laugh.

Louisa did not quite understand that last remark, but she must have sensed its meaning since she felt a spasm in her body that was more than embarrassment. She did not answer, but pushed a pile of the underclothes towards the girl behind the counter.

6

Louisa had learnt something about Franklin Delano Roosevelt in school, so she might have understood her father's lecture that afternoon if she had been able to concentrate on it: but her mind followed her eyes to the audience and she studied their faces and their reactions to what Henry said, rather than her father's face or what he said.

On this occasion the hall was filled with delegates. Some of them did not understand English, but there was a synopsis of the lecture for them to read in French, German and Spanish – and even the deaf could appreciate the American's distinguished manner and demeanour.

The gist of the talk was a measured accolade for the New Deal and its architect, Roosevelt – and a refutation of Hofstadter and others who maintained that Roosevelt's liberal and progressive measures were accidentally arrived at. It was consistent with Henry Rutledge's other works and, therefore, came as no surprise to the other delegates that he should admire and enjoin the pragmatic approach to social questions. Theorists, he argued, tended to be dogmatists and dogmatists liked to shape human beings to their dogma – their so-called surgery becoming butchery as they probed the open carcass of society for the imaginary corruption they had diagnosed. A President, said Professor Rutledge, should be like a judge, not an advocate, weighing the issues as they came before him. This was the theory behind the medieval institutions of king and parliament, and the underlying values remained valid today.

To the mostly European audience of this conference, Roosevelt's reputation was a remote and provincial preoccupation, but they drew from this lecture – or the summary of it – the kind of indictment of Communism they expected; some even read into it a critique of Gaullist policies; and they responded with nodding heads, grunts of approval (led by Bonnefois) and loud applause after the final phrases of the lecture.

Louisa smiled with delight at her father's success. Yves Bonnefois leaned over to her and said: 'That was superb' – which made her flush with pride as if she herself had just given the lecture. Then, as they rose from their seats, Bonnefois stooped and whispered in her ear: 'I've a surprise for you tonight.'

Eight of them now went on to dinner at Lapérouse – the Bonnefois, the Halbeströms, the Hindleys and, of course, the lecturer and his enchanting daughter. Louisa had been aware that some sort of celebration would follow the lecture: she had put on her new dress from the Galeries Lafayette and one set of her new silk underclothes. She had slightly shaded her eyelids and reddened her lips with a little lipstick.

And at the table among grown-ups she behaved like a grown-up. She sat straight and made conversation so effortlessly that the middle-aged Englishwoman, Mrs. Hindley whose tone was in general apologetic, leant across the table and asked Louisa if she were really only sixteen.

'Well, I'm nearly seventeen,' said Louisa.

'Oh dear,' said Mrs. Hindley. 'You make our daughter Sally seem quite retarded.'

'Perhaps it's boarding school,' said Louisa politely, imagining that all English girls went to boarding school.

'Oh, no, dear, not on Albert's salary. She's at Reading High.'

Louisa blushed and took a sip of her wine.

'She doesn't dress at all,' Mrs. Hindley went on, looking Louisa up and down, 'she just listens to those awful singers. I mean, do you like them? The ... the ... what was their name?' she turned to her husband.

'The Beatles,' said Professor Hindley.

'That's right. The Beatles.'

'Oh, well, I used to ...' Louisa began.

'She still does, don't worry,' said Henry, from the other end of the table.

For a moment Louisa's smile almost became a scowl, but then she looked down and said: 'Yes, I do ... sometimes.'

'And why not?' Yves Bonnefois said, spreading his arms out to demonstrate his open mind. 'Charlotte listens to Charles Aznavour, don't you, my dear, and she's a little more than sixteen, even. ...'

Charlotte was less able than Louisa to control her reactions: *'Mieux que toi dans le bain,'* she said, her face set straight. But they all laughed and continued to eat *langouste*.

When they were on to *crème au chocolat, fruits glacés* and their sixth bottle of Burgundy, Bonnefois began to complain about the anti-Americanism of the Gaullists. 'What I suffer for your sake, my friend,' he said to Henry, stretching his arm out in front of the self-effacing Mrs. Halbeström to rest it on the American's shoulder. 'Really, I have no influence any more. A recommendation from me, the professor of *sciences politiques* at the Sorbonne, is worse than nothing for one of my graduate students. Believe me, it's worse than nothing.'

'You should live in a neutral country,' said Halbeström, the Swede. 'There are so many Communists in the universities that if I, the only anti-Communist, did not exist, the government would have to invent me.'

(Louisa, bored, crumbled her bread on the white tablecloth.)

'Why's that?' asked Henry, leaning forward.

'To send to your conferences,' said Halbeström laughing. He turned to Bonnefois. 'You have to have a Swede, don't you, Yves? At any rate, you have to have some kind of neutral – you can't all be Nato.'

Bonnefois, who had drunk at least a bottle and a half of the wine on his own account, threw back his head and neck and laughed. 'My dear fellow, if only I could land a Russian – a real, live professor from Smolensk or Nizhny Novgorod! Ha, ha! That would really bring it in.'

'Bring what in?' asked Professor Hindley, peering out of his tweeds and blinking over his spectacles.

'The dollars, my friend, the dollars. We could make your allowance fifty dollars a day instead of twenty, and provide return tickets first class. Your holiday in Paris would be *grand luxe.*'

Hindley smiled at Bonnefois. 'Oh, yes, I see,' he said. Then he smiled at Henry – a different kind of smile, naturally, since he had not forgotten that Henry was an American.

'Those gentlemen in New York,' Bonnefois went on, 'who pay me to pay you and to take you to Lapérouse' – his arms went out to indicate the table, the white table-cloth stained with the splashes of heavy eating – 'they would be *inordinately* impressed by a Russian.'

'I don't know if I'd be so impressed,' said Henry.

Bonnefois turned to him and blinked. 'No,' he said, 'not you, Henry, I don't mean you – of course not. It's the others. You know who I mean. The others.'

Bonnefois then was quiet, and his mood changed from raucousness to one of stuporous silence. He allowed Charlotte to change the subject, and did not speak again until they had finished their coffee and liqueurs. Then he said, suddenly, in the same boisterous tone as before; 'We must hurry, because ...' and he stood up, 'at the request of Miss Louisa Rutledge, I have eight tickets for the *folies.*' With a flourish he produced what he had described – eight dark-blue tickets.

Louisa sat up and gripped her hands together.

Henry too leant forward. 'I'm not sure that Louisa ...' he started to say.

'It's not the *Bergères,*' said Bonnefois, leaning across to Henry. 'It's only the Casino de Paris. *Spectacles.* Dancing. You know....' He started to imitate the can-can with his fingers on the table-cloth. Henry turned to Charlotte Bonnefois with an expression of uncertainty still on his face. Her eyes met his and she smiled. 'It'll be nothing,' she said. 'Like a music-hall.'

Caught, then, between Charlotte's reassurance and Louisa's appealing eyes, Henry abandoned his misgivings. 'OK,' he said: and was cheered for it by the Hindleys, the Halbeströms and the Bonnefois.

7

They were in a box, or at least a portion of the circle divided from others like it by a thin wall. The seats were in four rows of two, rising in tiers to the back. The couples were mixed: Mrs. Hindley and Mr. Halbeström sat in front; behind them Louisa and Yves; then Mrs. Halbeström and the Englishman and, at the back, Charlotte Bonnefois and Henry Rutledge.

The curtain was raised and the dancing started – rows of girls kicking up their legs in the manner of the Radio City Rockettes, only they wore fewer clothes. Henry sat back in his plush chair, relieved that the spectacle was in an idiom his daughter would accept. As he did so, Louisa turned and gave him a look of excitement and happiness. He smiled back and watched, and allowed the alcohol in his blood to blunt his anxieties. He looked sideways at Charlotte – the beautiful Frenchwoman at his side . . . but then his attention was distracted by the show.

The dancing had stopped. A woman, naked but for a sequinned *cache-sexe*, stood in a hotel bedroom with a man, also as nude as was allowed by law. With titters and shy glances they began to get dressed. Henry looked down at his programme and saw that this sketch was called 'The Nudists' Honeymoon'. The audience laughed: Henry glanced at Louisa just at the moment when Yves, laughing, put his hand on her shoulder. Henry stood up. 'It's not really suitable,' he said. 'I'll take Louisa home.'

Charlotte looked up at him: Yves turned round. 'Really,' he said.

'It's all right, Daddy,' Louisa said.

'No,' said Henry. 'You're too young.'

The occupants of the box next to them started to grumble. Yves stood up. 'You wait,' he said to Henry. 'I'll take her back.'

'Don't bother,' said Henry abruptly, conscious of the smirk on Charlotte's face.

'Let Yves,' she said. 'It's his fault for bringing us here.'

'No,' said Henry, becoming almost confused. 'No. She's my daughter. I'll take her.'

Yves shrugged and sat down. By now there were thumps on the partition, and an usherette looked in behind them. *'Qu'est-ce qu'il y a?'* she said.

Henry and Louisa left the box: Yves came with them to the foyer. 'You'll join us later, won't you?'

'No, I don't think so,' said Henry, having recovered his easy manner. 'I'm rather tired. I'll call you tomorrow.'

Yves shrugged and returned to the theatre: Henry and Louisa took a cab back to the hotel.

'I didn't *mind* the show,' said Louisa.

'No,' said Henry. 'No, I know. But it was very silly. We shouldn't have gone there.'

'It was my fault, wasn't it, for telling Monsieur Bonnefois that I wanted to go?'

'It was no one's fault,' said Henry, taking his daughter's hand.

Louisa looked as if she might cry. 'I just wanted to say I'd been,' she said, her head falling against his shoulder.

'Well, you can now, can't you?'

She looked up at him with wet eyes and smiled.

8

Louisa was still in bed when Henry came into her room the next morning. 'How would you like to leave today?' he asked.

'Today?' She sat up and rubbed her eyes.

'I called the airline. If we left now, we could get down to the African coast – to Mombasa or Malindi. You'd like that, wouldn't you?'

'I'd just love it ... but don't you have to stay here? For the conference?'

'I don't see why I should. I gave my lecture.'

'But what about the Bonnefois?'

'I'll call them. . . .' He turned to go back to his own room. 'And you get dressed. The plane leaves at one-thirty.'

'I will,' said Louisa, jumping out of bed and flinging open

her wardrobe – all, almost, in one movement. She decided that this too was a day to wear her new petticoat.

Henry went back to his bedroom, but he did not call the Bonnefois: the calls he made were to the hotel reception to say that they were going, and to the airline to confirm the reservations from Paris to Mombasa that he had made half an hour before.

They flew so fast in the atmosphere across Europe, the Mediterranean, Egypt and the Sudan, that when they arrived in Nairobi and came out into air no warmer than it had been in Paris there was little sense of having travelled the five thousand miles, nor of reaching a new continent, but simply that of a day spent indoors or at the cinema.

The aeroplane arrived at Nairobi in the evening, but because they were now half-used to French time they were neither of them especially tired and so decided to take advantage of an immediate connection to Mombasa.

It was late at night when they landed by the coast and here, at sea-level, the air was hot and damp. Henry and Louisa were almost the only passengers on the flight and there was neither coach nor taxi at the airport to take them into the town. The official of the airline on which they had travelled – an Indian – telephoned for a car to take them into Mombasa.

'And can you call a hotel?' asked Henry, a feeling of helplessness coming over him as he stood, sweating, in the artificial light.

The official shook his head. 'Have you reservations?' he asked.

'As a matter of fact . . . no, we haven't.'

The official shrugged. 'It's very late,' he said.

'I know it's late,' said Henry, 'but we've got to sleep somewhere.'

The Indian picked up the telephone. 'Which hotel, please?' he asked.

'I don't know. Anything decent.'

'I will call my brother.'

Henry waited, watching Louisa who stood on the edge of her feet beside him. He damned himself for landing precipitately like this in Mombasa – at one in the morning, with no reservations. He was so used to being meticulous that this unaccustomed chaos – after so many hours of travelling – brought him almost to tears. Travel was too easy: it was absurd to skip from continent to continent and climate to climate as if going from room to room in a large house.

'My brother has room for you,' said the Indian.

'Fine,' said Henry, 'thank you.'

The Indian took them to the entrance to the hut which served as a terminal and a taxi appeared out of the dark, driven by a Negro. They climbed into the back seat, their luggage was placed in the boot and the driver was given instructions as to where they were to go. He drove them along the coast into the city. Henry and Louisa could discern the shapes of palm trees along the side of the road, and occasionally they could see fires with figures of men crouching over them set back from the road in the undergrowth. Then the town began: there were houses and dim street-lights, then bars, garages and hotels. For a moment Henry felt that they might enjoy themselves – however humid it might be – because it was exotic and strange-smelling and unlike anywhere else.

'Are you tired?' he asked Louisa.

'A little.'

'It's really four in the morning ... Paris time. I guess we should have stayed in Nairobi.'

'We'll have an extra day by the sea.'

'I hope it doesn't get too hot.'

'We'll get used to it, Dad.' She yawned and looked composed, though her clothes were damp from perspiration and the humid atmosphere.

'I thought they were all Negroes here,' she said.

'And Indians.'

'They mostly seem to be Indians.'

'There may even be some Arabs. Mombasa used to belong to the Sultan of Zanzibar, and he was an Arab.'

'Just think,' said Louisa. 'This morning we were in Paris and now we're on the Indian Ocean.'

'Better than the *Folies Bergères*?'

'Oh, yes,' she said, 'much.'

Their improved spirits deteriorated again when they reached the hotel. Its façade was seamy and the foyer was a covered courtyard, insufficiently ventilated, lit by dim electric lights, and furnished with dirty armchairs. They were led into it from the taxi by an old, black porter who seemed to speak no English but indicated, with a movement of his arms which held their suitcases, that they must sign the register before proceeding. Henry did this, then followed the porter across to the far side of the foyer and up two flights of wide stairs. Here the wet air had a strong smell of rot. On the second floor they came out onto a gallery – the doors of the hotel rooms opening onto it like monks' cells onto a cloister. Outside one of the rooms there was a wire rack, hung with grey underpants and socks – hanging fruitlessly to dry in the wet air. There were also noises from the rooms – slight noises, because it was night, but noises nevertheless, of heavy lungs and congested nasal ducts. As they passed one open door the porter gestured towards it, as if to indicate that it might be of use to them – what use, he had no need to explain, since the smell of latrines came from it.

Henry, the dapper millionaire, was appalled, but it was too late now to go anywhere else. He did his best, therefore, to relax his repugnance and resign himself to the squalor – but then a room was unlocked and it became apparent that it was the only room offered for the two of them. It was large, with a double bed, but was hotter – much hotter – than the air outside. The porter had laid down their suitcases and opened the shutters before Henry asked for the second room: but every interrogative gesture was met with the same dumb hand pointing towards the one room, the one bed. Before he left, the porter switched on a slow fan on the ceiling, as if this would make up for the inadequate accommodation.

There was no bathroom attached to the room, but a wash-basin in the corner. Louisa left the room to return to the lavatory that had been pointed out to them. While she was out, Henry opened his suitcase, took out his cotton pyjamas and sponge-bag. He removed his jacket and tie and went to wash his face and hands at the basin.

Louisa returned. 'Watch out for cockroaches,' she said: and she tried to smile but she could not, so she started to cry. Henry took her into his arms. 'My poor baby,' he said.

'Oh, Dad, it's so awful,' she said.

'I know,' he said.

'And Paris was so awful and I hated the Bonnefois.'

'So did I.' He patted her shoulder and her sobs changed to sniffs. 'We'll get some sleep,' he said. 'We'll feel better tomorrow.'

He took his pyjamas and went to the filthy lavatory, where

he changed into them since there was no screen in the bedroom. He waited in the gallery – listening again to the grunts and snores of the other guests – to allow Louisa an interval of time in which to change into her nightdress. But when he came back into the bedroom she still stood at the basin, washing, dressed in the cream silk slip she had bought in Paris.

She smiled at him when she turned after drying her face with a towel. Henry got into the wide bed and took up his book.

'That's a fancy thing you're wearing,' he said.

'I bought it in Paris.'

He watched her for a moment – her bosom fringed with lace, her long legs emerging from the flank of smooth silk. Then he turned his eyes to his book and Louisa half-hid behind the wardrobe to change into her night-dress.

'You don't mind, do you?' he asked, as she got in beside him. 'I guess I could sleep on the floor.'

'I don't mind,' she said. 'I thought you might.'

'Of course not.'

'I always used to ... remember? Climb in with you and Mother.'

Henry smiled.

'I guess we'll think it's funny, one day,' said Louisa.

He closed his book and turned off the light. They both lay down, facing away from each other, but though it was late now – by French as well as East African time – and both were tired, neither seemed able to sleep. For twenty minutes they both tossed around in the bed; it seemed even hotter than before.

Henry sat up to throw off the linen cover, leaving only a sheet to cover them. He did not know whether Louisa was awake or not; but then she whispered: 'It's so hot.' Her voice was touched with the hysteria of insomnia.

'Don't worry,' he said, and he put his arm round her, and she breathed more steadily (though the heat of her father's body might be thought to have made her hotter still): but Henry, instead of experiencing discomfort at his daughter's body next to his, began to feel it not as the little shape of his child but as the longer, fuller form of a girl – and, as she adjusted her position to sleep in his arms, her soft but solid stomach moved against his side. He felt this and became alert – body as well as mind – and sorely wanted to move his hands over the damp body of Louisa, to touch in the dark the cavi-

72

ties of her frame, to feel how, and how much, his daughter was now a woman.

In his mind there was, to say the least, an instinct against doing this – an instinct which grappled with his reason, with the repeated, insidious 'why not?'. And while the dispute pre-occupied his mind, his body inched towards its own way. But then he was struck with a sudden agitation at the enormity of what he was doing and, with a strong, irrational effort of will, he thrust himself from her.

Louisa, if she was asleep, was awakened by this sudden movement. 'Daddy,' she said. 'Are you all right?'

'Yes,' he said, 'I'm sorry.' And then – 'It was just a kind of dream.'

They both tried to sleep again – their bodies parted. Louisa's breathing became truly regular: Henry's was more a simulation, since he was kept awake for some time by his own feelings of remorse and self-disgust.

9

What he did not know – the next day – was whether Louisa had any idea of what he had done. If she had, she showed no signs of outrage or shame, nor made any allusions to it. She was, as it happened, unusually gay – making fun of the squalor of the hotel as they ate their breakfast in its immense, dark dining room, which had no windows to the open air.

Henry himself was careful, since his conscience – freed from fatigue and immediate lust – had resumed its usual position of strength within his personality. Eating breakfast, he was at that stage of remorse in which he was half-persuaded that the incident had been a dream. The self-deception, however, would not stick since they returned to the room where it had happened, to pack their bags – and there was the bed, and there was the basin where she had stood, mature and womanly in her silk shift.

They checked out of the nasty hotel that morning, and walked into the city of Mombasa. It was unpleasantly hot and humid so they went first to the airline office to arrange to go up the coast to Malindi that afternoon; Henry also made sure that there would be two rooms at the very best hotel. Then walked up to the Portuguese fort, which was almost all there was to see in Mombasa, then down again to look in at the shops. They were offered brass-studded chests from Zanzibar, but declined; eventually, Louisa found a sucked ostrich egg which she liked and Henry bought for her.

It was hot, too, in Malindi, but the hotel was directly on a five-mile stretch of beach and a breeze came in from the sea. Their accommodation was now luxurious: each had a small, thatched hut with a bedroom, bathroom and sitting room. As soon as they arrived, Louisa decided that she wanted to swim – though the sun had almost set – and she persuaded Henry to go with her by saying that it would cheer them up. So they changed into their bathing costumes and went down onto the long beach and into the warm sea. Henry came out first and sat on the sand – his slim stomach creasing with the curve of his back, his face looking down at the ground between his knees. Then he looked up and watched his long-legged daughter leave the water and lollop up to him – a solicitous smile on her face.

'Isn't it lovely?' she said.

He nodded.

'This is what I *really* imagined – palm trees, and this huge beach with no one else at all.'

'Yes.'

She sat down beside him. 'Are you feeling all right? I mean, you're not sick or anything, are you?'

'No. Why?'

'Well, you're kind of silent.'

He smiled. 'It's the change of climate.' He looked down at Louisa's slight stomach – then sharply away again.

'What were you thinking about?' Louisa asked, noticing the wincing gesture.

'When?'

'Just then.'

'What a pretty daughter I'd got.'

'Do you think I am – really?'

'Yes. Really I think you are.' He mimicked her and they both laughed: but Louisa took the compliment and blushed slightly too.

They went in and changed and met again in the bar in the main building of the hotel. The other guests were all Europeans – Belgians, mostly, and Dutch. Henry had already ordered a martini for himself when Louisa joined him.

'What would you like?' he asked.

'A whisky sour,' she said, sweetly, naturally – and he ordered it for her although he would not normally have allowed her to drink alcohol. But then she was dressed in a simple, grown-up dress and her hair was up in a way she rarely wore it.

At dinner she sat very straight and talked a lot, since her father was mostly silent. 'The Laughlins aren't really happily married, are they, Daddy?'

'I don't know. . . .'

'Well, Bennie says they're always screaming at each other.' She paused, then – 'I don't understand why people do get married, really, since a lot of them don't seem to work out at all. . . .'

'Ours is OK, isn't it?'

'I guess it is. But I don't know, do I? I mean, I'd be the last to know if you and Mother didn't get on. Because people often stay together because of the children, don't they?'

Henry smiled. 'I can promise you that your mother and I don't stay together just because of you and Laura.'

'No, but . . . like coming on this holiday and Mother staying at home. You wouldn't have done that ten years ago.'

'That doesn't mean we're breaking up.'

'No.' Louisa picked at the sleeve of her dress. 'But it's kind of loosening up.'

'That's not necessarily a bad thing.'

'Well, I *know*,' said Louisa. 'I know. I didn't mean it was.'

Henry seemed uncomfortable, and Louisa was disconcerted to think that she might have made him so, but she had made up her mind to converse, seriously, on this particular topic.

'Did you love any girls before you met Mother?'

'Yes,' said Henry gently. 'Yes, one or two.'

'What were they like?'

'Well, I used to go out with several girls at Yale.'

'Yes, but . . . you know . . . particular ones.'

'There was one called Helen.'

'Why didn't you marry her?'

'I went into the army.'

'Anyone else?'

'There was a girl in Germany . . . a German.'

'A German?' Louisa was slightly shocked.

'She was very nice.'

'Yes, but . . . I mean, whose side was she on?'

'She worked for us.'

'Oh.'

'Her husband had been killed.'

'Oh. I see. She was married.'

'A widow.'

'A widow.' Louisa nodded – impressed. 'And what happened to her? I mean, why didn't you marry her?'

'You don't marry someone just because ... because you like them.'

'I guess you split up when you came back.'

'Exactly.'

Louisa drank her wine. 'And then?'

'Then I met your mother.'

'Where?'

'At a cocktail party in New York City given by your great-aunt Fanny.'

'That isn't very romantic.'

'I'm sorry. Where would you suggest?'

'I don't know ... in the park, or a museum.'

'Or the subway?'

Louisa smiled. 'How long was it before you got married?'

'Not long.'

'A year?'

'Less.'

'How long?'

'I can't remember ... five or six weeks.'

'That was romantic.'

'Yes.'

'And then I was born?'

'You were.'

Louisa relaxed a little, smiling to herself as the narrative reached this point – her own birth.

'Why did you wait for years before having Laura?'

'Well, sometimes it just happens like that.'

'I guess it does.' Louisa thought to herself for a while. 'Why did you marry Mother and not that German woman?'

'I loved your mother more.'

'And she loved you?'

'Yes.'

'I think I'll love so much the first time that I'll never love anyone else.'

'You'll be lucky if you do.'

'It is better, is it?'

'It's very rare.'

'I think it'll be like that with me.'

And, for the first time that evening, her eyes left her father's face and stared into space as she imagined her first and only love.

They were both tired, having travelled, swum and slept badly the night before. They left the restaurant and walked back towards their huts. Louisa put her arm round her father's waist and he put his on her shoulder.

'Its nice, isn't it?' she said.

'Very nice.'

'I'd like to stay here a long, long time.'

'Yes.'

Then, as they reached her door, Louisa turned to him and said: 'They're huge beds, aren't they? Bigger than last night, even. . . .'

Henry looked down at her.

'I mean . . .' she began.

He let go of her. 'Good night,' he said, and he turned without kissing her and walked towards his hut.

10

Thereafter their friendliness deteriorated – since her elegant body was always there before his eyes, in summer frocks and night-dress, her legs casually apart, her bosom in a T-shirt, inflicting a pain as real and severe on the father as any knife or club or hot iron; and hurting him, too, in his mind, where the ordinary, decent American was humiliated by his shaming desire for his own child.

When Henry was alone, he could manage – to think of other things, and to think like a parent of Louisa; but whenever her lilting figure came into his room – to hug and tickle and pose in innocent yet knowing ways – his ordered, sober thoughts were shaken up and smothered in his physical reactions.

His only defence was to reverse the amatory course they seemed to have taken – to become more the father and less the lover. The charm which he had always like to exercise on Louisa he now placed in abeyance: he limited her to a single glass of wine and told her to be in bed by ten. And in Addis Ababa, where they went next, he befriended an Italian woman of his own age, staying at the same hotel. Louisa was sent away at night, was ordered to leave them drinking at the bar which she did, grumpily, feeling – quite rightly – that there was much, much more, behind his reimposition of parental authority.

The greatest insult, to her, was being sent with a family of English children – and their nurse – to see the Emperor's lions. Henry said that he would rather go to the museum.

'So would I,' said Louisa.

'What nonsense. You want to see the lions.'

'No, Dad, no. I'd rather go with you to see the museum....'

'Well, you can go some other time.'

'Why can't I go with you?'

'I'm going with Signora Lambrelli, and you can go with the Butler-Clarkes.'

Louisa's face set in rage. She said nothing more; and she went with the English brats who were younger than she was, anyway, except the girl, who certainly might have been since she wore her hair in plaits.

Louisa's childish anger made it easier for her father, since she bothered less with her clothes now, and never looked him in the eye with the wary, tentative expression that – with her prettiness – had so nearly brought him to scandalous sin.

When they left Addis, they were alone again – but though there was no Signora Lambrelli and no English family, their relationship remained formal. In Gondar, as they looked up at the angels painted on the ceiling of the Debre Berhan Selassie Church, Henry spoke to his daughter at length, but it was only to tell her about the Coptic Church and the seventeenth-century civilization in Ethiopia. At dinner, however, he even laughed and Louisa smiled, so they were back to some sort of intimacy – but on his part it was measured, and on hers it was cautious, wary of a second humiliation.

They flew next to Lalibela – a village high and remote, in spare hills, accessible only in dry weather when the small plane could land on the mud strip ten miles or so from the town. Louisa, used to jets, was a little afraid on the jerking, bumping DC3; but her father seemed at ease, so she felt no real fear, nor was she sick like some of the other passengers.

The attraction of Lalibela was in the churches, which were carved in one piece out of the soft rock. They were thus situated in pits, connected to each other by caves and tunnels. For the convenience of tourists who came there, there were guides and also, here in the wilderness, a new hotel with all the taps, basins, sheets and soap that travelling whites expect.

Henry and Louisa were driven there from the landing-strip in a Land-Rover – an hour's drive up donkey-paths. They checked in at the hotel, washed, and then set off at once to see the churches, since they only planned to stay one night.

They did indeed see the sights – the honey-coloured churches – but these were not all that there was to be seen, for lining the mud streets were the beggars – emaciated men covered with sores, feebly holding out their hands; tubercular children and babies, in the arms of the wizened mothers, their faces covered with dribble, flies feeding on their open skin.

Louisa was more concerned with these than she was with the churches or the Ethiopian landscape. 'But you must give them something, Daddy – you must!' And Henry, awkward at alms-giving like all Anglo-Saxons, did reach into his pockets and hand to one wretch a few cents in the country's currency. But there were, of course, more – and there were the same beggars again as they retraced their steps to see a church they had missed – and each time they passed them Louisa urged her father to give until, as he put it, he had no more change.

'Then give them bills,' said Louisa.

'Don't be silly.'

'Why not? You can afford it.'

'Of course I can't. Not to feed and clothe the whole damned lot of them.'

Louisa was silent: she looked dumbly at the churches and heard her father's cultural explanations, though she hardly listened to them. Then, at dinner, she turned to her father: 'You could feed and clothe them, if you wanted, couldn't you?'

'Who?'

'The people out there.'

'No . . . I don't know.'

'We're rich, aren't we? I mean, one of our paintings is worth fifty thousand dollars. You could buy a lot of food and clothes for that.'

'Yes,' said Henry patiently, 'but they'd eat it all, and then there'd be no picture.'

'Is it better to have a picture than to feed people?'

She looked at him directly now – the same, direct look she had always given him, but with a harder edge to it.

'It's very complicated,' said Henry.

'Well, I wish you'd explain it.'

'I will some time.'

Louisa sighed. 'I mean, I'm more interested in that . . . really . . . in people, than I am in churches and things.'

'Perhaps you should have stayed with your mother, then.'

Louisa blushed. 'I don't mean to be ungrateful, Daddy. I'm having a really good time. But foreign countries are people, too, aren't they? Not just monuments?'

'Yes,' said Henry, 'Yes, of course. I'm sorry.' And he did feel apologetic towards Louisa – for his contradictory moods of sternness and indulgence. He felt more sure of himself now that she was firmly a child again, and would have liked to resume his role as a spoiling father: but Louisa was now the severe one of the two.

'Are you going to tell me?'

'What?'

'About not giving money to people who haven't anything to eat.'

'Well,' said Henry kindly, 'money can buy food, but it can also buy instruments for producing food and clothes and other things. Now our money, or most of it, is invested in business which provides work and, in the end, food and clothing for a lot of Americans and South Americans . . . perhaps, even, some Africans. I don't know. But there isn't enough of my money, or anyone else's as yet, to provide work and food for everyone in the world.'

'But all our money isn't in business, is it?' said Louisa, 'because we've got those pictures and . . .'

'Pictures are culture,' said Henry, 'which is just as important, in its way, as feeding people.'

'And we spend a lot of it,' Louisa went on.

'Yes,' said Henry, 'but even doing that gives people some work and some wages. The people who run this hotel would be out of work if we weren't here. And those ten-dollar bills you wanted me to give to the beggars out there will provide work for someone, some time.'

Louisa was silent for some time. 'Well,' she said at last, 'I guess that *explains* it. But I don't really understand how.' Then she added: 'If I had any money, I'd give it, I think.'

11

Axum, the last of their stopping-places in Ethiopia, lay on a hilly plateau in the mountains bordering on Eritrea. It had, for the tourist, prehistoric tombs and ugly stele–stone needles sticking up into the sky. Louisa was unimpressed, and bored by what her father told her about the older church – that it was on the foundations of a cathedral destroyed by Judith the Pagan but built, so it was said, by the Queen of Sheba. The eyes of the American girl were for what she saw – only dull tombs, costume jewellery (in the museum) and a modern church built by the present emperor, Haile Selassie, which was more like the Harvard basket-ball stadium than anything else.

'I guess I really don't understand,' she said to her father. 'I mean, to spend all that money on this great big church for a little dusty town like this, when they've already got an old one. Is that what you mean by culture being more important than feeding people?'

'Well,' said Henry, 'not exactly. People build churches to satisfy their religious needs, not their cultural needs.'

'But we're not looking at churches for our religious needs, are we, because we don't have any.'

'No. That's right. But religious art also has cultural value – and so does secular art . . . like Picasso.'

It was hot as they tramped around Axum and, in the heat, Henry could not think clearly – or so he told himself. Louisa, on the other hand, found the heat no impediment to the working of her mind – rather the opposite.

'What has cultural value in the States, Daddy? I mean, Picasso isn't American, is he?'

'No, but there are plenty of American painters.'

'We don't go and see churches, though.'

'No, but there are fine examples of architecture like the Lincoln Centre . . . and then culture isn't just aesthetics. There's learning, and Harvard, after all, is a good example of that kind of culture.'

'Learning . . . yes.' Her voice was sceptical.

'Isn't that important?'

'I can see it's important if it helps people. . . .'

'As it does.'

'You'd think, though, that you'd try to feed people round

the world before you started to learn and teach and every-thing.'

They were back to that. Louisa had certainly been affected – even shocked – by the wretched of the earth in Lalibela: but equally astounding to her was Henry's soft, petulant re-action to their demands, the giving of small change, the with-holding of the bills.

All other things being equal, she might not have noticed his inconsistency – for children tend to accept their parents' be-haviour and not question it – but coming at a moment when, for reasons of his own, her father was re-imposing his pater-nal authority after a decade of indulgence, it gave her a weapon to fight for what she had gained. And every time she struck with it, she found the same soft, defenceless area of flesh. And so her questions continued as they travelled on – through Asmara and Cairo to Rome – and by the time they reached New York Henry was bored by it all, and he said so, irritably: and Louisa was in the odd mood of someone who finds she has won a contest she would really like to have lost.

12

They spent the remaining weeks of the summer on Martha's Vineyard with the rest of the family. The two 'Africans', as Lilian called them, were now able to go their own way and they did – Henry reading and writing, trying to complete a few more chapters before term began, while Louisa lay on the cooler, fresher beaches of the Atlantic and told her friends, casually, that her tan came from the East African sun.

There was a boy on this fashionable island off the coast of Massachusetts called Danny Glinkman. Louisa knew him vaguely from one or two parties in Cambridge – his father taught at MIT – and she now began to see a lot of him, not on dates or anything romantic like that, but just on and off around the place, swimming, or in the small drugstore in Oak Bluffs. There was no question of romance, because he was ugly, smaller than she was, and marked with the usual mis-fortunes of adolescence – spots, gaucheness and a croaky voice. What that voice said, however, did interest her much more than necking with boring beach-boys like Bennie Laugh-lin: for Danny Glinkman had read a lot of books she had only heard of, by authors like Marx and Plekhanov. 'You've really got to read these people,' he told Louisa, trotting beside her as they walked into Oak Bluffs.

'But they are Communists, aren't they?'

'Sure.' Danny shrugged and smiled up at her with a touch of bravado.

'But they're wrong, aren't they?'

'Who says they're *wrong*?'

'Well . . .' she flapped her hands helplessly, '. . . everyone.'

'I don't,' said Danny. 'I actually read the *Communist Manifesto* and it doesn't sound all that wrong to me. In fact it sounds a whole lot right.'

Louisa shook her head. 'I don't know . . . really, I don't.'

'And you should read Proudhon. "All property is theft." I kind of like that.'

Danny was very cool, and Louisa was impressed because she had not read that sort of book. Again, if she had not seen and felt the question of social injustice, she might have been as bored with Marx and Danny as she would be now by some other boy whose topic was Jung and the collective unconscious: for thus our psyches affect our experience and our experience our ideas.

'I hate having money,' she said to Danny, in a secret tone of voice. 'I really feel bad, sometimes . . . I mean, do you know, Danny, in Africa there were babies . . . little *babies* and children who had nothing . . . *nothing* to eat? And no homes? No Band-Aids? Nothing. And there we were, staying at all those hotels and eating ourselves sick and having servants brush our clothes. . . .'

'That's it,' said Danny. 'And it's like that over here, too, except they hide it.'

Louisa appeared alarmed. 'Over here?'

'Children die on the Indian reservations, just like they do in Africa, because they don't have the right kind of food. . . .'

'Do they?' asked Louisa.

'And in West Virginia, even, white children grow up all misshapen, some of them, because of not having protein. . . .'

'In West Virginia . . . ?'

Danny nodded, his face set serious 'It's always been the same. The rich just don't care about the poor and America's run by the rich.'

'But Communists don't help the poor more than we do, do they?'

'Sure they do. They don't let people starve.'

'But they kill people, don't they?'

'Yes.'

'That's bad, isn't it?'

'I don't think it's worse to kill the guilty than to let the innocent die. I think it's better.'

13

'It's intolerable,' said Lilian to Louisa – the family alone, sitting at supper. 'Jeanie tells me that Bennie asked you to go with him to the Napiers' barbecue, and you said you'd rather go alone.'

'Well,' said Louisa, 'I would.'

Laura laughed. 'So would I.'

'I just don't know what you girls have against Bennie,' said Lilian. 'You both used to like him.'

'He's kind of dumb,' said Laura – smiling her placid child's smile at no one in particular.

'He's not dumb,' said Lilian, 'is he, Harry?'

'Well,' said Henry, 'not specially.'

'Just because,' said Lilian, 'he likes to talk about the Red Sox instead of Jean-Paul Sartre. . . .'

'It's not that, Mother,' said Louisa. 'I don't mind people being dumb, anyway. It's just that he's not even ... well ... very nice.'

'How can you say that,' said Lilian, 'when he's the son of Harry's oldest friend? Or do you think, perhaps' – her tone became sarcastic – 'that Bill isn't very nice, either?'

'He's nice, all right,' said Louisa. 'But he sure is reactionary.'

There was a moment's silence.

'He's what?' asked Lilian.

'Reactionary.'

'What's that mean?' Laura asked her father.

'Ask Louisa,' said Henry, smiling.

Laura turned her wide eyes to her sister. 'What's it mean?'

'It means ... it means being old-fashioned,' said Louisa – a little confused.

'Huh,' said Lilian – hampered in this conflict with her daughter by the quantity of bourbon in her blood.

'Is Bill old-fashioned?' Laura asked.

'She means politically old-fashioned,' said Henry.

'Is he, Daddy?' Laura asked.

'I wouldn't have thought so,' said Henry, 'but then I guess I'm a reactionary too.'

14

The Rutledges returned to Cambridge after Labor Day and the new academic year began with the routine of Henry's lectures and seminars, Lilian's dinner-parties and ladies' luncheons, and school for the girls. But what had started that summer continued on its course, imperceptible in itself as a malaise, its immediate manifestations easily ascribed to a stage through which the girls must grow. Laura became vaguer and more silent, while Louisa seemed to develop backwards, taking less and less interest in clothes and boys – going more in a gang with Danny Glinkman and one or two others among the intellectually precocious children of Cambridge academics.

Though they lived in the same house, the parents and children saw little of each other, and such family holidays as the week's skiing in Vermont with the Laughlins became a trial of patience for them all. Louisa's relations with her mother were quite normally bad: a thousand mothers and daughters bitched at each other in the Bay area. With her father she behaved like what, in a sense, she was – a woman spurned – and Henry was as exquisitely confused as a man might be who had almost deflowered his daughter and now only staved off the compulsion to do so with an aloof and artificial exercise of paternal authority. He smiled and was benign and played, with some style, the bit-part of father and Professor of Political Theory. He was fortunate, too, in the rôles that the others chose for themselves – for instead of finding himself a King Lear on stage with a Lady Windermere, he was given cues by his wife and daughter which made it clear that they were acting in the same piece. When Louisa asked him, for example, about Vietnam – what and why and how – she did so in the tone of suppressed hostility befitting the rebellious daughter: thus Henry could disguise his inadequate answers with the patient manner of the goaded father who knew – but could not say – that there was more behind her protest than the mere logic she supposed was on her side.

By the summer of 1965 – a year after his holiday in Africa – Henry had all but forgotten the hot night in Mombasa: the smell of Louisa's body, that had seemed to cling to his fingers as Duncan's blood to the hands of Macbeth, was now gone – washed off not by the multitudinous seas of the summer resort, not the fluoridated water of his Cambridge washbasin but by a strong and persistent determination to shut the matter out of his mind. He became, once again, a moral man who could talk of America's commitment to freedom around the world, and tell Louisa that appeasement of dictators was a sure and certain way to worse and wider wars.

Part Three

1

Two days before Christmas, 1965, Louisa was eighteen years
old. She was by then fully grown and a girl of uniquely American beauty, with a face of English freshness and Irish anima-
tion, and legs so long that only an admixture of German
blood with a dash from the Ivory Coast could explain them.
Her nose alone was un-American, for instead of the pert,
indeterminate nugget of flesh that demonstrates the synthesis
of different nationalities in most American girls, there was a
sharp, aquiline bone over thin, distended nostrils.

She dressed tidily now, but without elegance, and she would
not have a birthday party because, she said, her parents would
not like her friends – and, she added, her friends would not
like them. Whereupon Lilian snorted and Henry smiled and
agreed that everyone did not have to get on with everyone
else – that human beings could be different, thank God, in
free societies. And that evening he asked Louisa into his study
to discuss her plans for going to college, because it would
soon be time to apply.

Louisa became excited and, for a time, polite. She really
wanted, she said, to go to Berkeley. Henry nodded and said
that he agreed – that it might be a good idea to get away
from home, though Radcliffe was a good college. And had
she thought of some of the other colleges in the East? Sarah
Lawrence or Barnard or Swarthmore?

'No, Dad. I really want to go to Berkeley, I really do. Not
just for college, but because it's California. I want to see what
it's like out there. I mean, I've been to Europe half a dozen
times, but I've never been further west than Albany. . . .'

'You'd be a long way from home,' said Henry.

'Sure,' said Louisa – and, for a moment, her caustic manner
returned, for she said: 'But it's not as if we can't afford the
air fare.'

For the next eight or nine months, Louisa lived in a California of the mind. She had seen films and photographs of its
beaches and vineyards: she had read that it was the matrix of
America, with a way of life for which the Eastern states would
have to wait fifteen years and the rest of the world a generation. She was sick, now, of Cambridge and the East Coast,

of being Professor Rutledge's daughter and having all that respectable money and European taste. She was caught by the image of sun and freedom, and saw in California a rough soil where she could earth the static that had built up around her. She fairly sparked with excitement when she filled in the computer cards (January) or heard of her acceptance (May) or packed her bags to leave (September). She would know no one out there – Danny had a scholarship to Harvard – but that caused her no concern. She wanted to be alone, anonymous, her own Louisa Rutledge – and start from the start.

Of course it was not quite so easy to escape. 'The Vollards will meet you at the airport,' her father said, as he drove her to Logan Airport. 'And they've arranged a room for you in a house with some other girls.'

'Great,' said Louisa. 'Thanks, Dad.'

'I don't know Vollard all that well,' Henry said, half to himself, 'but he was at Princeton when we were there. He did a good piece on Chile in *Foreign Affairs* a month or two ago. You might tell him that I saw that.'

'I'll be coming home at Christmas, won't I?' asked Louisa, momentarily nervous at leaving home for the first time.

'I hope you will,' said Henry. 'And call us as soon as you arrive.'

2

San Francisco – the clean, pastel-coloured houses she passed as they drove from the airport were in such contrast to the grime of Boston. The Vollards were of a type she knew – obsequious – so Louisa half-ignored their conversation and looked out of the window. Her excitement had been justified: it was quite different, much brighter. They came into the city and her eyes fell on launderettes, shops and restaurants as if they were rare and extraordinary sights. They drove up and down some of the steep streets. Louisa hardly heard the banalities of her driver, Professor Vollard, and his wife: her mind was on the new life she would lead. Then they left the city and drove across the Bay Bridge and here indeed was a wonder of the world – this mesh of steel across the water.

The Vollards drove her first to their house, since they insisted on feeding her, at least, if she would not stay the night. Louisa remembered to call her parents. Professor Vollard winced involuntarily at the girl's slow-speaking over long distance, but then he remembered who she was and left her to speak to them, her eyes peering out of the window of the house above Berkeley, studying the first lights on the other side of the bay. 'Yes,' she said, 'I'm fine. I'm really glad to be here.' She became impatient. Her father's voice was an irrelevant intrusion. She said good-bye and rang off.

After dinner Professor Vollard drove her down into Berkeley to an apartment on the second floor of a clapboard house near the campus. The two other girls were there, and were easy and friendly, and told her, when Vollard had gone, what a gas it all was, living there in California. Louisa sensed at once that these girls were dull: she made up her mind not to let them get in her way.

She went with them, the next morning, to be shown around the campus, and then they took her down Shattuck Street and all the excitement Louisa had felt the day before returned to her at the sight of so many various people – the bedraggled, picturesque, black and Asiatic. It was not that she was a country girl, but what passed before her eyes here – the people's faces, the incense and shawls in the shop-windows, the obscene and radical magazines on the news-stands – was all quite exotic set against her limited experience of Harvard Square.

It was two weeks before she met Jason Jones: the first of these weird faces she could talk to and touch. She had gone with one of the girls to a party given by a lecturer in biology. There was wine and Scotch, and several people were smoking pot. Jason Jones was one of these: he was sitting on the floor when he first saw Louisa, leaning back against the wall. He looked at her, laughed, slapped his knee, and laughed again. Louisa blushed slightly and looked away, but she had already become fascinated by his appearance. His clothes were filthy and his hair was long. He wore leather trousers, stiff with dirt, a moustache, and a paisley-patterned shirt. Around his neck was tied a thong which held at his chest an emblem of peace in hammered bronze.

It was not this costume which made her curious, nor his long hair, for she had seen varieties of both before: but the way he laughed, the cool look in his eyes when he slapped his knee, was quite strange, as if he were remote from his own humour. She looked back at him (she knew no one else to talk to) and he nodded to her to sit down at his side. She glanced around to see if she was observed or not: then went to him and sat on the floor.

'What's so funny?' she asked.

He laughed again. 'You.'

'I don't see why. . . .'

'Your accent, for one thing.'

'Well, I think yours is pretty strange. . . .' She pronounced 'strange' at its most nasal.

'Haven't you ever been to Iowa?'

'Uh uh.' She shook her head.

'I bet you've never been West before.'

She shook her head again.

'That's what I was laughing at.'

'You could tell?'

'I could. I mean, you're so *neat*. You could've come out of a Fifth Avenue store.'

'I'm sorry,' she said, blushing.

'Never be sorry,' said Jason Jones and he smiled. 'Here, try this.' He handed her his cigarette and she inhaled it inexpertly so that Jason Jones laughed again and taught her how. The drug in her blood had little immediate effect, but later in the evening she felt gay and relaxed, hungry and loving. She talked to Jason for two hours: then he disappeared and she went home alone.

She attended classes the next day, but the admirable concentration with which she had started the term had already left her. She dwelt on Jason Jones – his thin face, his narrow body and the knowing, sardonic flow of words. She could not imagine that she would not see him again and she walked around Berkeley in the four or five days that followed in a pleasant state of expectancy: and, sure enough, on the fifth day, a hand fell on her shoulder as she bought her *Ramparts* and he was there beside her.

'Where've you been?' he asked.

She shrugged and smiled. 'Around.'

With a weasel's smile he said: 'You'd better buy me some coffee.' They left the bookshop and went to a drugstore and she did buy his coffee: he turned out his pockets to prove that he was broke.

'How do you eat?' she asked.

'Oh, I bum a quarter here and there or I get a girl to cook me something.'

A girl. She, Louisa Rutledge, badly wanted to be that girl – to see him eat food she had cooked.

'I guess I could rise to hamburgers,' she said.

He nodded. 'I like them fat,' he said.

'Yes,' she said. 'When?'

'I can't tonight,' he said.

Her spirits fell.

'I guess I could tomorrow.'

They rose again. 'Will you come to us?'

He looked up. 'You live with a couple of grey girls, don't you?'

She had told him that. She shrugged apologetically.

'Better come over to my place.'

His room, on Pratt Street, was as dirty and bizarre as its tenant. He had lived there, clearly, for some time. The walls were covered with scarlet felt, tacked to the plaster with brass upholsterer's nails. Onto the felt were pinned a variety of posters and pamphlets – political and psychedelic, coloured and drab, black and white. His bed was just a wide mattress, covered with an Indian printed cloth There was a chair and a table, and rush matting on the floor, but no wardrobe nor chest-of-drawers which were, indeed unnecessary, since he wore the only clothes he owned. In one corner of the room, on the floor, there was what seemed to be a shrine with a small, brass statue of the dancing Shiva and an Arab pipe. A stick of incense, standing in a jar and alight, sent fumes into the room that camouflaged other smells that might have come from other sources. Had it not, Louisa would not have noticed them. She was excited and delighted by this louche, romantic habitation: it confirmed what she thought of the man. With ease she sat back on the mattress (the only place to sit) and threw down the string bag containing ground beef and ready-chopped onions and buns. 'This is really great, Jason, really. . . .'

Instead of seeming pleased that she liked his room, Jason frowned. 'It's just a place,' he said.

She shut up, cursing herself for being so raw as to admire anything: and admiring Jason all the more for being so cold and off-hand about his scarlet walls.

'Have you got plates?' she asked.

He did not answer, but rummaged in the box on which his Shiva was placed and came out with a frying-pan, two plates, two forks and two mugs. There was dried fat and egg-yolk on the plates and forks.

Louisa took them out onto the landing, where there was a small sink, kettle and hot-plate. She took all the neat packages containing the ingredients for the hamburgers and unwrapped them: she mixed them together on one of the plates and then patted the substance into thick slabs and set them to fry. She washed the plates and forks, cut open the buns with a fork and put coffee powder into the two mugs. At one moment, she glanced through at Jason: he had put on a record and looked bored. She smiled happily and returned to the hamburgers.

When they were cooked she took them through. Jason ate them without comment: there was even no expression of like or dislike in his eyes – but, from the way his lips touched the bun and the way his teeth bit into the meat, it was clear that he enjoyed them.

'You get that here?' he asked Louisa, nodding at the loose, paisley smock she was wearing – a pattern not unlike his shirt, only its colour was blue while his shirt was green.

'Yes,' she said.

'It's nice.'

She said nothing, but her heart beat faster as they finished their food and coffee for she knew, or thought she knew, what would happen. Jason himself seemed almost nervous. His hand shook as he scraped a nugget of cannabis resin into the tobacco of an opened cigarette and re-rolled it in a new paper. The record came to an end. Louisa crawled forward to choose another and, as she did, she knew his eyes were on her legs so she took her time but eventually put on the second side of the same heavy, mystic beat. She lay back next to him on the mattress and they smoked the cigarette down to its last eighth of an inch. Then he leant over and kissed her – a proper, American kiss that she had experienced before – though never with a moustache to brush against her nose. But then he went further, as she knew he would: with none of the timorousness of a high-school date his hand went under her loose dress and prowled at will around her body.

3

Jason came from Iowa, and dressed and wore his hair in a way that was unorthodox there but quite normal in Berkeley. He had been in California now for three years, and he had never been home meanwhile. His face – thin and cynical – was constitutionally grey, even after exposure to the Californian sun, yet there was dignity as well as fascination in its immobility.

He was political. He had been active in the Free Speech Movement in his first year, and had been arrested several times. He had told Louisa, when he first met her, that he was a revolutionary, yet he was never in the centre of things and, while he talked as if he participated, it became apparent that he talked enough to leave little time for action.

Louisa knew about most of the political issues: she had talked to her father about Vietnam, and to Danny about Marx. With Jason, however, her political attitudes ceased to be just attitudes and ideas and took on the intensity of her love. Her mind belonged to revolt as irretrievably as her body belonged to Jason: indeed, her dedication was interchangeable, for she liked to think that she would gladly die to change the world and America.

Unfortunately, Louisa's new lust for social justice did not revive the militancy in Jason, who had reached the tail-end of his commitment. A month after their affair had started – four weeks of frequent sexual bouts and Louisa's rising joy – he told her to shut up about fucking Vietnam. It was, of course, a moment of post-coital gloom, and Louisa was not surprised or offended by his abrupt language, since it had never been anything else.

'I'm sorry,' she said. 'I do go on.'

'No, no,' said Jason, lying back on the mattress. 'You say it. I mean, it's your thing, but you've got to remember that I've been *through* all that.'

'Where to?' she asked, tentatively.

'To me,' said Jason. 'You can't know who you are until you've been through it all – pot, black power, politics, all that. I'm nearly there, but I've been at it for quite a time. It can't happen all at once. I mean, when I first came West I was like you – all heated up about the war and all that. But then . . . well, just about when you met me, I began to realize that it just wasn't me.'

'But . . . but aren't you against the war?'

'Sure,' he said, 'sure. I don't want to get drafted, so I'm against the war. I like to say what I like, so I'm for Free Speech: but once you get into those things – I mean really in – then they take hold of you like anything else, and try to make you something you are *not.*'

He lay back, his hands clasped behind his head. Louisa –

dressed now in jeans and a T-shirt, still too inhibited to lie naked as he was – leant over and rested her arms on his chest.

Jason Jones continued his monologue. 'I want to be me, that's all. I don't know what that is yet. I may never know. But I know one or two people who I am not. I'm not my father's idea of Jason Jones; I'm not my mother's, either. And I'm not Lyndon Johnson's Jason Jones, nor Edgar Hoover's nor General Hershey's nor Bobby Kennedy's.'

'You're my Jason Jones,' said Louisa, smiling.

'I am not your Jason Jones,' he said, not smiling. 'I'm going to be my own man. Do you know what that means? Your own man?'

'Well ...' Louisa began.

'You don't know,' said Jason. 'Of course you don't. You're a girl, and they cling. That's all they want to do – cling and make you into a fucking father and citizen and all that crap. ...'

'Well,' said Louisa, smiling more ecstatically, 'why don't you throw me out?'

'I will,' he said, 'don't you worry. But you've got something for me just now. This whole East Coast thing ... I've got to work it out ... in me. You ... I don't know ... your voice ... all that Harvard stuff ... it makes me feel kind of funny, somehow. And your father being loaded. That kind of thing.' He sat up. 'You know,' he said 'I sometimes feel your tits' – he did what he said he sometimes did, his hand under her T-shirt – 'and wonder if they're worth their weight in gold. Did you know that? I really do. I hold them both, weighing them up, and wonder ... well, if gold's three sixty-seven to the ounce. ...'

'You brute,' said Louisa, readjusting herself on the bed and laying her cheek on Jason's unwashed shirt where it lay on the bed.

'I never met one of your sort before,' he said. 'I knew your kind was around, though. I went to New York once and walked around Madison and Park Avenue and saw some real classy girls: but you're more like the country product ... those fancy estates up the Hudson. ...'

'My grandparents,' said Louisa.

'That's right. I thought so. You get that kind of thing out here in Kent County, but it's not the same. Everything's new here.'

'Daniel Rutledge signed the Declaration of Independence,' said Louisa.

'That's what I mean. You've got history, and I haven't been through that at all. Out in Iowa, no one's got any kind of history. It's like the people and the corn are interchangeable. Mind you, my folks aren't farmers. Dad's got a car dealership in Rock Rapids: but hell, tractors ... I mean, he'd have been hammering wagon wheels a hundred years ago. That's not history. That's just another crop of corn.'

'What difference does it make?' said Louisa.

'It doesn't make a damn difference. I mean, don't think I don't know that, because I do. But it's just something I've got to go through ... the East Coast thing. Like you're doing your West Coast thing.'

'I guess we can help each other,' said Louisa kindly.

'No,' said Jason, turning to her with angry mouth and eyes. 'I don't want you to help me. That's just what I don't want. It's something I've got to do on my own, because if anyone helps me I just become a piece of them.'

Louisa shrugged. 'OK, OK.'

'People are always trying to wipe themselves off on other people, making out they're helping them,' said Jason. He shuddered and Louisa sat up.

'Do you want some coffee?' she asked.

'Yes,' he said. 'You make some.'

Louisa lifted her graceful body off the bed. She went to the landing and stood by the kettle waiting for it to boil, happy to be naked beneath her clothes.

4

When it came to the middle of December, and the end of her first term at college, Louisa felt herself to be a changed person. She remembered, however, that she had promised to go home for Christmas and her nineteenth birthday and, though reluctant to leave Jason in his rented room, she was curious to try out her new character on her parents.

The costume in which she chose to travel – jeans, beads and a shawl – was enough in itself to show that Berkeley had made her different. Both her parents were at Logan Airport to meet her. As she waited to pass through the barrier, Louisa watched her father's face attempting to smile, and then her mother's eyes which had quickly switched to Henry when she had seen her daughter's clothes. But Henry did manage to smile and he held it as Louisa kissed him (first) and then Lilian: and she kissed them both with feeling, as if to reassure them that her affection for them had not gone with her East Coast clothes.

She spoke quickly, with excitement, as they left the airport and drove through the Sumner Tunnel. 'Dear old Boston,' she said. 'Really, California's so different. Everything's much greener.'

'Don't forget it's winter here,' said Henry.

'Sure, well, we get a kind of winter too.'

She told them about California as if they had never been there; and, indeed, her parents did not know her California – the California of freedom and revolt. Louisa was discreet, of course, about several areas of new experience, but those aspects of her life that she tactfully selected seemed to provoke a certain sullenness in her parents. Henry began to interrupt her – to ask her if she had seen this or that art gallery or exhibition. Her answers were always no.

'Well, I guess that leaves Disneyland,' said Henry.

'I haven't been *near* Los Angeles.'

'You hardly seem to have been to San Francisco.'

'I'm at college, Dad. Not on vacation.'

They crossed the Charles River and entered Cambridge in silence.

Lilian showed more interest in Louisa's life when the two women were alone in the kitchen, but by then the daughter felt humiliated and started to sulk. Her mother's contrived curiosity irritated her, and everything about their house and Cambridge seemed intolerably close. She left the kitchen and went up to her room and, while she was on the stairs, Laura came in: she, at least, seemed glad to see her sister.

'What's it like?' she asked Louisa, as they went together to Louisa's room.

'Fantastic,' she said.

They settled down, and Louisa started all over again about Berkeley and this time her audience listened hard and asked for more detail and more fact. 'Do you have friends?' Laura asked.

'Sure.'

'What kind?'

'Well' said Louisa, smiling modestly and giving the look, of someone embarking on a confidence, 'there's this boy. . . .'

'Oh,' said Laura, her eyes widening, 'what's his name?'

'Jason,' said Louisa.

'And what's he like?'

'They wouldn't like him,' said Louisa, nodding down towards the kitchen and study.

'I would, wouldn't I?'

'He's got long hair and a moustache. . . .'

'Great,' said Laura.

'And he's really free. I mean, he just does *anything*.'

'Oh, said Laura, sighing with dreamy excitement. 'And is he . . . I mean, is he yours?'

'Sure,' said Louisa. 'We kind of live together.'

'Not *really*?'

'Out there it's just normal, Laurie.'

'Well,' said Laura.

'But you mustn't tell.'

'Oh, no, I wouldn't.'

'He's really great. You *would* like him.'

'Does he smoke?'

'Pot?'

'Yes.'

'Of course. Everyone does at Cal.'

'We do a bit here,' said Laura modestly. 'Some of the kids from school . . . I kind of like it.'

'Yes . . . it's great, it's really great.'

'What about acid?'

Louisa looked askance at her sister for a fractionary moment. 'Er . . . not yet,' she said.

'I'd kind of like to try it,' said Laura.

On the second evening after her return – the eve of her nineteenth birthday – Henry asked Louisa if she would like to go with them to a cocktail party.

'Must I?' she asked.

'No, of course not,' he said. 'I just thought you might like to.'

Laura was out with friends, so when her parents had gone Louisa was left alone in the house, sealed in by a black, wet evening. She felt sorry, in a way, that she had not gone – then remorse that she had refused her father so abruptly: and, feeling remorse, she started to justify her behaviour to herself – an interior debate which broke up in confusion just at the moment when her parents returned.

'I don't know how you can stand it,' she said, as she sat with them in the living room. 'All those false people gassing on about their little Harvard things – whether so-and-so's *published* or if somebody else will get *tenure,* and all the time their sons, or not *their* sons, of course, but other people's sons, are getting their brains blown out in Vietnam. . . .'

'I assure you,' said Henry, pouring himself some vodka and tonic, 'I assure you that there was no absence of talk on Vietnam.'

'Oh, yes, I guess it's fashionable now.' Louisa sat back in a comfortable chair and lifted one of her legs over its arm.

'Would you like a drink?' her father asked.

'No, thanks. I don't *drink*.'

Henry shrugged, crossed to a chair and sat down. 'There were some interesting people,' he said. 'Howard Platt, for instance. . . .'

'Who's he?'

'A chemist. He won the Nobel Prize last year.'

'Huh.'

'It doesn't impress you?'

'No, it does not.'

'I'd say his work is of some benefit to humanity.'

'Well, why didn't you say that? I mean, it's so typical of this whole Harvard-MIT scene to talk about doctors and professors and Nobel Prizes and Presidential Medals. You never say he's saved a human life with his discoveries, or so-and-so's invented a new protein that's going to feed starving people in India. . . .'

'No,' said Henry. 'There's a certain amount of truth in that.'

Lilian, rather drunk, came in from the kitchen. 'Is that what they teach you out there?' she asked. 'About the starving people in India?'

'It's not what they teach you,' said Louisa, 'but it's what you learn.'

'Well, I wouldn't call it very specialized knowledge.'

'It's more important than most of the crap they try to teach you. . . .'

'You seem to have learnt a few other things besides. . . .'

'What?'

'Never mind.'

'Come on, Mother. If you want to say something, you say it.'

'Look,' said Henry. 'Let's just have a drink and . . .'

'No,' said Louisa, 'I want to hear it. It's not fair just to imply things and then not say them.'

'You learnt how to be a little bitch,' said Lilian casually. 'That's what I was going to say.'

'Well,' said Louisa, furious and rising in her seat, 'Well, you said it, and since you brought it up, let me say that I learnt a thing or two in California that make you both look pretty . . . pretty damned phoney.' She was erect now, and white in the face.

Henry raised his hand. 'Please . . .' he said.

'Let her blow,' said Lilian. 'Let the poison drip from her fangs.'

'Well, what the hell do you think you are, you two,' shouted Louisa, 'sitting here in this swank house, collecting paintings like postage stamps and swilling down the gin . . .'

'We've heard all that before,' said Lilian. 'I thought you'd learnt something new. . . .'

'It wouldn't make that much difference,' said Henry, calm between the two women, 'it really wouldn't make that much difference if we sold them all.'

'Well, I don't know,' said Louisa, her fury collapsing. 'I can't argue. But I wish Jason were here. He could.'

'Who's Jason?' asked Henry.

'Oh, he's a boy I know in Berkeley.'

On Christmas Day, Louisa sent a cable to Jason Jones. Henry, sitting in his study, could hear her read it out over the telephone: 'Happy Christmas Jason. How I miss you. Returning twenty-ninth. Can't wait. Louisa.'

5

She told her parents, before she left, that she loved Jason Jones, and they suggested that she bring him home in the spring. They would pay his fare. She put this to her lover as she sat, clasping his hand, in a cab driving along the edge of San Francisco Bay into Berkeley.

'Yes . . . well, why not?' he answered. 'We might stop off and see my folks on the way.'

The cab took Louisa to her room, where they dropped her suitcase: then she went with Jason to his, where they made love and she stayed the night.

Their life thereafter returned to the happy routine of the previous term. Louisa saw no one beside Jason, and Jason seemed to have only one close friend, a poet called Ned Rampton. He was a large, heavy man and at least ten years older than Jason. He was a failure as a poet because his verses, like his life, was derivative of the Beat Movement of the 1950s. He lived in a converted loft in San Francisco and while, before Christmas, he had come across to meet Jason in Berkeley, they now went to him because Louisa had the Volkswagen her father had given her for her birthday.

She would buy some food and cook it, on those February evenings, at one end of Ned's loft while the two men talked to each other at the other. Ned's hair was sparse and black, and his nose had the texture of pumice-stone; his appearance was as soiled as Jason's, but what Louisa found attractive in Jason she found repellent in Ned; she suspended her instinctive dislike, however, from loyalty to Jason, who grew angry if she asked even a neutral question about the value of his friend.

'Hell, you wouldn't ... you *couldn't* understand him. He's onto things that *I* can hardly get hold of.'

One of the things Ned was onto, which Louisa sensed but never mentioned to Jason, was Louisa. He watched her movements with his slow eyes and every now and then put solicitous but irrelevant questions to her, or complimented her cooking – only to leave half his food on the plate. She decided, however, that lecherous looks were little to have to tolerate for Jason's sake, and she knew, from listening to them talk, that Jason respected, almost revered, his friend.

Their conversation ranged over poetry, politics and religion – the younger man asking plaintive questions, the older answering in ponderous tones of self-conscious wisdom. It appeared that Ned was a Buddhist, or a Hindu – Louisa was never quite sure which. He postulated a detachment from self which Jason evidently longed for, but could never achieve.

Their life continued like this into March. Louisa followed her courses conscientiously and joined Jason in his room in the afternoon. He rose late, and never went to lectures or even seemed to study much, holding all the courses to be irrelevant to what mattered. He read a certain amount – Castro or Buckminster Fuller – while listening to music: the sitar, Bach or the Vanilla Fudge. In the evenings they would eat, drink tea, smoke pot, talk or make love, and all the time Louisa became increasingly happy because he was wild and sullen but stayed with her, seeming to need her: and, alone together on his mattress, he held and touched her body, not sizing up its value in gold but revering it as something very much more precious, and then taking it, and using it, with a force and desperation that moved her to an oblivious pitch of feeling.

It came nearer to the time when they were to go East again. With her monthly allowance of five hundred dollars came the extra sum from Henry to pay for two return tickets to Boston: then, suddenly, Jason decided that they should get married. He did not propose in any accepted sense, but simply said that it might be better if they were engaged so far as their families were concerned. 'I don't know about your folks,' he said, 'but mine might get kind of steamed-up if we just roll in like that.'

Louisa, who loved Jason so very much, felt a delight she hardly dared show – thinking for a moment that this off-hand observation was his way of declaring his love, his way of saying that he wanted it to last for ever. But then she noticed that Jason's contemplation of marriage was a wholly introspective process: he did not look at her when he suggested it, but sat cross-legged with his eyes on the floor.

'But are you sure, Jason,' she said. 'You always said you didn't believe in marriage.'

'I don't believe in it,' he said, irritated. 'But I don't not believe in it, either. I think people should do with it what they like.'

There remained enough of the sentimental child in Louisa to make her feel that this was not quite the way in which a lover should court his bride – and, for a time, she hesitated, but she could think of no convincing answer to Jason's 'Why not?' Why not indeed? She loved him. They more or less lived together. She could see no reason why they should not continue to do so indefinitely: she could conceive of no life without him. That, in a sense, was a marriage already, so why not ratify it, make it acceptable to those who might find their present state immoral?

It was when she thought of them – those who might dislike her living with Jason unmarried, his parents and hers –

that she prickled inwardly: for while Henry and Lilian might dislike Jason as her lover, she doubted that they would like him any better as her husband. She felt nervous spasms in her stomach when she thought about Jason and her father in a room together; Lilian, she knew, could take him.

But it was her life, after all, and so why not? The intuitive caution waned before this negative logic and the girlish sentiment – her love – that reinforced it. Thus she accepted Jason Jones with his own words: 'Yes, OK, why not?' And when she said it, he looked up at her with his angry, weary eyes and crossed to kiss her with that serious expression of affection which made him so dear to her.

6

Having made up their minds to get married, Jason and Louisa decided to do so forthwith. There was some talk of stopping off in Nevada or Idaho on their way to Iowa and Massachusetts, but Louisa felt that this would be gratuitously cruel to her parents: and, anyway, she wanted to be married from her own home. She therefore wrote to Henry and Lilian, telling them of their decision and asking them to arrange for a quiet wedding in Cambridge sometime in April when they would be there. She thought a letter would be better than a telephone call, allowing her parents time to get used to the idea before facing her or Jason Jones. She was nervous, nevertheless, until she heard from Lilian, whose reply was concise, polite but agreeable.

Jason too was nervous – not about her parents, but about his. He never spoke about them to Louisa but she noticed that the day before they left he went to a barber: and though his hair remained long, and his moustache drooped over the sides of his mouth, it was all cleaner and tidier than it had been before.

They flew from San Francisco to Sioux City, and from there they took a bus to Rock Rapids, a small farming town in the top left-hand corner of the state of Iowa where Jason had been born and raised.

'We're a long way from the ocean,' said Jason, as they arrived in the town.

'Sure,' said Louisa, looking out of the window of the bus

at the parallel and dissecting streets, tree-lined and neatly laid out.

Jason had told his parents of the day they would arrive but not the time, and so no one was there to meet them. The bus had left them in the centre of the town and now, with Louisa, and carrying their two suitcases, he walked out of town again in the direction of Luverne and the Minnesota state line. His parents' house was one of the last on the row. In front, the grass was well cut: behind, there was a clear view of the cornfields.

While Mr. and Mrs. Jones had not seen their son since he had left for Berkeley, they seemed to know what he had become and showed no surprise at his long hair and necklace. They were both of medium height with square faces: the original Welsh blood had been watered down to a small fraction of their predominantly Scandinavian stock. They shook hands with Louisa and nodded to Jason, and both seemed to hold their breath while they were in the house – not so much in a physical sense (though this might have been justified, since their son did smell) as in terms of emotional expression, treating them both with unusual reserve.

'How've you been?' the father asked his son, but then did not listen as Jason made some kind of rambling reply.

At dinner after their arrival, Jason told his mother and father that he was going to marry Louisa.

'Oh, yes?' said his father. 'Well, that's just fine.'

The mother said nothing, but stared at Louisa.

'You got folks?' she asked eventually.

'Yes,' said Louisa .

'We're on our way to see them,' said Jason.

'Where's that?' asked Mrs. Jones.

'Cambridge,' said Louisa. 'Cambridge, Massachusetts.'

'That near Springfield?' asked Mr. Jones.

'No,' said Louisa, 'Near Boston.'

'Her pa's a professor,' said Jason.

'Oh yes?' said the father. 'I guess that's not a bad thing to be.'

There was a silence; then Jason said: 'One of her ancestors signed the Declaration of Independence.'

'Oh, yes,' said Mr. Jones. 'Way back, then?'

'As a matter of fact,' said Louisa, 'they were collaterals.'

Mrs. Jones rose to clear away the dishes. Louisa rose too,

to give her a hand, conscious of her rôle as a future daughter-in-law, but the mother turned and said: 'Oh, no, you sit' and Louisa did as she was told. She sat in silence, glancing around at the simple, ugly furniture – the plastic-covered sofa and the framed postcards of the Grand Canyon.

'You finished studying yet?' Mr. Jones asked Jason.

'Sort of,' said Jason.

'I think Barry's coming around after dinner. Said he'd like to see you. You remember Barry, don't you?'

'Yes,' said Jason. 'Of course I do.'

'He's *been* in the army,' said Mr. Jones.

'He out already?'

'He was wounded.' The father lifted the palm of his hand and covered his right cheek. 'Got the side of his face blown off,' he said.

'Christ,' said Jason.

'Yes,' said Mr. Jones. 'But he'd like to see you.'

Barry, the boyhood friend, came to the door at nine. His face had indeed been shot away, though by now the reconstruction of the army's plastic surgeons had almost healed, leaving a tracery of red lines between the pieces of grafted flesh, like the joints of a jig-saw puzzle.

'You got a nice girl,' said Barry, looking at Louisa, 'but you sure shouldn't marry her until you're through the army, because you might come back looking like this, and that wouldn't be fair.'

'I wouldn't mind,' said Louisa.

'No?' Barry laughed. 'But it might not be his face, you see. You never know where they're going to hit you.'

Jason turned white.

'Did you get your draft notice yet?' his father asked him. 'I guess I sent on a few letters from the board.'

'Yes,' said Jason, 'but I was deferred, see?'

'Yes, but you won't be deferred any more, not after you've finished college.'

'I don't know,' said Jason. 'I guess not.' He looked from side to side.

'There's nothing else you're going to do, is there?' asked Mr. Jones.

'No, not in particular.' Jason looked at Louisa. 'She's still studying, though.'

'Yes, well, I guess *she* won't get drafted,' said Barry – and he laughed again.

They slept in separate rooms in Rock Rapids for the two days they were there and so were only alone when, on the first afternoon, they walked into the town.

'There's nowhere to go,' said Jason. 'It's all cornfields. It drives you crazy.'

'It's green and nice, though,' said Louisa. 'Didn't you like it?'

'I didn't. No. I never did. It's too far from the ocean. It's too far from anywhere.'

Louisa did not mention his parents, but she noticed that since the evening before Jason's face had set into an expression yet darker than it already was. 'We shouldn't have come,' he said, as the Sheriff's car drove slowly past them – the driver stunned and suspicious at such curious pedestrians in the parish of Rock Rapids. And, when the patrol-car had driven on, he said: 'I hate them, the pigs! Christ, shit, I hate them.'

7

The two days they spent in Iowa, however, turned out to be better than the three weeks in Massachusetts. Lilian fetched them from the airport: she said 'Hi' to Jason: her face expressed nothing. The confrontation with Henry took place in the evening, upon the professor's return from his seminar. He barely looked at Jason before turning his eyes on his daughter as if she were mad. Whereupon Louisa started to cry.

Jason Jones had no idea of why Louisa was in tears: he was himself as wound up to do his best as he had ever been. He had shaved his face cleaner than usual and his shirt was almost clean. True, his sneakers had holes in them, but they were not so dirty as to leave marks on the Rutledges' carpet.

Both Henry and Louisa recovered themselves almost immediately: the professor offered them both a drink – and, out of politeness, they accepted: but then he started on the advantages of long engagements and Louisa saw at once what he meant to say.

'Now long was your engagement, Dad?' she asked.

'Mine? I don't know. Not long. But that was different.'

Louisa looked sour and sullen and went to help her mother in the kitchen .

'How long were you engaged?' she asked her.

'About three weeks.'

'I thought so.'

Laura sneaked in after Louisa. 'Hey, Louisa,' she said. 'I like him. He's weird.'

'You can say that again,' said Lilian.

'Oh, Mother, don't,' said Louisa. 'I love him.'

'Don't worry,' said Lilian. 'I like him a lot. He's like a Saluki. And don't worry about Harry. He'll get over it.'

'I hope he does.'

'You are both kind of young, aren't you?'

'I'm nineteen. That's not young these days.'

'These days, no. I guess it isn't.' Lilian started to stir the dressing. 'You sure you love him?'

'Oh, yes, Mother, yes, I do.'

'And he loves you?'

The briefest falter. 'Y . . . yes. Yes. I'm sure he does.'

Lilian said nothing: she continued to stir the oil, vinegar, salt and mustard in the bottom of the teak salad-bowl.

'He'll get straightened out,' said Louisa.

'What's he going to do?'

'He's got to get finished at Cal. first. We'll go back and live there.'

'What about the draft?'

'Yes, well, there's that: but they haven't drafted him yet. Perhaps they won't.'

When they returned to the living room, Henry was showing Jason his collection of pictures. The older man's face was taut with the effort, and it tightened still more when his lovely daughter re-entered the room, lovely even in the hobo's clothes she now wore. He looked at his wife: her face was expressionless until she caught his glance, when her lips turned up into a slight smile.

After dinner, Louisa and Lilian sat down to make out a list of a few guests to be invited – the grandparents on both sides and some of the family's closer friends.

'What about the Laughlins?' asked Lilian.

'No,' said Louisa, glancing across at Jason who sat looking ill at ease on the other side of the room. 'No, it's not worth bringing them all the way from Washington.'

Though Louisa was involuntarily excited by the arrangements for her wedding, she could not entirely apply herself to them with Jason at a loose end in the same room. Lilian noticed this, left the room for a moment, then returned and sat down. A few moments later Laura came in. She sidled up to Jason and asked if he played cribbage.

'Yes,' he said. 'Yes, I used to.'

'Like a game?'

'Sure.'

Thus the fifteen-year-old Laura sat down with her sister's future husband and played him, and beat him, at cribbage.

Though cribbage kept Jason quiet in the three weeks that followed, Louisa could see that he seethed within – at her parents, their house, their friends, their conversation. Henry, too, became more and more on edge, though he spent most of the time in his rooms at Harvard. At those moments in the evenings between coming home and going out again, he was polite to Jason, and both seemed to agree to keep off contentious topics in their conversation, including the marriage. If ever their discourse touched so much as the outer limits of this subject, they all combined to steer it clear. There was no man-to-man talk about the marriage, no mention of a settlement, no discussion of their future.

Henry remained calm like this and, when the day itself arrived, he put on a suit quite unperturbed. He smiled at his daughter as she appeared at the top of the stairs, her beauty marred by styled hair and a wedding dress. The company of guests and relations shuffled as Henry led his daughter into the living room, where Jason walked forward – shaved, washed, brushed and dressed in a brown suit. Then the Justice married them. Afterwards came congratulations from the bride's parents, grandparents and friends. There was no one present on the bridegroom's side.

Henry, the host and father, remained polite and benign throughout the reception that followed the ceremony. His face had been still as he heard Louisa's soft voice give assent to the powerful and absolute vows, but it relaxed again after that. It was towards the end of the reception, when Lilian went up to help her daughter change into a different dress and looked through the door of her own bedroom that she saw her husband, leaning against his chest-of-drawers, weeping into his hands.

8

The guests waved in the conventional way as Louisa and Jason
– Mr. and Mrs. Jones – left the reception and drove off to
Cape Cod in a rented car. A honeymoon had been arranged
for them in a weather-worn house on the beach, lent to the
young couple by friends of the Rutledges.

It was a bad wedding night – as bad as any. The weather
was cold, and though the house was heated its summer fur-
nishings gave an impression of discomfort. Jason, who had
been silent in the car as they drove down, slumped straight
into a cane chair when they arrived.

'I want to eat,' he said.

Louisa went to the fridge and took out some Strasbourg
pâté and Dom Perignon champagne that had been left there
for them with a little card by the friends whose house it was.
Jason glared at these delicacies when they were placed before him with slices of brown bread-and-butter.

'I can't eat that shit,' he said.

Louisa said nothing. That was all there was in the house.
She sat down on the other side of the table.

'What a load of crap, what a load of fucking crap,' said
Jason – not now referring to the victuals.

'Darling . . .' Louisa began.

'Please . . . *please* don't call me that.'

'OK,' she sighed.

'All those crass bastards. . . .'

Louisa was silent.

'Your fucking family. . . .'

'I know, I know,' she said, shrinking into her pretty cotton
dress. 'I'm sorry.'

'Now,' he said, 'now I know what it's like to be black. At
last I really know what it's like to be a coon.'

'Well, it's not my fault,' said Louisa, her voice rising.

'It's not your fault,' no,' said Jason, his voice whining with
affected irony. 'Except that they're your fucking family.'

'Your family weren't so great.'

'At least they didn't treat you like a bit of trash.'

'You imagine that.'

'The hell I do.'

'You just *want* them all to be like that.' She was angry now,
and tired. 'It was you who wanted to get married out here.

I'd have been happy to get married in any old city hall. But you're the one with a thing about the East Coast establishment – not me.'

'Yes,' said Jason bitterly, 'I had this thing about the East Coast . . . I *had* it. . . .'

Then, either because she was angry or because she did not want to hear any more, Louisa snatched up the bottle of champagne and went out onto the beach. It was dark and cold, but she went down to the water all the same. She fumbled at the wire and foil of the bottle but kept her eyes on the dim white of the waves. The cork blew off into the sea. She raised the bottle and drank from it, and as she brought it down again she started to cry. She stayed on the beach for half an hour or so until she was quite damp and cold. When she came back into the house she found that Jason had dropped off his suit and was asleep in the bed.

9

They returned to California after two days on Cape Cod without seeing her parents again, and Louisa rented a small house in the hills above Berkeley. Her allowance was apparently increased: they had quite enough money for rent, food, the Volkswagen and pot. She hoped that they might pick up now where they had left off – that the East Coast episode, their marriage even, might be forgotten. They talked and made love as before, but Jason never recovered the temporary solicitude he had shown in the weeks before they had married. In his head he seemed more knotted than ever.

Louisa put this out of her mind. She was delighted with the house, which had a garden and a kitchen in which she could cook with more daring and imagination than had been possible on Jason's hot-plate. The house was unfurnished, but its rooms were painted white and they brought up from Jason's room his mattress, posters and dancing Shiva. Louisa bought other furniture, including a bed for the mattress, and rugs and posters and put flowers in the house. She made what she thought was a very nice home, though she would admit to Jason – when he pointed it out to her – that it lacked the atmosphere of his red-walled room.

It was in this house, in June, that some communication arrived from the draft board in Iowa, forwarded by his father.

Jason looked white and afraid. 'Hell,' he said, 'they won't get me.'

Louisa saw that he was shaking. She went across to hug him, kiss him, and murmur that they would go to Canada or Europe, or have a baby, but he remained rigid. When, a week later, she told him that in all probability she was going to have a baby, his face twisted up even more.

'I hate it,' he said, 'all this...' and his hands waved in the air to indicate a vague notion of domesticity.

'But you want a baby, don't you?' Louisa asked. 'You won't get drafted.'

'Who in hell wants a baby?' he shouted at her. 'Sucking at your guts and then coming in here and carving into my life. I don't want it. I don't want anyone.' He then left the house and, taking the Volkswagen, drove off, leaving Louisa alone with the dinner she had cooked until late that night.

10

When Jason stayed away, as he did every now and then, Louisa knew that he was with Ned Rampton, who seemed the exception to his misanthropy. She never asked Jason where he had been, but she knew that this was where he went. It was also clear that his conversations with his friend calmed him down, for sometimes she would go with him into San Francisco to see them together. As soon as Jason set foot in Ned's loft, he seemed to relax. There followed then the long, slow conversations between the two men lasting so late into the night that Louisa found it hard to keep awake. But, driving home across the Bay Bridge, Jason would at least talk to her. 'It's the country,' he would say to her. 'It's this fucking America of ours. If I'd been born anywhere else, it'd be fine, just fine....'

'Yes,' said Louisa. 'I guess that's it.'

'Ned thinks we should go to Mexico. The Indians there... they just sit chewing peyote. No wars. No property. They're just high and beautiful from when they're born until they die.'

And sure enough they did leave Berkeley – but not for Mexico. Ned Rampton was evidently more important to Jason than his advice, because, after a night spent away from their home, Jason told Louisa that they were giving it up and going to live with Ned in San Francisco.

'No,' said Louisa, 'No, Jason, we won't. We can't.' She was horrified, feeling averse to her husband's friend but not daring to say so.

'Why the hell not? I'm sick and tired of driving back and forth and just at this moment I need Ned, I really do.'

'But,' said Louisa, 'but that loft's just one big room. We wouldn't even have a room of our own, would we?'

'We'd build a partition.'

'Can't he come here? I mean, we've at least got a spare room.'

'He can't come here to Berkeley. Hell, it's not him who needs me, Louisa, it's me who needs him.'

'No,' said Louisa, 'I just won't. I want to stay here. I've planted flowers and done all sorts of things.'

Jason shrugged. 'Well,' he said, 'It's your life. You stay if you want to, but I'm going.'

Now Louisa's distaste for Ned Rampton was strong, but it was insignificant in her own mind compared to her love for Jason Jones. She had also to admit to herself that she was uneasy about her husband's mind and so, when she saw that he was really determined to go, she agreed to go with him.

The loft in San Francisco was forty yards long and had concrete walls, floor and ceiling. It was on the fifth floor of a warehouse, and the floors beneath were still used for storing goods. The entrance was at one end: at the other, in one corner, there was a shower and a wash-basin, and opposite a kitchen sink and gas-cooker. The lavatory was down a flight of stairs. Ned moved his bed away from the entrance towards the kitchen end of the loft, so that Jason and Louisa could have some privacy. Between his bed and theirs he erected a shoulder-high wall of suitcases and cardboard cartons, and he 'wouldn't peep over' he said to Louisa and, for the first few days of their cohabitation, he kept his promise – even averting his eyes when she walked on the old carpets the length of the loft to the shower.

In the afternoons when she came back from her classes she kept to their end, by the entrance, and sat reading while Ned and Jason murmured together in soft voices about life. Louisa showed no interest in their discussions, which irritated Jason: he informed her of this, because it was a ground rule of Ned's way of life that everything should be said – spoken out frankly – lest it fester within.

Louisa replied – frankly and forthrightly – that she was not interested, that she did not need a new philosophy of life, that maybe America was poisoned, but she was not.

'But you are,' said Jason. 'We all are. We're all utterly corrupted by the system.'

'Unless,' said Ned, his heavy eyes turning onto his disciple, 'unless we get out of our own ego. Then we are liberated from ourselves and from our environment – America. We shed loose our scabs and squeeze out the poison.'

'That's it,' said Jason. 'That's it. If only. . . .' and he banged his fist into the palm of his hand.

Louisa shrugged her shoulders.

Ned's diagnosis of Jason's malaise was this: that he had had a personality foisted onto him by a corrupt society, a personality which was not 'him'. That was why he was so unhappy and dissatisfied with himself.

Louisa's opinion was a variant on this: 'Perhaps you'd like yourself a bit better if you didn't think about yourself so much.'

'But Louisa,' said Ned, 'you've only got yourself, that's all there is.'

The first measure of therapy which Ned proposed – whereby Jason's true self would be freed from its artificial form – was a medium dosage of the hallucinatory drug lysergic acid diethylamide.

Jason swallowed and clenched his fists.

'It's just like pot,' said Ned, 'only more so. I think that if you'd taken a trip earlier, you'd never have got yourself into this.'

'Yeah, OK,' said Jason.

'What do you think, Louisa?' Ned asked.

She shrugged. 'I don't know. I just hope he doesn't have a bad trip and jump out of the window.'

'He won't,' said Ned, 'because we'll both be here.'

'Yes.'

'Unless you'd like to go with him?'

'Uh-uh.' She shook her head.

Jason swallowed his lump of sugar at four in the afternoon. He started to shake, but Louisa gripped his hand and, in time, he relaxed. His eyes became glazed and his face assumed the beatific expression that had first attracted her to him. Later he rose and walked around the loft – as quiet and gay as a happy child. He spent more than half an hour rattling the door-handle. Then he went to the bookshelf and played his fingers up and down the spines of the books, as on a piano. After it was dark, he went to the window and looked out over the roofs to the small corner of the bay that was visible through them – to the line of lights on the other side.

'Look,' he said to the others, 'look at the lights.'

'Yes, Jason, they're lovely lights,' said Ned.

Louisa was bored.

Jason noticed this and came up to her. 'You', he said, 'you don't care.'

'I do, Jason darling, I do.'

'Don't *call* me that.'

'She loves you, Jason. She loves you very much,' said Ned. 'She loves you more than anything.'

Jason turned away from them both. Louisa turned to Ned with an expression of some kind of gratitude.

'I've got a few goodies for us too,' he said, smiling, and bringing from his pocket a tobacco-pouch. 'Real Mexican super-hash.'

They both went and sat on Ned's bed and rolled cigarettes, smoking pot into the night, keeping their vigil over the far-gone, themselves half on the way. But, even in her placid intoxication, Louisa felt some irritation at the monotonous journey of Ned's eyes up and down her body.

11

The night passed. Jason came back from his trip, swearing it had been a success, a liberation, but outwardly as morose as ever. There were more interminable talks with Ned and at the end of the week he came to Louisa, as she lay waiting for him in bed, with the proposition that she should spend that night with Ned.

Louisa frowned, very slightly, constraining her immediate reaction of disgust, no longer free within herself to express her feelings to her husband. 'But I don't want to, Jason,' she said, slowly and quietly, conscious that Ned could probably hear them from the other side of the barricade.

'I think,' said Jason, 'I think you should.'

'It's you I love,' said Louisa.

'Look,' he said, his face tightening like a cow that feels grit in its cud, 'you've got to get off this suffocating you-me thing. It's very, very nasty.' He paused. 'We're all part of the same big ... big ... thing. You've got to be peaceful and passive and relaxed and just float into it. You love me. OK. That's fine. But it's not enough. You've got to love other people, and Ned is there, and he wants you. You know he wants you. He's in *pain* because he wants you, so how can you *deny* him ...?'

'Jason,' said Louisa, in slow, definite tones. 'Jason, I'm expecting your baby.'

The tightness became a frown. '*My* baby? It's not my baby, Louisa, because I don't have anything that's mine. I'm all over that primitive, ownership thing. It's evil, Louisa. It's the basis of all evil – that ugly, possessive ... thing. That's the extermination of Indians. That's Vietnam. Having and keeping and grasping. If you've got something, you should give it: and you have got something. You've got your body. You gave it to me: now let Ned have it for a time. You've got to, you've got to. ...'

He said this last, looking strangely into her eyes.

'I don't know if ... I could, Jason,' said Louisa.

'Then get out of here,' he said, 'because I can't stand ... any more ... people ... you ... if they're not free from all that ugliness and all the poison. ...'

Louisa said nothing: she was stretched away from Jason, at the edge of the mattress, almost on the floor, staring not at him but at the blankets between them.

'Go on,' he said. 'You go. Get out. Go back to where you belong.'

She stood in her night-dress.

'Go back to your father and mother, and their house and their pictures and books and objects. ...'

She stood back, hovering at the edge of their corner of the loft. Her eyes, wide open, looked at the suitcase she would have to pack; and through her mind passed images of their empty house, of aeroplanes, airports, her parents and Jason as no more than a memory. At this she opened her mouth to speak again, but she saw her husband crouched, self-absorbed, meditating with a contorted face. Thus she brought her lips together again without uttering a further sound: she turned and walked down the loft, away from him.

Ned lay on his bed reading. He looked up at Louisa as she came: 'That's right,' he said, 'that's right!' He took her hand and she knelt down at his side feeling dizzy and cold and sick.

'It's winter for you now,' he whispered to her as he touched her first, 'but in spring you'll bud, you'll see, and in summer you'll blossom.'

She was undressed and he smothered her body with his alien smell and consistency; his panting breath was loud, loud enough for Jason to hear its quickening, and she gave some sort of cry as he entered her, but thereafter she was silent, and she wished he would be – for the sake of her husband.

12

Louisa awoke in the morning. Her mind fought for some moments to ward off consciousness but all at once it came upon her and she held her breath as she sensed the sleeping form next to her. Then she slipped out of bed and stood naked next to it, wondering if Jason was there, wanting to rush to him but convinced, in some irrational faculty, of her own guilt. So she retrieved her nightdress from the bedclothes, pulled it over her body and went to the stove. She brewed coffee, standing there, watching the flame on the aluminium, waiting for the water to rise and splash against the small glass window at the top of the pot. Only when the coffee was made did she dare to go beyond the trunks and packing-cases – as if to tell her husband that it was ready. He was not there.

She went quickly to Ned, who was waking.

'He's gone,' she said.

'Don't worry,' said Ned. 'He'll be back.'

They sat at the kitchen table drinking coffee and at nine Jason came in. 'I just went out,' he said, with a shrug. He looked tired and drawn, but there was no telling how long he had been out and Louisa did not dare to ask. The three of them sat together in silence, drinking coffee. The frankness, the openness, which was once the way of the two men in the loft, was suddenly gone. There was no mention of the night before: no discussion of the various, adjusted, relationships. Louisa looked at Jason many times, as a prelude to talking to him, but his face was now quite closed to her.

The three of them went to a movie in the afternoon. Louisa cooked curry for supper and after that she returned to Ned's bed as if there were no question about it. The lamp went off on Jason's side of the barricade, and Ned took from his shelf a copy of *The Kama Sutra of Vatsyayana* 'I want you to read this,' he said to Louisa in soft, serious tones. 'It's a kind of

Hindu book of sex instruction, but it was written fifteen hundred years ago.'

She took it: it fell open in the centre of the volume where the pages had been well pressed down.

'It's just what we need in the West,' said Ned, 'as an antidote to the repression we have in us all after two thousand years of Christianity. I think ... I think, if we went through some of these rituals and positions, it might waken you up to a new kind of awareness and help you with some of those New England hang-ups.'

There was nothing but seriousness in his tone of voice. Louisa looked up at the massive man above her, at the sagging stomach covered with black hair to be seen through his open pyjamas. He leant down and took the book from her.

'People,' he said, 'sexually speaking, are divided into types. Now you, I'd say, are a mare, and I know I'm a horse, which makes us what's called a high union. . . .'

He lay down beside her. Louisa edged away but, with a gesture of impatience, Ned took hold of her and there began her education in Hindu copulation.

13

The next morning Jason was gone again, and he did not return that night. Ned and Louisa did not mention his absence to each other, but the *Kama Sutra* was put back on its shelf and they slept.

Three days later Jason still had not returned and in the afternoon Louisa found herself alone in the loft. She dithered for a time, uncertain of what to do, but eventually, around five, she drove in the Volkswagen to Berkeley. The house was empty: Jason had not been there. She drove back to the campus and parked the car. She then walked around the streets, looking into shops and drugstores where she thought she might find her husband. She did find him. He passed her in the street. He saw her, recognized her, and passed on. Louisa stopped and turned but did not cry out or follow him.

She was back in the loft when Ned returned in the evening. 'I've got to lose this baby,' she said, 'I mean. . . .'

Ned stretched out his large hand and felt the small, hard growth in her stomach. 'Yes, well, I guess it can be arranged.'

'Can you?'

'The money . . . that's all it needs.'

'I've got that.'

'Then it's off to Mexico,' he said. 'It's as simple as that.'

They drove down California, around Los Angeles, then across to Arizona. It was July now, and hot. They stayed in motels on the way, sweating together at their lessons in sexual technique: by the time they reached the Mexican border at Nogales they were well on with the Congress of the Crow. From there they only had to drive a hundred miles south to a village beyond Magdalena. There, amidst the peasant hovels, was a clean, well-equipped clinic. A polite doctor, speaking precise English and wearing a clean, white coat, took care of Louisa – showing her first to the office where she paid her thousand dollars in cash, and then to a private room where she changed into a hospital smock.

Ned waited in the village for the two days they kept her there – they were careful and thorough – procuring what marijuana he could find. When it was all over, he fetched Louisa and drove her north again, back into the United States. They spent a night in Tucson, and there Ned asked Louisa where she wanted to go.

'Where? I . . . I hadn't thought.'

'If you want to drive east, just take me to the airport.'

'No,' she said, 'No. I'd like to come with you . . . if you'd like me to.'

'Sure,' said Ned. 'Sure I do. There's a lot of nice things you've still got to learn. Baby, soon you'll really *blossom* out.'

She did blossom, as the summer went on, in the way he meant the word. The girl's modesty and timidity – to him, her inhibitions – were sucked out of her like the pap of a fruit until their sexual exchanges obsessed her as much as they did her instructor. She played at it and talked about it with the same coy glee. She eyed him in company with a gross complicity, and discussed all other subjects in his puny vocabulary of venereal and hallucinatory metaphor.

But after the summer comes autumn – the real season coinciding this time with the symbolic. Louisa returned to the loft one afternoon to find Ned and another girl on his bed, *The Kama Sutra of Vatsyayana* open beside them. And in the frank and open discussion of their relationship that the three of them had afterwards, it was agreed that the thing between Ned and Louisa was over, so she might as well move out. The lease on the house in Berkeley had terminated; Jason was gone; and it was thus, just a year after she had first come to California, that Louisa returned home to the East Coast.

14

Henry and Lilian had heard little from Louisa during the summer, and were confused by her unheralded arrival in Cambridge. She told them, with no explanation, that she and Jason had broken up and that she had dropped out of the University of California. The parents, in their perplexity, could not bring themselves to ask why to either of these statements.

'What do you want to do now?' was the only thing Henry could think of to say.

'I guess I'll get a job in Boston or something,' said Louisa, 'and perhaps go back to college next year.'

'Well,' said Henry, 'This is your home. You can stay here as long as you like.'

'Thanks,' said Louisa, 'but I think I'll get an apartment.'

'If you want help with a job . . .' Henry began.

'No,' said Louisa sharply, 'no thanks. I want to do it on my own.'

Though she would not come to her parents for advice, Louisa did deign to use them for the purpose of gathering information. She found an apartment in Boston, but then called her mother to ask about a divorce.

'They're difficult in Massachusetts,' said Lilian. 'You should have stopped off in Nevada.'

'Yes,' said Louisa. 'I guess I could go back, though. Before getting a job.'

Two days later she received a letter from her father's lawyers explaining just how to set about obtaining a divorce, in the states of Nevada and Idaho. The only requirement was three weeks' residence. She had by then, and on her own initiative, started to visit, twice a week, a psychiatrist in Cambridge, Dr. Fisher. She talked a lot and he listened and agreed, mostly, with her ideas on what had gone wrong in her relationship with Jason, Lilian, Ned. . . .

With a certain weariness, at the end of September, she went yet again to the airport and took a plane to New York, and from there to Reno. The flight was going on to San Francisco, and she clenched her fists for fear she might find herself there again. She did not, however, but descended at Reno just as she wanted to be – alone, independent, taking the strands of her shredded life and knotting and weaving them together again. She checked in at a modest hotel and, next morning, filed her application for a divorce. Then she sat down to wait. On the third day she took a trip to Lake Tahoe, and walked along the edge of the water, returning to Reno that night. After the end of the first week, she heard from the lawyers in Reno that Jason had been located and would not contest the divorce. There was no comment on how or where he was, and she felt no curiosity. She spent the mornings and after-noons reading novels and the evenings watching television. The lady at the desk of the hotel was quite friendly – full of stories of girls waiting for a divorce: otherwise Louisa was alone.

It was on the evening of the tenth day that she suddenly felt the urge to see a movie – an urge whose power alarmed her, for there was more to it than her dissatisfaction with the entertainment provided on the smaller screen of the television. Between five and six, she walked up and down in her room. twisting her hands together, trying to remain where she was: but the arguments for going out seemed strong. She would get some fresh air, and could look at the stills outside the cinemas to see if there was anything worth seeing.

The air was cool, the streets flashing with lights and sounds. She stopped in front of the cinemas and looked blankly at the posters, but her mind was on the pounding of her heart. At the third cinema, she paid for her admission and went in. She sat down and faced towards the screen, taking nothing in. Then, gradually, her face turned and she looked around her and saw, in the row behind her, a man. It was not too dark to tell his age or kind, but she looked at him more than once as if to make something out: and, as if to assist her, this man left his seat and came round and sat next to her. Louisa did not look at him, but when his hand came onto her lap she gripped it and covered it as it went under her skirt.

Some minutes later they both left the cinema. Still she did not look at his face, but led him back to her hotel and, when they were in her room, she clutched him to her maniacally and moaned and begged until he stripped and fucked her.

Then, after a moment of quiet, her eyes opened. He was black, and he caught his breath and said 'Wow.' She could not move her body because he was still on it, but she turned her head and opened her mouth, hoping to be sick on the pillow.

She was not, so she said 'Please go': and he did, zipping up his fly and humming. 'Any time, ma'am,' he said as he left.

The days that were left were a painful load to be born until she was free of Jason: but it was carried easily since she knew it was to be lifted from her – that in the dissolution of that marriage would also be dissolved that episode in her life, that aspect of her personality.

Thus when she felt again, after five days, that compulsion which shook her body – the need, as she described it to herself, to 'find a buck', to have herself besmirched and split and sated by any man she could find – she gave in to it leniently. She knew that in another week it would all be over.

15

She was happy as she flew back to Boston, and she went the next day to Sunday lunch with her family in Brattle Street. She was still guarded with Henry and Lilian, though much kinder than she had been for a year or so. She talked with Laura after lunch and warned her, with the full authority of an older sister, not to fool around with acid.

That evening she went back to her apartment in Boston and on the Monday went to see Dr. Fisher to tell him that she felt a whole lot better after the divorce and was happy to be living on her own and had only to find a job for everything to be perfect.

On the Thursday afternoon she had nothing much to do so she put on a record and sat down to read a book. Her body was no sooner settled, however, than she felt within it what she had hoped never to feel again. She tried to read: she tried to listen to the music, but neither her eyes nor her ears were a match for the flawed instinct which welled up in her and drew them and all her other senses into its vortex.

She stood. She walked up and down the room. Her hands gripped and twisted together as if trying to hold her there but she could not help herself. She left her flat and went walking in the streets of Boston until she saw a man she thought might meet her needs whom she followed onto the Common.

Part Four

1

There were seven students in Professor Rutledge's seminar on Political Theory. They were all third-year students, except for Danny Glinkman who was in his second year and Alan Gray, the Jesuit priest, who was reading for a higher degree.

The seven had been chosen from more than a hundred applicants from Harvard and Radcliffe: in consequence, they were all particularly intelligent and well-informed in this branch of their studies. Their intelligence, varied, of course, so did their levels of maturity. Danny was, perhaps, the most brilliant among them: his mind however was like an ungeared motor, turning at high speed but pulling no load. The priest, on the other hand, had an extra decade of experience with which to temper the inspirations of his intellect: and the Mexican-American, Julius Tate, though only twenty-one, showed a judiciousness in his approach to the subject equal to that of the priest.

The physical appearance of Julius Tate reinforced this quality of mind. He was tall with straight, heroic features and strong, graceful limbs. All this, with a melancholy mouth, black hair, dark skin and the flash in his eyes was enough to confuse the two girls in the seminar, Debbie Cooper and Kate Williams, and though they recovered their composure after the first two or three sessions, they listened throughout the term to his few words with double the attention they accorded to Danny's heated stream of brilliance.

What five of the members of the seminar had in common – the priest, Alan Gray, Julius, Danny and the two girls – was a radical point of view. Julius and Danny both belonged to the Harvard chapter of the Students For a Democratic Society. Alan had, at first, tried to disguise his own views as just sympathy for revolutionaries: but, as the term progressed and the seminar, which followed no formal order of study, left Hobbes and jumped to Marx and Mao Tse-tung, this sympathy spilled over into undisguised advocacy of revolution which surprised Henry Rutledge since he had heard of such priests but never met one.

Radical is a loose term for even these five students, since Americans do not categorize themselves as readily as Europeans. The girls, for example, represented quite different aspects of what might be called progressive views.

Kate Williams was from Maine and in her general character was conservative. She dressed neatly and might have belonged to a sorority, had there been one at Radcliffe. Her father, like Lilian's, was a judge, and one could imagine that he was, or had been, a liberal himself. Kate's views were no more than extreme liberalism – agitation on behalf of the victim, whoever he was. If she had reached her present age five or so years before, she would certainly have been among those who went into the Deep South to agitate on behalf of the blacks: as it was, she did it for the draft-dodgers and war-resisters in Cambridge.

Debbie Cooper, on the other hand, was an anarchist more than anything else, and believed in a freedom which far transcended any political context. She was plump and voluptuous, and doubtless was easily persuaded to be free with all that. She was as much against the laws against drugs as she was against conscription: these two issues could be coupled together so far as she was concerned and thrown in with the Mann Act, the police, Hitler, Stalin and the State laws against abortion, as a corpus of totalitarianism which she, Debbie Cooper, was definitely against.

The two students who were not caught up in this wide net of the Left were Mike Hamerton and Sam Fowler. It was not that these two were right-wing: theorists of fascism or even conservatism were not to be found in Cambridge – hardly, indeed, in the North-East. Mike Hamerton did, as it happened, come from Chicago, and he felt some disdain for his weird contemporaries at Harvard, not, however, because they were radical but because they were hot and neurotic. He thought that Political Theory should be a branch of mathematics: he was majoring in maths and his stated ambition was to go into computers. He believed, calmly, that there was nothing these contemporary counting-beads could not achieve in all fields of human endeavour. If he studied political thought, and took courses in Art History and Philosophy, it was only so that one day he could programme a team of computers to come up with the definitive political system, work of art and philosophical truth.

Mike was thin: his hair was sparse and his face pockmarked, but this unprepossessing appearance did not diminish his self-confidence. He sat at the back of the room and, when he spoke, he spoke clearly and with the exactness of the computers he so admired.

Finally there was Sam Fowler who, in terms of Left and Right, was *hors catégorie* because he was black. He was particularly conscious of being the only black in the seminar, and reserved a mildly hostile tone for all the others except Julius, who was brown. Many conflicts went on behind his proud eyes as he sat at the back of the room in the opposite corner to Mike Hamerton. They were betrayed, to a degree, only when it came to his turn to write a paper (on Plekhanov) and read it to the seminar, for he demonstrated a superb talent for analysis and exposition, warmed by a concern for the humanitarian content of political ideas but spoiled, ultimately, by an unnatural forcing of every concept to the parochial plight of his black brothers in the United States.

This at any rate, was Henry Rutledge's evaluation of his single Negro. He once pointed out to Sam, politely, that not all the exploited in the world's history were Negroes.

'No,' said Sam vehemently, 'but here, and now, they are.' Then he added: 'and brown,' with a look of uncertain camaraderie towards Julius.

Julius shrugged and said: 'Yes ... I mean professor, you've got to admit that.'

And the professor admitted it and the class agreed, and the subject was dropped.

The relationship of this class with their professor was a curious one, for he was a liberal and they all, for different reasons, would call his liberalism complacent or hypocritical or unrealistic. And not only did Henry Rutledge hold certain ideas which they all condemned, he was also, in America at large, their most celebrated protagonist. At least he had been. By the fall term of 1967 he was more cautious and academic, discussing the political thought of others rather than pronouncing any of his own. Nevertheless, a professor must comment, and his comment remained what it had always been, a description of the error of all systems that were not democratic in the Western sense. It might be questioned, then, how it was that his students, most of them revolutionaries, came to his class at all: and when they were there, listened to him with an attentiveness that could almost be called respect.

The answer lay in his manner, for he practised a kind of self-effacing friendliness that caught his students unawares, in the seminar as well as in the lecture hall. They had all imagined, for instance, that the famous Professor Rutledge, millionaire and class-mate of Senator Laughlin, would expect a lion's share of the talking-time; but when a session of the seminar came to an end, it would invariably be found that he had talked very little; that Danny had said most, or that Kate, who was shy, had been coaxed into giving her views while the professor held back his own.

This kindness and tolerance might not have been enough to beguile the more militant: but there was a further quality which the young sniffed out like pigs after truffles and which the priest, too, came to recognize and admire. This was the small opening in his mind through which he was prepared to admit new ideas, even those which conflicted with his own opinions. The gap was indeed small: like most men of his age he had made up his mind on the world, and was reluctant to upset it; but while the majority of his contemporaries – those who, in the view of Danny and Debbie and Julius Tate – now governed America would ignore or deny facts which did not fit their theory, persisting in their errors to the misfortune of those who were the subject of their policies, Henry Rutledge, the ideologist of this establishment, would consider and ponder such facts, patiently considering the revolutionary hypothesis, never contradicting but only asking questions to expose the snag.

There came a session of the seminar, however, when this chink in his mind seemed to have widened – indeed, to have opened so wide that the light it let in dazzled him. In the previous class they had talked about Adam Smith, and the professor had diverted their attention from Smith's political thought to his moral philosophy. There had been some exchange between Henry and Alan Gray, who was informed on *The Theory of Moral Sentiments;* then they had returned to the political and economic aspects of the subject, but thereafter the teacher had been distracted and had left the discussion entirely in the hands of his pupils.

Most of them ascribed this to an 'off day'. They hardly mentioned it amongst themselves as they dispersed after the session: only Kate said to Debbie that the professor looked unwell. But at the next session, which was to have been on Bakunin, the professor looked even worse, white and distracted, and seemed unable to concentrate on what anyone was saying. None of them knew as yet about his daughter's attempt to kill herself. Danny knew the family, but it was a long time since he had seen the professor outside his rooms at Harvard.

There arose an atmosphere of embarrassment in the seminar and eventually Alan, the abrupt, thick-set, close-cropped priest, asked the professor if he would not like them to go.

'No,' said Henry Rutledge. And then he added: 'Why?'

'You don't look well, sir,' said Alan.

'No,' said Henry quickly. 'It's all right. I'm not ill.'

They went on for a while about Bakunin, but then Henry suddenly interrupted Julius, who was reading the paper, with the question, 'What's the use?'

The barometer of embarrassment, which was Debbie's fidgeting buttocks, Mike's doodling pen and Kate's stillness, rose at once as the older man facing them behaved at variance to his norm. The question was general, not directed at Julius: its delivery was violent, not polite. Henry Rutledge had lost his reflex charm.

'What do you mean, professor?' asked Alan.

'I mean,' said Henry, his body shaking 'I mean, what's the use of learning about Bakunin or Marx. It'll never come to anything.'

Sam Fowler's eyes widened: the white man had lost his cool.

'Well, I'm *majoring* in Political Theory,' said Debbie, worried suddenly about her credits if the course was to come to an end.

Henry's twitching face relaxed a little and he smiled at the girl. 'I meant,' he said, trying to recover from his outburst and make it seem normal, 'I meant to question the ... practical application of anything that we learn. What effect can it have on our lives?'

'You learn facts,' said Mike, after a silence. 'And you form opinions.'

'And your opinions govern your actions,' said Julius. 'At least, they should.'

'They should, yes,' said the professor, 'but I can tell you that they don't. I've been teaching Political Theory for twenty years, and America isn't one jot less rotten than it ever was ... nor is it likely to be.'

The class that had started to relax was electrified again, not with embarrassment but with excitement: their professor had never called America rotten before.

'You're young,' he said, 'but, believe me, kids like you leave this class every year and they know it all, or they should know it all, but nothing happens. Our society goes deeper into every known kind of evil mess. . . .'

'You *said* it,' said Danny amazed at this sudden light in his professor's mind.

'It's a mistake I'd like you to avoid,' said Henry, 'but I dare say you won't. You'll convince yourselves that theory and action are quite different things. If you do that, you'll get trapped in the academic world and lose every chance of affecting real political power.'

'But I thought,' said Kate, 'that you did have some power.'

'How, then?'

'With Senator Laughlin,' she said, embarrassed.

Henry stared hard at her. 'Not at all,' he said. 'I used to decorate his band-wagon, that's all. Why, if I had had any influence, that man wouldn't be the reactionary he is today.'

2

It was clear to Alan that his professor's expression of such an opinion was prompted by something more than the belated conclusion that he had been wrong all his life. The communistic priest had thought for some time that Henry Rutledge might not be a happy man: he had deduced it from the man's known belief in those American values which were turning so sour at the time. When that session of the seminar was over – Julius' essay on Bakunin was left unfinished – Alan remained behind. He went up to the professor and asked him whether he should prepare his paper on Proudhon for the following week, or whether they would go back to Bakunin.

Henry's eyes hovered over the priest's face – his mind finding it difficult to concentrate on the question. 'I don't know. . . .' he said. 'Yes . . . no, we'll let Julius finish first.'

'OK,' said Alan and he made as if to go, afraid to seem curious yet anxious for the professor – the priest's reflex to provide comfort if he could. 'You wouldn't have time for some coffee, would you, professor?' he asked suddenly.

'Sure,' said Henry, almost automatically, and they walked together out into the darkening, autumn afternoon, and crossed the campus to the Faculty Club.

'I've never really understood,' said Henry, who seemed to

have recovered, tentatively, his self-possession, 'why you want to study political theory at all?'

'It's not so far from theology,' said Alan, and the two men laughed.

'How do your superiors like the idea?'

'Well, they pay the fees.'

'Then they don't disapprove?'

'Perhaps they're just glad to get me out of the way.'

'I dare say . . . with your ideas.'

They sat down in the comfortable chairs of the Faculty Club and drank their coffee.

'You got the kids very excited this afternoon,' said Alan.

'Did I?' Henry smiled. He was slightly ill at ease with the priest, either because he was a priest who wore a black suit and a dog-collar, or because there were fewer years between them than he was used to with his students.

'Certainly you did,' said the priest. 'Kids of that age don't really believe in their own ideas themselves, I should say. They're just trying them on. To hear someone like you come out and *agree* with them. . . .'

'I hardly remember what I said,' Henry replied.

'Well, you said that Senator Laughlin was a reactionary.'

Henry laughed. 'I hope they won't quote me in the *Crimson*.'

'It'll be *The New York Times* or nothing,' said Father Gray. They both laughed again.

'But you're not a child,' said Henry. 'You're not just trying them on, are you . . . your ideas?'

'No,' said Alan. 'No. I believe in them.'

'How do you . . .? I've never asked you before, but Communism and Catholicism are usually considered to be contradictory beliefs.'

'Yes,' said Alan, admitting this, 'but they're not.'

'Well,' said Henry, 'Marx was an atheist.'

'Yes, I know. And most Communists are. But I think that that's fortuitous. I'd say they think you have to deny God to see a meaning in history: but Christ used history, didn't he? The history of the Jews, anyway.'

'Yes . . . yes, indeed.'

'I see Communism as a political science, professor, not as a religious belief.'

Henry nodded. 'Yes,' he said. 'Yes, I see how you do it.' He adjusted himself in his chair. 'And I think certain precepts apply to both, don't you? Such as self-knowledge. Christ enjoined it, so does Mao Tse-tung.'

'It's important,' said Alan.

'It wasn't aimed at you. I was thinking more of myself, when I was your age, when I had very strong ideas of what was practical or Utopian or reactionary; but in fact our notions of all these things tend to come back to the subjective circumstances of our lives.'

The priest nodded.

'I mean,' said Henry, 'it's easier for a priest or a hobo to be a Communist than it is for a millionaire.'

'Yes,' said Father Gray, 'I guess it is.'

'But then, sooner or later, it catches up on you. You're made to see that your idea of scientific truth isn't scientific truth at all.'

'So you say to yourself – what's the use?'

Henry looked at the priest and nodded. 'Yes. And really, what *is* the use? This endless teaching of kids who just go on and teach more teachers in their turn: and then, in the end, you find that what you've taught them is all wrong anyway.'

'The test of theory ought to be action.'

'Exactly and if, after all our teaching, the pupil goes out into the world and falls flat on his face in the first year. . . .'

Father Gray was silent, because he did not understand who it was the professor was referring to.

Henry went on; his voice became thick and strained. 'Did you ever work in a parish?' he asked.

'For two years in New York.'

'Did you ever hear of a girl who went out to pick up men? Older men? And take them back to her apartment?'

'Yes,' said Father Gray. 'It happened.'

'Why? Why did they do that?'

'Different reasons, I guess.'

'But it's abnormal, isn't it? I mean, boys going after girls . . . that's one thing. But a girl . . . and a middle-aged barman . . .'

'There's usually something wrong in the family.'

'What though?'

'It depends on the family.'

There was silence for a moment between the two men. The priest did not like to pursue the conversation nor did he feel that he should change the subject. He just watched Henry Rutledge's hands as they twisted together.

'Have you ever met my daughter Louisa?' Henry asked at last.

'No . . . no, I haven't.'

'She tried to . . . well, kill herself, last week . . . and . . .', the professor heaved himself up and sighed, 'and we thought she'd been raped, but it emerged . . .' he tried to smile but his expression disintegrated further, and he finished his sentence only with effort, '. . . it emerged that she was the one who had . . . made the proposition to this . . . this slob . . . this middle-aged bum.'

Alan said nothing. He just sat quite still and waited for the other man to speak or keep silent.

'You just don't know,' said Henry, with a shrug of despair. 'You just don't know how, or why, it got to this. It must be something we did wrong . . . as you say, there's usually something wrong in the family. . . .'

'Yes,' said the priest, 'but it used to be factors such as poverty and overcrowding.' He smiled. 'I guess that's not what it was in her case.'

'No,' said Henry, his expression remaining serious, introspective and preoccupied. 'I don't really know what it was.' He looked up at Alan. 'I hope you don't mind this . . . this confession?'

The priest shook his head.

'We're really an average family,' said Henry, 'behind all that public image. 'I'm not trying to evade my responsibility for what has happened to Louisa, but I don't think her trouble is unique. I know two or three other girls in Cambridge who were divorced before they were twenty. . . .'

'She's divorced?'

'Yes. And she only married six months ago '

'Who did she marry?'

Henry sighed. 'Some Californian dropout. Your average, confused hippie. There was nothing special about him.'

Alan thought for a moment, then said, 'I would agree with you, professor . . . it's a social phenomenon.'

'I wish,' said Henry, 'I wish I could understand it.' He took up his cup and drank some of the coffee, now cool. The young priest followed suit.

'Do you?' asked Henry.

'No, not entirely.'

'Which category does it fall into? Politics or religion?'

'Politics, I'd say.'

'She's not a sinner?'

'Well,' said Alan, smiling again, 'you never know.'

'You mean she might just be depraved. . . .?'

'It's unlikely. Depravity doesn't happen just like that.'

'Unless it's inherited.'

'Congenital depravity?'

'Why not?'

Alan shook his head. 'No. We all get a fresh start.'

'You're talking of morals now, not science.'

'Perhaps.'

'If she's not a sinner, then what is she? A lunatic?'

'No, 'said Alan. 'A casualty.'

'Of what?'

'Of a . . .' Alan hesitated. 'What did you call it this afternoon? A rotten society?'

'Yes.'

There followed one of those silences that take place when only two people talk together: then Henry said: 'You've got things clear in your head, haven't you?'

'Yes,' said Alan simply. 'Just now I have. They may get muddled again.'

'I guess I was clear-headed once,' said Henry.

'And will be again, perhaps?'

'Maybe.'

Their coffee was finished: neither wanted more, nor did they wish to end their conversation. Henry hesitated, however, to continue his sceptic's interrogation of the sure.

'You come down to it in the end, don't you?' he said eventually. 'What can we do about this rottenness of our society?'

'As a citizen, do you mean?'

'As citizen and political scientist?'

'Well, just like a doctor. You diagnose the disease and prescribe the cure.'

'What's your diagnosis?'

'The capitalist system.'

'And your cure?'

'Revolution.'

3

Henry Rutledge asked his wife whether they ought not to cancel their party, arranged for the middle of October.

'Because of Louisa, you mean?' she asked.

'Yes,' said Henry, glancing up to the ceiling of the kitchen where they stood as if afraid that the subject of their conversation might hear them.

'No, I don't think so ... unless you're frightened of unleashing her among your students.'

Henry did not wince at this, as he might have done: 'No, it's not that. I just don't want to drive her out of the house if she doesn't feel like seeing a lot of people.'

Lilian said nothing and, as the two adults pondered the question, Laura breezed in and went to the fridge to pour herself a glass of milk.

'Hey,' said Lilian, 'you're the interpreter around here. How do you think your sister would react to a party for her father's egghead students?'

'Like we always have?'

'Yes.'

'I guess she wouldn't mind.'

'You'd better ask her.'

Laura shrugged. 'She's not in.'

'Ask her later, then.'

'Where is she?' asked Henry.

'With Dr. Fisher, I guess.'

'Her fifty-dollar friend,' said Lilian.

'Perhaps he's the one to ask,' said Henry.

It was Louisa herself who asked her psychiatrist, after Laura had put the question to her.

'Well, how do you feel about it?' asked Dr. Fisher, sitting in his black-leather button-backed chair while Louisa sat looking out of the window of his opulent consulting room.

'I don't know,' she said: then she smiled. 'I might try to pick up one of his students.'

'You might, yes.'

'I mean, if it's true what you say, that I'm just trying to hurt Dad for preferring Mother to me, then it's likely, isn't it, that I might rape one of his students in our living room.'

'I doubt it, though,' said Dr. Fisher, mistrustful of Louisa's ebullience that morning.

'Kill or cure,' she said, laughing.

Fisher glanced at her nervously.

'I expect it'll be cure,' she went on. 'I feel so good right now, I don't know if I even need to go on seeing you.'

She turned and smiled at him. She was indeed looking well, fresh-faced and lively, in spite of her broken rib.

'You said that before, Louisa,' said Dr. Fisher, gently scratching the smooth skin over his jaw.

'Yes, I do know,' said Louisa, looking down darkly at her lap. 'But then it was a kind of calm before the storm.'

'And now?'

'Well, now it may be too, but at least I know what to expect.'

'What do you expect?'

'Sudden gusts of lust, I guess.' She gave an almost mocking smile at her psychiatrist.

Dr. Fisher heaved himself up in his chair and glanced at Louisa's long legs. 'I really wouldn't advise you to ... to at-attach yourself to a student,' he said.

'Better than a truck driver.'

'Not much. You need a more stable relationship. . . .'

She did indeed feel better, to be teasing Dr. Fisher who, she knew, was going to say next, as he did: '. . . with some mature and understanding man. . . .' meaning himself, but not daring to spell it out or make a pass because it would be against professional ethics, and an unstable girl like Louisa might, just possibly, report him, *post coitum*, instead of doing herself in.

'And you'd feel sick at yourself afterwards,' said Dr. Fisher.

'That's what I've got to get over,' said Louisa. 'All that guilt.'

'Yes, well, you have to do that too, but you shouldn't put yourself in a position of feeling guilty until you're sure you know how to manage it.'

'Practice makes perfect,' said Louisa.

Dr. Fisher glanced up at the electric clock on the wall, Louisa's hour was up. He did not like to leave her in this flip-pant mood, but Mrs. Furenstein would be waiting.

'Will you promise to ... er ... to wait until after next Thurs-day?'

Louisa stood up. 'To please you, Dr. Fisher, I promise.'

She smiled. He sighed and shrugged and showed her out.

4

Louisa told Laura, who told their parents that they could go ahead with the party: she even started to look forward to it. She was, after all, only nineteen – young enough to begin again as the professor's daughter, flirting in her party-dress with his handsome students. She went so far as to accompany her mother into Boston to Bonwit Teller's and ask her advice about a new dress. Lilian was amenable to this daughterly approach and did not notice the touch of cynical self-mockery in Louisa's choice of childish styles.

'It's too young,' she said, as her daughter held out a pink-and-white pinafore dress. 'Anyway, you'd look terrible in it.'

'What do you suggest then?' asked Louisa.

Lilian went through a row of dresses on the rack, ignoring the advice of the woman who was trying to serve them. 'This,' said Lilian at last, pulling out a simple dress – grey and clean-cut.

'Widow's weeds,' said Louisa.

'Highly suitable,' said Lilian.

Louisa blushed. 'OK,' she said.

The dress had no sleeves and when worn over a blue silk blouse, as it was on the night of the party, it made Louisa seem that Lilian thought she had best make herself out to be – a girl who was young but experienced. She came down from her bedroom wearing it when one or two of the guests had already arrived – Alan Gray, the priest, and Mr. and Mrs. Weldon, neighbours of the Rutledges insufficiently eminent for the second party nearer Christmas.

'Why, Louisa,' said Mrs. Weldon, 'how nice. I thought you were in California.'

'No,' said Louisa and nothing more.

Henry came forward. 'Louisa,' he said, 'this is Father Gray. He's in my seminar.'

'Call me Alan, please,' said the priest, shaking her by the hand.

Louisa looked up and noticed the purposeful look in his eyes: she ascribed it to his odd profession.

'You're in the seminar?' she asked shortly.

'Yes,' said Alan.

Louisa said nothing else, but moved across the room to get a drink from Laura. 'He's a bit old, isn't he?' she whispered to her younger sister.

'Who?'

'That priest.'

'You get old students sometimes, I guess.'

'Spooky.'

They both laughed. Louisa sipped at her orange-juice. In

spite of her clothes, she felt herself getting younger and younger, slipping back into her childhood, as if she were high.

'I hope they're not all priests and middle-aged,' she said to Laura.

'You wait,' said Laura, smiling.

'Have you met any of them?'

Laura nodded.

'Have you *dated* any?'

'Uh-uh,' said Laura, which meant no. 'But there's one I think you'll like. He's really a dish.'

'Not him?' asked Louisa as Mike Hamerton entered the room.

They both laughed again, not caring whether the bland but ugly boy associated their laughter with his appearance. 'No,' said Laura, 'not him.'

It was nearly eight-thirty. Others arrived and were given wine or whisky, or vodka and lime. Then Danny appeared, the only one of the students who knew the family already. He had heard that Louisa was at home, and it might have been thought he would be curious, but he simply said 'Hi' quite flatly, and started to drink. His face was fixed in the way of someone who is trying to contain pain or emotion.

Kate Williams came across to talk to Louisa. Louisa was polite, but though the girls were of the same age and similar backgrounds they hardly shared anything else and, by then, Louisa's eyes had fallen on Julius Tate, whom she recognized at once as Laura's 'dish'. Her half-attention to Kate's conversation now went completely; her eyes, fixed on Julius, widened: 'A buck,' she murmured to herself, 'a real buck.'

'What was that?' asked Kate.

Louisa refocused on the other girl. 'Who's that?' she asked, nodding towards the Mexican-American.

'Oh, that's Julius.'

'Is he in the seminar?'

'Yes . . . I guess all the kids here are.'

Louisa had started to feel a kind of vertigo now, as her nerves and bowels reacted to the presence of Julius, while all the time she continued to talk politely to the prim girl from Maine.

Julius, on the other side of the room, could not be expected to understand the effect he was having on Louisa, but he did notice the pretty girl whom he supposed to be the professor's daughter because of her similarity to her father. He also noticed that her eyes were on him and so thought he might talk to her. She was a pretty girl.

He crossed the room with an empty glass and Louisa took the opportunity, for the first time that evening, to play the part of the host's daughter. She offered him a drink.

Kate, whose glass was also empty, moved away across the room leaving Louisa and Julius alone together.

'What would you like?' asked Louisa.

'Oh ... Scotch, if there is any,' said Julius, in his slow, almost abstracted, tone of voice.

Louisa took his glass and filled it. He followed her for a few paces and stood behind her, his eyes glancing at the Bonnard. He had never met Louisa before, but he felt that acquaintance that exists between men and women who have exchanged interested glances. He was not at a loss as to what to say. 'Which one are you?' he asked her as she handed him his drink.

'Which one of what?'

'I heard that the professor had two daughters.'

'That's right. I'm the elder. That's Laurie over there.' She pointed out her younger sister.

'She looks kind of dreamy,' said Julius.

'She's probably high.'

Julius nodded.

'How do you like the seminar?' asked Louisa.

'It's all right,' said Julius. 'It's really all right. Your father's an interesting man.'

'Yes,' said Louisa sourly, 'he writes books.'

'I don't mean like that. I mean that there's more to him than that.'

'You tell me.'

'These last couple of classes, he's been acting kind of crazy.'

Louisa looked down at her glass of orange-juice and changed the subject. 'Where are you from?'

Julius' face became vague 'Oh, the South-West.'

'New Mexico?'

'Yes ... sort of,' he said, as if disclosing a secret.

'You're an American, aren't you?'

'Sure. Why not?'

'Well, you might be Mexican.'

'Do I sound like a Mexican?'

'No, but you look like one.'

'My father came from New Jersey.'

'Mr. Tate?'

'That's right.'

'What does he do?'

'Again Julius became evasive. 'Kind of odd jobs,' he said.

Louisa thought she would keep quiet now. Julius was looking away from her across the room, as if bored or seeking someone else, and she did not want to scare him off with abrupt, aggressive questions. It was not his secrets she wanted.

'What do *you* do?' he asked, after a while

'I was at Cal.,' said Louisa. 'Berkeley. But I dropped out.'

'Why did you do that?'

Now it was her turn to evade the question. 'I just did,' she said.

Julius nodded. 'What are you going to do now?'

'I don't know. Get a job, and then pick up somewhere else next year.'

'The professor can get you in anywhere, I guess,' said Julius with a smile.

'Sure. He has his uses.'

Louisa was remarkably calm and cool, standing next to Julius, since his proximity had in no way diminished his attractiveness. On the contrary: she had particular uses lined up for every aspect and feature of Julius Tate. His soft black hair, which fell over his face, she would twist in her fingers; his round, stubbled face she would squeeze into an oval between her hands, and she would tap her fingers along the strong, straight ridge of his nose and kiss his child's lips and draw a look of longing from his vague brown eyes. But, for the moment, she just tapped her foot on the ground and sipped at her orange-juice.

Then there was a commotion in the middle of the room. Danny, who by now was drunk, started to shout – at Mike, initially, but then at all the guests and all Americans. 'You just don't care,' he said, his narrow and intelligent face crumpling at last. 'You don't know and you don't want to know, but we did it just as much as the Romans killed Jesus Christ . . . oh God, oh God.'

He sat down on the sofa and hunched over his drink. Everyone else in the room had stopped talking, and all were equally confused and embarrassed. Lilian came into the living room from the hall where she had been standing. Her face was set in a determined expression, as if to say that she knew how to deal with students who could not hold their liquor: but she was drunk herself and stumbled over the carpet which, though she did not fall, seemed to deflect her from her mission or make it seem absurd.

'Oh God, oh God,' Danny kept repeating to himself.

Henry and Alan both approached Mike. 'What is it?' Henry asked.

Mike, whose face was quite as calm as it always was, said: 'He's just upset, professor.'

'What about?'

Danny heard this and looked up, his desolated, tear-stained face now angry again. 'What about?' he repeated, shouting as before. 'You ask what about? Don't you read the papers or watch television? He's dead. Che is dead and we killed him, our mother-fucking CIA did it, so we did it, and he's dead.'

He collapsed again.

'Che Guevara,' said Mike. 'In Bolivia. It's him, all right. Castro's confirmed it.'

Henry nodded and was silent.

'And you didn't even notice it had happened,' said Danny. 'You didn't even notice.'

'Yes,' said Henry quietly, 'yes, I did.'

5

Louisa took advantage of the fracas around Danny to say to Julius: 'Let's get out of here.'

He followed her without answering.

'What was it all about, anyway?' asked Louisa as they walked down Brattle Street towards Harvard Square.

'The Bolivians got Che.'

'They killed him?'

'Yes.'

'And that made Danny go crazy like that?'

'Yes,' said Julius. 'He really feels things like that. Politics, I mean.'

'I used to once.'

'Not now?'

'Not so much. I'm on Danny's side, but I don't get uptight about it.'

'No.'

'What about you?'

'Well, I'm kind of active.'

'In New Mexico?'

'No. Here. In the SDS. But I'm not really that taken up in it. Like you, I guess.'

'There are other things,' said Louisa.

Julius nodded, but he did not question her further to find out what the other things might be. 'What were you thinking of doing now?' he asked Louisa.

'I don't know ... I mean, if you want to get on ...' she began, suddenly considerate at this late stage.

'No, no,' he said. 'I'm not going anywhere particular.' He looked at his watch. 'I'm hungry,' he said. 'Let's get a sandwich or something.'

They went into a drugstore beyond Harvard Square and sat there together at a table, eating cream-cheese sandwiches and drinking coffee. They were a striking couple – both good-looking, long-legged and well dressed. Louisa's clothes were only worn for the party, but Julius was always well dressed. He now loosened his tie as he leant over his coffee-cup.

'You certainly are pretty,' he said, in the off-hand manner which was always his opening line with girls of Louisa's age: the casual delivery enabled them to swallow the sticky compliment.

'So are you,' said Louisa, straight off, her eyes staring into his which was not a riposte he had met with before from girls just out of high school. He did not, however, change tack.

'I nearly didn't come to the party,' he said, 'and then we wouldn't have met. Think of that.'

'We would,' said Louisa.

'How's that?'

'I don't know ... in the Square.'

'Yes, but that wouldn't have been a *social* meeting.' He smiled knowingly.

'No,' she said, half turning her head, not quite sure of where they were or what was their understanding. 'Look,' she said suddenly, 'I've got to go to the bathroom.'

'OK,' he replied, sitting back to let her pass.

Louisa rose from her chair and went to the squalid lavatory where she peed as she did indeed want to, staring down at her bared thighs, almost amused to see them in this banal context. They reminded her of the precautions she ought to take. She took her contraceptive out of her bag, covered it with spermicide and pushed it in between her legs. She stood up, wiped her hands on the towel by the basin, rearranged her clothes and pulled the plug. Then she looked at herself in the mirror. She pulled a wisp of hair further over her face and undid the top button of her blouse.

Julius had finished his coffee, and she did not want hers. 'Let's watch the late show on TV,' she said.

'OK,' said Julius. They walked out of the drugstore. 'Do you want to come to my place?' he asked.

'Where's that?' asked Louisa.

'Fifty-nine Elm Street.'

'Do you . . . er . . . have an apartment there?'

'Yes.'

Louisa said nothing for a moment, not caring to ask if he shared it or lived alone.

'We'll take a cab,' said Julius.

They walked towards Harvard Square and, as Julius hailed a cab, Louisa said: 'We could go to my place in Boston.'

Julius turned. 'OK,' he said, quite easily.

'I mean to say,' said Louisa, 'it's almost as near as Elm Street.'

'Don't you live at home?' asked Julius.

'Well, I do at the moment,' said Louisa, 'but I took this apartment in Boston. I mean, I plan to take a job there.'

'Yes,' said Julius. 'Yes, of course.' His features retained his usual expression – amusement and disdain – but anyone who knew him well – his mother, for example – would have sensed his nervousness. He pulled at his fingers as they say in the cab, driving alongside the Charles River with Boston on the opposite bank. He said nothing, and neither did Louisa. She was already taken up in the mood of what she had in mind.

He paid for the cab: Louisa had no money on her anyway. She was, however, sufficiently self-possessed to have the keys to her apartment. She led the way.

'I haven't been here for days,' she told Julius as they came into the small hall-way. She glanced into the bedroom: everything seemed to be in order.

'It's a really nice place,' said Julius. 'Do you have any room-mates?'

'No,' said Louisa as casually as possible, 'I don't like to share with other girls.' She went into the kitchen. 'You go ahead and switch on the TV,' she said to Julius pointing towards the living room.

She joined him again a moment later with some Scotch, ice and glasses. Julius glanced at them but did not comment.

'I lived with two girls in Cal.,' said Louisa. 'It was OK, I guess, but it's better to be on your own.'

'I guess so,' said Julius.

Louisa poured out two glasses of whisky, handed one to Julius, took one herself and sat down in the armchair.

'What's on?' she asked.

Julius had not switched on the television. 'I don't know,' he said, leaning forward to do so.

'Let's not,' said Louisa, her eyes widening. 'Let's talk.'

'OK,' said Julius. He sat down on the sofa and watched Louisa. The room was warm and pretty. She had kicked her shoes off onto the floor and had lifted her legs up onto the chair. The skirt of her dress had slipped up her stockinged thighs and her blouse, too, was pulled apart by the way in which she held her shoulders back: because its top button was undone, Julius could see a certain amount of her bosom – enough, at any rate, to want to see more.

Louisa saw what effect she was having on him – the desired effect – but she was impatient, she had no time. She started to fidget, languorously, and then stood again on the floor.

'Can I come and sit there?' she asked Julius, pointing to the place next to him on the sofa. She asked in exactly the tone of voice of a child who is trying something on and Julius heard and appreciated what it was.

'Sure,' he said, but he half-choked on the word: and when she did sit next to him, her flank brushing against him as it descended, he gulped down his drink and said: 'I've got to go.'

'No,' said Louisa, suddenly nervous. 'No, please.'

'Yes, I've got to. This isn't right.'

'It's OK. It is, really.'

'No . . . I mean, you're the professors' daughter.'

She had nothing to say to that.

'And anyway,' said Julius, 'It just isn't right like that . . . anyway.' He want out into the hall. 'I'll see you, though,' he said.

Louisa did not reply. When she heard the door to her apartment close, she stood up but not to throw herself out of the window. She simply stalked around the flat, her lips pursed and her feet itching to stamp themselves through the floorboards like Rumpelstiltskin's. She lay for a time on her bed, her fingers hovering over her body, but in the end she sat up and left and took a cab back to Brattle Street.

6

The next session of the seminar did not discuss Proudhon or Bakunin but was taken up by the recently assassinated Guevara, in deference to Danny's feelings and the general interest of the class.

'We've got to make up our minds what we think about him,' said Henry, his voice quiet and calm, 'because Che did throw down the gauntlet not just to the liberal reformists all over the world, but also to the established Communist parties.'

'I don't really understand what he was trying to do,' said Debbie, with a nervous glance at Danny Glinkman.

There was a silence while they all waited for Danny to answer.

'Well,' he said at last, doing his best to remain calm like the professor, 'well, I'll tell you. He was trying to do in Bolivia what Castro did in Cuba – that's to start a guerrilla type of revolution with just a few men and gradually get the peasants to join them.'

'I guess it isn't a democracy out there?' said Kate, interrogative and apologetic.

'It sure isn't,' said Mike, with a short laugh.

'It's a military dictatorship,' said Alan, speaking clearly but with as much suppressed feeling as Danny had shown. 'Like almost all governments in this hemisphere, it's a military dictatorship which protects the interests of the landowners and capitalists. And, of course, the interests of the United States.'

'The corporations,' said Julius.

'Look here,' said Mike. 'If we weren't in there to mine their copper, then they'd never get it out of the ground.'

'The hell they wouldn't,' said Danny, furious again. 'Or the Russians would help them without taking ninety per cent of the profits. . . .'

'There you are,' said Mike with a shrug. 'It ends up with the Russians. Now, if you really want the Russians. . . '

'Let's get back to the theory, if you don't mind,' said Henry. 'Not that the practice isn't important, but I think we ought to deal with the theory first.'

Kate Williams picked up her pen to take notes.

'We'll begin with Marx,' said the professor. 'Now he postulated a revolution of the working classes against the bourgeoisie, but he only talked in general terms of how this would happen.'

'But he did say, didn't he,' asked Mike, 'that revolution could only take place in a fully industrialized society?'

'That's the way he thought it would happen, yes. As it's turned out, revolutions have only occurred in semi- or non-industrialized societies – the proletariat joining with the peasantry. This is what happened in Russia, and Lenin's concept of revolution – the sudden seizure of state power – remains, by and large, the European and North American Communist strategy. It is only when we get to Mao, in China, that the idea of revolution develops into that of the guerrilla war – the gradual, local concept of revolution. The revolutionary situation which Marx and Lenin considered a pre-condition, a necessary pre-condition, is now not something you wait for but something you bring on by direct, military confrontation with the power of the bourgeois state.'

The class was silent now, as they listened to their professor.

'We have reached here, as I see it,' he went on, 'a psychological theory of revolution. The strength and inevitability of the revolutionary movement is not now in massive numbers, obedient to immutable economic laws, but in the political consciousness of individual revolutionaries – what one might call morale. Mao Tse-tung's thoughts are not so much political or economic maxims as psychological insights into human nature and its relation to political power. He says, so to speak, that a single controlled and determined man is worth a hundred who are confused; that the man who is prepared to sacrifice himself to a strong, practical ideal which he fully understands will always beat an adversary who fights only for money or from fear.

'In Cuba, this psychological theory was put to the test in laboratory conditions. A handful of determined men showed that they could defeat Batista's soldiers if they attacked them piecemeal. This was sufficient to convert an incipient revolutionary situation, an oppressed peasantry, into a real one, a politically conscious peasantry, prepared to fight and die for the revolution.

'Che fought with Castro but he wasn't a Cuban. He was an Argentinian and an internationalist. Like Rosa Luxemburg, he felt that national entities were irrelevant, which is why he called for a plurality of Vietnams. The struggle of the Vietcong was not, for him, the *Vietnamese* revolution but the world revolution. It is the same attitude, you will remember, as that of Burke who wrote his reflections on the revolution *in*

America, not the *American* Revolution. From his conservative point of view, revolution was a universal phenomenon, as likely to break out in one country as another.

'Che was right in at least one respect: Vietnam is the crucial test of the modern, psychological concept of revolution, for there a modest number of highly motivated Vietnamese are fighting an equal if not greater number of their fellow countrymen, and half a million Americans as well. On paper, or rather in the computer, the odds are hopeless, but there is that essential element of morale going for the Communist side, because the ARVN and the US Army are both, when you come down to it, herds of unmotivated men brought face to face with their "enemy" only through the complicated and cumbersome machinery of a state. As individuals, they have no vital interest, indeed no interest at all, in fighting the Vietcong: as individuals, therefore, they are reluctant to risk their lives. This is the flaw in our position in Vietnam, and the one which may lose us the war.'

The class murmured in agreement.

'I want to return, though, to Che, and the theoretical aspect of this kind of revolution,' Henry went on, 'for if the hypothesis continues to be proved true, as it was in Cuba and may be in Vietnam, then why not apply it to any and every non-Communist country? Why not bring on the revolutionary situation by getting up a group of dedicated revolutionaries in the hills – a *fuoco*, as it is called – to ambush first small and then larger units of the government's forces? This, it seems, is what Che tried to do, and we have no way of knowing as yet what went wrong.'

He paused. The class remained quiet, all the members looking silently at Henry, reassembling his words in their minds, to make their own sense of them. Henry himself leaned forward pensively on the table at which he sat, his eyes staring at its surface, his left hand fidgeting with his lower lip.

'Practical failure,' said Alan at last, 'does not mean, necessarily, that the theory is wrong.'

'And it's only one failure,' said Danny. 'It went all right in China and Cuba, and they're still fighting in Vietnam.'

'I don't see,' said Kate. 'I don't really see why. I mean, revolution is violent and people get killed. . . .'

'Wouldn't you have been against Batista?' asked Danny.

'I guess so,' said Kate, still uncertain, 'but not all non-

Communist countries have Batistas. I don't see why you have to have a revolution everywhere.'

The class turned towards their professor but the expression of lucidity had left his face. 'It's difficult,' he said. 'It's very difficult. It could be that radical change is violent by its nature, because it means making people do things against their will. As to whether radical change is in fact necessary or worth the pain and disruption it causes, that's up to each individual to decide. I think that sitting here in Cambridge it can seem as if the world isn't such a bad place: but that might be because we're in the eye of the hurricane. If you go onto the fringe of our world, into South America or Africa or even into the slums right here in Roxbury, then the word "injustice" begins to take on a more substantial meaning. Or something might happen to you, or to someone you know, which makes the concept of a sick or corrupt society really mean something to you. . . .'

'But what has that got to do with capitalism?' asked Kate.

'It's in the interest of capital,' said Alan, 'to make men vain and greedy and ambitious.'

'I guess it's something you see or you don't see,' said Kate, shrugging her shoulders.

'I see it all right,' said Mike, 'but I don't agree with the interpretation. It isn't capital that defines human nature like that: it's human nature that invents something like capital to serve a purpose. And capital, I'd say, has done us pretty well. The world was stagnant, economically speaking, from the beginning of history until around 1760 when capitalism really got on its feet. Now we can put men into space and keep people alive with drugs and machines who would otherwise have died.'

'Yes,' said Julius, 'but now we know how it's done we don't need to do it the same way. You're like the Chinese guy who thought you had to burn down your pig-sty if you wanted roast pork because that was the way he first came to cook it.'

They all laughed except Mike who said, in a scathing tone of voice: 'Communism isn't so damned efficient. Show me a Communist country that's done better than we have.'

'Relatively,' said Danny, 'they've done better in Russia and East Germany. . . .'

'Capitalist countries have double the rate of growth of Communist countries,' said Mike. 'Look at Japan.'

'Yes,' said Danny, 'but what about the poorer countries?'

'They do better with American aid than Communist ideology.'

'They do not,' said Julius, 'because our aid goes straight into the pockets of the corrupt politicians.'

'You can't pour new wine into old casks,' said Alan.

'That's right,' said Julius.

'Well,' said Debbie, 'I don't agree with Mike but I don't see why you have to use violence like Che did. I mean, what about Gandhi? He got rid of the British without any violence, didn't he?'

'You gotta use violence,' said Sam, suddenly and vehemently. 'The blacks in this country have been kept back for a generation by the idea of non-violence. People just walk over you if you lie down like some bitch on heat. . . .'

'You, Sam, you . . .' Debbie began, taking these last words personally.

'The example of Gandhi,' said Henry, interrupting Debbie but smiling at her at the same time, 'may turn out to have been the exception that proves the rule. He was, after all, dealing with a weak imperial power. He was also working within the context of a Hindu society which valued passivity in a way that the rest of the world does not.'

'We have to recognize, I think,' said Alan, 'That force and authority are closely linked. Force can even create an effective semblance of authority. The value of Castro's early ambushes, surely, was to show the Cuban peasants that counter-force could be used effectively. The advantage of the guerrillas was not in the number of soldiers they killed or arms they captured, but in the humiliation of Batista. Loss of face meant loss of authority and loss of authority meant loss of political power.'

Alan hesitated, then went on: 'One might even postulate a law of nature, that moral authority must have force in reserve. A husband must be able to dominate his wife, physically if necessary, and parents their children.'

Henry smiled. 'That sounds like Saint Paul,' he said.

'Well, it isn't much like Jesus, is it?' said Debbie. 'He didn't believe in force.'

'No,' said Alan, 'because his kingdom was not of this world, whereas revolution is very much of this world.'

'But could you,' Henry said, 'could you, now, take a gun and kill someone – which is what it comes down to – as Castro did?'

'Yes,' said Alan, 'yes, I could, now, take a gun and shoot Lyndon Johnson, for instance, with a perfectly clear conscience.'

Henry shook his head. 'I couldn't,' he said.

'I could,' said Danny.

'Well, why don't you?' asked Mike sneering.

'I just might,' said Danny, his neck reddening, 'and he'd only be the first.'

'What about you,' Julius?' asked Alan.

'Well yes,' said Julius. 'I'd shoot Lyndon Johnson ... but I'm not planning on doing it.' He laughed.

'Why not?' asked Alan.

'Well, because I'd never get away with it, for one thing.'

'One might,' said Alan, 'if it was well planned.'

'I'd shoot Wallace,' said Sam. 'If he came through that door and I had a gun in my hand, I'd shoot him.'

'It wouldn't change anything,' said Henry. 'You can't kill prejudice by shooting the man it throws up.'

'No,' said Alan, 'but you can make an example.'

'An example to whom?'

'To those who suffer from his ideas and actions. Why should Johnson, because he's President, be individually exempt from the dangers of the war he makes others fight?'

'You wouldn't stop the war by killing Johnson.'

'Perhaps not. But it might encourage those fighting on the other side: and it might teach those who so lightly took us into Vietnam that there are those who regard them as criminals and hold them personally responsible.'

This was said forcefully and Henry hung his head as if he had no answer to it. Then Kate raised her hand.

'Professor,' she said, 'I don't want to interrupt anything but I'm afraid I have to go.'

Henry looked at his watch and saw that it was far past the time for this session of the seminar to end. 'OK,' he said, 'we'll go on with this next time.'

7

Louisa was sitting in the living room when her father returned that evening. They said hello to one another and she watched him as he poured gin into a glass jug for the first Martini.

'Do you want one?' he asked.

'No, thanks,' she said, with an emphasis that should have

provoked a pained expression on Henry's face but did not. He just added the usual dash of vermouth, swirled the jug around and poured out his drink. Then he crossed the room and sat down in an armchair to read the *New York Review of Books* as if no one else was there.

Louisa had nothing to read: in fact, she was bored and rather hoped for some sort of dramatic conversation with her father. So she said to him: 'I think I'll stop seeing Dr. Fisher.'

'Good,' said Henry, without looking up. 'Where's your mother?'

'She's over at the Clarkes.'

Henry nodded.

'She's worried about Laurie,' Louisa went on.

'Why?'

'I don't know. She hasn't been in all day but that doesn't mean much. Mother thinks she's been acting kind of funny lately, and staying out a lot, and Mrs. Clarke always thought Eddie was with us.'

'Where are they, then?' asked Henry.

'They don't know. She's gone over to the Clarkes to try and find out.'

Henry continued to read his journal.

'I've got an idea where she might be, though,' said Louisa, in an attempt to arouse his curiosity.

'Where's that?'

'Well, there's this guy who teaches at BU called Tony. He lives over in Boston somewhere. I guess that's where they go.'

'How did they meet him?' Henry asked.

Louisa shrugged her shoulders, which Henry could not see because he had returned to his reading, but he seemed content with no answer because he did not repeat the question.

Louisa saw that there was going to be no conversation with her father, so she got up and left the room. She hesitated in the hall for a moment and then went into the kitchen. She wanted to stamp her feet again and she had wanted to for a few days now: this, her father's benign indifference, on top of . . . of everything. She had a good mind to jump out of a window again.

Her trouble was, she told herself, that she had no friends of the right kind in Cambridge. The girls from Buckingham School who had not left the area were quite out of her world now – or rather she was out of theirs. Danny had become much too earnest. It was clear that she would have to meet some new people, perhaps through Laurie and her circle who seemed a cool lot. The image of Julius slipped into her mind: she clenched her teeth as she thought of her humiliation.

Lilian came into the house through the kitchen door. Her face was thin and severe with anxiety.

'Did you find them?' Louisa asked.

'No. The Clarkes don't know where they are, or where they've been going.'

'I shouldn't worry, Mother,' said Louisa. 'Fifteen's quite old these days.'

Lilian fidgeted with the vegetables she intended to cook for dinner. 'I'm sure she'll be home,' she said, 'but she's become very strange. She never talks to any of us, just walks in and out like a little ghost. She wears that same cotton frock without a coat or jersey in weather like this. . . .'

'She just gets high, that's all. You don't notice things like the cold when you're high.'

'What do you mean – high?'

'You know. Pot.'

Lilian snorted. 'I wish you kids wouldn't,' she said.

'It's harmless, Mother, really it is. Alcohol and cigarettes are far worse.'

'So they say,' said Lilian. 'I just hope she isn't taking anything else.'

Louisa became thoughtful as this idea struck her. 'Look,' she said to her mother, 'I think I know where she might be. I'll go and look for her.'

Without waiting for an answer she left the house and took the Volkswagen. She drove down to the river, along Memorial Drive and over onto the Massachusetts Turnpike, throwing her dime into the basket of the automatic gate. She left the Turnpike a mile or two later, at the Prudential Centre, and crossed over into South Boston, coming to a stop outside a house on Warren Avenue which Laura had once pointed out to her as being that of her friend Tony.

A faint mauve light came out of the windows on the first floor. Louisa climbed the steps up to the front door and rang the bell. She could hear the drone of music, and she studied the blistered brown paint on the door in front of her as she waited for it to be opened. No one came to do so, however, so she rang again and then peered round into the front room on the ground floor. There was a mattress on the bare floorboards, and an upturned tea-chest. It was a familiar scene.

For a moment she felt uneasy, not because of those within but for fear of the curious occupants of the slum houses on either side. Being dressed as a middle-class American, she felt a fear of being robbed, but at that moment the door was opened by a grey-faced, middle-aged man with flared, fuzzy hair.

'Is this Tony's house?' Louisa asked.

The man lifted his eyebrows as if to ask for a reason why he should even answer her.

'I'm Louisa,' she said. 'I'm Laurie's sister.'

'Yep,' said the man, 'come in.' He allowed her to pass through the door as if Louisa had shown him a ticket or a membership card. 'She's upstairs,' he said. 'On a trip,' he added.

'What kind?' asked Louisa.

'Acid,' said Tony.

Louisa nodded. She had never taken it, but she remembered Jason's experience and for a moment, she felt the unfamiliar emotion of alarm on another's behalf.

The stairs were narrow and the whole house smelt of incense and marijuana. This atmosphere was thickest in the room on the first floor to which Louisa went, searching for her sister. Tony had gone in ahead of her but the light from the mauve bulbs was faint and for a time she could not make out the identity of the five or six people sitting and standing there. They all seemed to be drugged in one way or another; some were talking disjointedly, others contemplating the posters on the wall – photographs superimposed on a paisley pattern, an optical trick for the hallucinatory high. As her eyes became used to the dimness, Louisa noticed Laura's friend Eddie shuffling around alone in a corner to the heavy rhythm of the music. His trousers and underpants were down round his ankles.

Unable to see Laura, Louisa crossed to him and asked him where she was. She had to shout because the music was loud and echoed in the unfurnished and uncarpeted room. Eddie, alas, did not seem to hear her even when her voice was at its loudest: he smiled into the air in front of her. Louisa took hold of his face with both hands and forced it to hers. 'Where the hell is Laurie?' she shouted; but the sixteen-year-old boy simply laughed and released a small squirt of urine from his bladder which hit her skirt and then dribbled down onto his own sodden pants.

'Beautiful,' he whispered, his face taking on the ecstacy of one totally fulfilled.

The host, Tony, now crossed the room to Louisa. 'She's upstairs,' he said. 'She's on a bad trip, so we took her upstairs.'

'Where?' shouted Louisa.

Tony beckoned to her and then ambled out of the room. Louisa followed him and at the top of the stairs was directed into a small attic room. There, on a pile of army surplus blankets, was Laura. She wore, as described by her mother, only a thin dress, but she was obviously unaware of the low temperature in the room. Her position was almost that of an artist's model – contrived, in the manner of Ingres. She sat on the blankets but her body was twisted and her head lay against the wall. The hem of her skirt had risen up to her waist, leaving her delicate legs uncovered. Her eyes, an inch from the plaster, were open: her hands propped up her body.

Louisa knelt down beside her. 'Laurie,' said she. 'Are you all right?'

The younger girl said nothing, but her eyes moved and, even in the small space between them and the wall, Louisa could see their demented expression.

'Come home,' said Louisa, taking her sister by the hand, 'Come on home.'

Laura allowed herself to be half-turned back into the room, but then she growled like a dying animal and hit her head several times against the wall as if nailing it to its previous position.

'Come home,' said Louisa again, pleading now.

'Look,' said Tony, standing behind her at the door, 'you can't take her home like that.'

'Well, what the hell do we do then?' asked Louisa. 'You aren't going to call a doctor, are you?'

Don't panic,' said Tony. 'She's been on trips before.'

'Like this?'

'No. They've been good ones. But she'll come down. You'll see.'

'When?'

'In a couple of hours.'

'A couple of hours?'

'Just wait. You'll see.'

'Well, I'm not leaving her here.' Louisa picked up a blanket and put it round Laura's shoulders.

'Look,' the man said, standing squarely in the doorway, 'you can't take her home because your people'll call the cops.'

'I won't take her home then,' said Louisa. 'I promise. But I've got to get her out of here.'

Tony stood aside. He was apparently alarmed himself, as Laura now started to whimper, and he stood back to let them pass 'I had to shut her in there,' he said to Louisa as they went down the stairs. 'You never know what might happen on a bad trip.'

'What about Eddie' Louisa asked.

'He's OK,' said Tony with a grin. 'He's doing what he likes to do.'

'And what does Laurie do? On a good trip, I mean?'

'She sings.'

Louisa got her sister sitting next to her in the Volkswagen and set off towards Cambridge without any clear idea of where they should go. It seemed that the horror in Laura's fantasy had abated: she watched the lights of the city as they drove through its streets. Louisa would not have hesitated to break her promise to Tony but decided that it would be better not to take Laurie home. She thought of Dr. Fisher, but somehow his slippery words seemed no solution. There was her own apartment, but she did not want to be alone with Laura. Then she thought of Julius. She remembered his address – 59 Elm Street – and so she drove through Cambridge in that direction without any clear idea of how he might help Laura.

She reached Elm Street, and Julius opened the door of his apartment. When he saw Louisa at the door he looked embarrassed.

'No,' she said, to reassure him. 'It's Laurie, my sister. She's in the car.'

'What's wrong with her'

'She's on a trip – acid.'

'Oh God,' said Julius. He came down with Louisa and together they brought Laura into the apartment. They carried her to his bedroom and helped her down onto his bed. Immediately she started to moan, saying 'oh-oh-oh' and doing her best to hit her head on the wall. They managed to quieten her down, however, and later she lay quietly, her eyes open and staring at the ceiling. Louisa and Julius covered her with blankets and came back into the living room

'We'd better call a doctor,' said Julius.

'No,' said Louisa. 'No. There's nothing they can do, anyway. If we just keep an eye on her until she comes down.'

'OK,' said Julius, 'if that's the way you want it.'

They sat silently together, and then Louisa became embarrassed in her turn as she remembered the circumstances in which they had been together the last time. 'I'm sorry to . . . kind of burden you like this . . .' she began.

'Forget it,' said Julius. 'I mean to say, we're old friends, aren't we?' He smiled with amused irony, and she smiled back and then started to cry.

'Hey, hey,' said Julius, but rather than comfort her he went to make some coffee. When he brought it in, he put his arm round her shoulder and told her to take it easy.

She did calm down and drank her coffee. Then she said: 'Can I call my parents'

'Sure,' said Julius. 'What are you going to tell them'

'I don't know. I'll just say it's all right.'

She dialled their number, and the telephone was answered by her father. She told him that she was with Laura, and that they were staying at a friend's place for the night. Henry seemed to accept this, so Louisa rang off without giving any further explanation.

Then she said she was hungry, and Julius went out for some hamburgers. They ate them while watching television, and at eleven Louisa went to sleep on Julius' bed, lying next to her sister. Julius slept on the sofa in the living room.

8

Louisa and Laura woke to the smell of coffee and bacon and came into the kitchen – both looking awkward in their own way and for their own reasons.

'How do you feel' Julius asked Laura.

She looked at him and paused, as if concentrating hard on the question. 'I'm all right. . . .' she said, and sat down.

The two girls were both wearing the clothes they had slept in: they looked crumpled and tired, but Laura was at least in full possession of her faculties and Louisa seemed relieved at her sister's recovery.

'What do you like?' asked Julius, standing at the stove. 'Eggs? Coffee?'

'Thanks . . . er . . . coffee,' said Louisa.

'I'd like some eggs and things, I think,' said Laura.

'You have them, then,' said Julius. 'And bacon. They'll do you good.'

And so the three of them sat down to a good-sized breakfast. They talked at first about anything except the events of the night before, but when they had finished the food and were left only with their cups half-filled with coffee, Julius looked across at Laura and said: 'That was pretty bad, wasn't it, last night?'

Laura swallowed and nodded. 'Yes,' she said.

'I shouldn't go on with it,' he said, with the kind manner of an older brother.

'No,' said Louisa, 'I really wouldn't, Laurie. It's dangerous.'

Laura nodded again. 'I know,' she said. 'It's just that ... well ... it seemed like worth trying.'

'Sure,' said Julius.

'And the first time it was fantastic.'

'It's fine, as a trip,' said Julius, 'but it's just a trip. It doesn't take you anywhere. It's only an escape ... a way of going crazy if you're not crazy already. And you're not, I'd say.'

'No,' said Laura. 'I sometimes wish I were.'

'It'd be easier,' said Julius. 'And if you want to go out of your mind on pot or acid or sex or anything, then there's not much anyone can say to stop you.'

'No,' said Laura. 'I don't want to but ... but ...'

'I know,' said Louisa. She turned to Julius. 'It's just that sometimes you get so low and depressed that you've got to get out of yourself – and it's better to blow your mind than commit suicide, isn't it?'

'Sure it is,' said Julius, 'but you've always got to come down again, and your life isn't going to get any better while you're up there. If anything, it's going to get worse. . . .'

'I know,' said Laura.

'You've just got to hold on and wait and make things better when you can,' said Julius.

'But it's so big,' said Laura. 'I mean, things like the war. . . .'

'You've just got to keep cool,' said Julius. 'Do what you can and keep cool. . . .'

'I guess so,' said Laura.

'There's a lot that's good in life,' said Julius, 'if you wait for it. I mean, there's love and having kids and books and music and painting and ideas. I guess we lose those things sometimes, and they get kind of poisoned for us here in the States, but they're there ... you wait and see.'

'OK,' said Laura. She smiled and then stood up.

'Do you want to go?' asked Louisa.

'I think I'd better,' said Laura. 'I want to see if Eddie's all right.'

'Well, I'll come too,' said Louisa, standing.

'No,' said Laura, 'no, I'll be OK.'

'Are you sure?' asked Louisa.

'Sure, sure. I'll get a cab or something.'

'OK,' said Louisa. She sat down again.

'I didn't have anything with me, did I?' Laura asked.

'No,' said Julius.

'Well, good-bye.' She held out her hand and Julius stood and took hold of it. 'Thanks,' she said, and then turned and left them.

Louisa, now alone with Julius, all at once felt awkward. She drank down the tepid coffee that was left in her cup.

'I guess I'd better be going too,' she said.

'Don't hurry,' said Julius, who also appeared ill at ease.

There was a moment of silence: then Julius asked: 'Do you think she'll be all right?'

Louisa shrugged. 'I hope so. She's kind of sensitive, though.'

'And aren't you?' asked Julius with a smile

'Yes,' said Louisa harshly. 'Only with me it's not drugs, is it?'

The smile vanished. Julius' face darkened with embarrassment. 'Love . . .' he began.

'Huh,' said Louisa. 'I've had all that.'

'There's got to be some kind of love,' said Julius.

'You sound like "Dear Abby".'

'Maybe.' Julius scowled, and to hide his scowl he turned away from Louisa and looked out of the window.

'I'm sorry,' said Louisa. 'Just think of me as a nut. We're all sick in the head around here. If the disease were physical, then you'd see spots on our skin or our yellow faces . . . It takes a little time to notice, if it's in the head.'

'Yes,' said Julius.

'I guess you've noticed by now, though,' said Louisa.

'Don't you go to a shrink?' asked Julius.

'Sure I do,' said Louisa caustically. 'But what can he do? He's just as sick as I am. Here in Cambridge it's like the bubonic plague. Everyone in America's got it except . . . well, except you don't seem to have it.'

'Don't I?' asked Julius – a question with a trace of mockery in its tone.

Louisa studied his face. 'No,' she said, 'I don't think you do.'

'Why not?'

'I don't know. Something to do with being Mexican, I guess'

Julius gave a slight snort, as if he had provoked this answer. 'I'm half-Yankee,' he said.

'I know,' said Louisa, 'but there must be some kind of immunity on the Mexican side. Indian blood, perhaps. You don't seem to keep asking what you're doing and where you're going and if you're happy, like ordinary Americans do the whole time. You just are what you are. I guess that's why I brought Laurie here ...'

Julius did not answer, and Louisa became confused by what she had said. 'I hope you didn't mind ... my bringing her here,' she said.

'No,' said Julius. 'I was glad.'

'Are you sure?'

'Sure I'm sure.'

'So we could be friends, could we, even if you don't want to ... well ...'

Julius smiled. 'We could be friends.'

'Then tell me something about yourself.'

'What?'

'Anything. After all, you know a certain amount about me because you know Dad. All I know is that your father ... well, you said he did odd jobs.'

'Did. Yes.'

'What's he do now?'

'He's dead.'

'Dead? You never told me that.'

'No,' said Julius.

'I mean, you said he was alive.'

'Well, he isn't.'

'When did he die?'

'When I was four years old.'

'Well I guess that's awful,' said Louisa – voicing an accepted emotion in a dry voice as if unconvinced that life would be so bad without a father.

'I had my mother,' said Julius.

'Of course.'

'And my uncle. My father's brother.'

'What's he like?'

'He's taken care of me,' said Julius. 'He comes ... he used to fly out to see me every year for my birthday.'

'Doesn't he live down there?'

'No. In Washington.'

'And he went to Albuquerque? Every year?'

'Yes.'

'Quite a guy.'

'He bought my mother's house for her, and he's paying for me to be here.'

'You owe him a lot, then.'

'I couldn't have come here otherwise.'

Louisa stood up. 'Can I make some more coffee?' she asked.

'Sure,' said Julius.

She crossed the kitchen and took the kettle to fill it with water from the tap; she then put it on and waited for it to boil, her back turned to Julius, the weight of her body resting on one leg.

Julius rubbed his face with his hands and through his fingers studied Louisa's long body.

'I hope you didn't think,' he said, 'because of what happened ... you know ... that I didn't like you.'

Louisa turned and smiled. 'No,' she said. Then she added: 'Just racially prejudiced.'

They laughed. The kettle boiled. Louisa filled their two cups with instant coffee. Then she sat down and they both seemed unable to think of anything to say, yet had no wish to leave each other.

'Your uncle,' said Louisa at last, 'he must be very proud of such a brilliant nephew.' An expression of affectionate mockery came into her face.

'He may not be too convinced of that.'

'You wouldn't be in Dad's seminar if you weren't good.'

Julius shrugged his shoulders.

'Not that you'll learn much from him,' said Louisa – her tone suddenly embittered.

'I've learnt a lot already,' said Julius.

'I can't imagine he'd teach you anything ... well, worth knowing.'

'Why not?'

'Well ... he's so kind of ... hopeless.'

'How do you mean?'

'He may be able to tell you about other people's ideas, but he hasn't really got any of his own.'

'We can't all be Karl Marx.'

'No, I don't want him to be a genius or anything. But I think he ought to have some sort of principles.'

'He hasn't any?'

'Not really, no.'

'And you?'

Louisa looked up at Julius. 'No,' she said, 'but I need some.'

Julius avoided her eyes. 'Where are you going to find them?'

'I don't know. From someone who's got some, I guess.'

'Don't look at me,' Julius said with a laugh.

She did look at him. 'I know you've got some but you don't want to tell me what they are.'

'You should try Danny,' said Julius. 'He's full of principles.'

'Danny. Yes. I know.'

'You saw how he went on about Che.'

'I saw, yes. But my mind was on other things at the time, wasn't it?' She smiled at Julius: and suddenly he leant over and kissed her. For an instant all the muscles in Louisa's body contracted: but then her body and mouth relaxed.

Their faces parted. Julius stood up again. For a time they looked at each other – eyes fixed on eyes – the girl sitting, the man standing. Then Louisa looked down at her lap and said: 'I've got to go.'

Julius stood back as she got to her feet. He saw her to the door.

9

The next morning Louisa drove from her parents' home to the less fashionable area of Cambridge over towards Somerville and stopped her car outside a small house darkened by chestnut trees. She knocked on the door and waited for some minutes until it was opened by a thin woman of around fifty.

'Hello, Mrs. Glinkman,' Louisa said.

The woman stared at her for a few moments.

'Don't you remember me?' Louisa asked.

'Louisa?'

'That's right.'

'Of course,' she said.

'I was wondering,' said Louisa, 'if you'd tell me where Danny's living these days.'

'He's living right here,' said Mrs. Glinkman. 'Come on in. He's upstairs.'

Louisa entered the house which was small and warm and smelt of Dr. Glinkman's pipe.

'Bruno,' said the wife, calling to her husband in his study, 'it's Louisa.' Then she added in a lower tone: 'Say hello to Bruno. I'll see if Danny's out of bed.'

Louisa pushed open the door of the study which she had known quite well a couple of years before. She prepared herself for the black spectacles which covered Dr Glinkman's functionless eyes.

'Hello, Doctor,' she said, her voice loud to make him aware of her presence and position.

'Louisa,' said the blind academic – a large, dark man rather older than his wife – as he turned in his armchair to face in her direction.

'How are you?' asked Louisa.

'Me? Well, the same. And how are you? We haven't seen you for such a long time.'

'I've been in California.'

'In California. Yes. I know.' His voice was sad as if he knew it all.

'I'm looking for a job now,' said Louisa. 'You don't need a secretary, do you?'

'Aha.' He laughed. 'If only I did.'

Louisa glanced at the piles of braille books by his chair. 'You're still teaching, aren't you?' she asked.

'Teaching . . . yes . . . what I can.'

'That's good.'

'And Danny's in your father's seminar.'

'I know.'

'It was kind of your father to accept him when he's only in his second year.'

'Everyone says Danny's very clever,' said Louisa.

'Please, please,' said Danny with mock modesty, coming in behind Louisa and tucking his shirt into his trousers.

'Is that you, Danny?' asked Dr. Glinkman.

'That's right, Pop,' said Danny.

'You see,' said Dr Glinkman to Louisa, 'I'm getting deaf now.'

'Not really, Pop,' said Danny.

'Not really,' his father repeated, an ironic echo.

'I'm sorry if I dragged you out of bed,' said Louisa looking at Danny's uncombed hair.

'Our genius might go a little further,' said Dr. Glinkman, 'if he could get up a little earlier in the morning.'

'Winston Churchill read his state papers in bed,' said Danny.

'And so you model yourself on Winston Churchill, do you,' said Dr. Glinkman. 'I thought it was Che Guevara.'

Danny blushed. 'Come on,' he said to Louisa. 'Let's get some coffee.'

'Drop in again,' said Dr. Glinkman to Louisa.

'Sure,' said Louisa. 'Sure, if you'd like me to.'

She followed Danny into the kitchen. His mother was upstairs or had left the house.

'You don't mind if I eat some breakfast, do you?' asked Danny.

'No, go ahead,' said Louisa sitting down at the kitchen table.

'How are you?' he asked.

'OK,' she said.

'Really?'

'Better than I was, anyway.'

'I'm sorry about you and that guy . . . Jason.'

'It's OK.'

'It just didn't work out?'

'No.' Louisa's eyes wandered round the kitchen – studying the old ice-box and gas oven. 'It's nice here,' she said. 'It hasn't changed.'

'No,' said Danny. 'It's all the same on the outside.'

'And on the inside?'

Danny shrugged. 'I don't know.'

'You haven't changed, have you?'

'I'm older.'

'I know, but you still have the same ideas.'

'They've developed somewhat.'

'Of course.'

'Are you living with your people?' Danny asked.

'On and off. I took this apartment in Boston but . . . well . . . sometimes I like to live alone and sometimes I don't.'

'I know,' said Danny.

'You're amazing, though,' said Louisa.

'Why?'

'You're the only boy I know who just goes on living with his parents without having bust-ups or nervous breakdowns.'

'We have our quarrels,' said Danny.

'Don't you ever want to move out?' asked Louisa.

'Sure,' said Danny, 'but it's cheaper living here. And I think Pop likes it. We talk a lot.'

'He's not like the others.'

'I know. He's blind.'

'No. I mean he's different in other ways, too.'

'He's got a lot to say.'

'You're lucky.'

Danny took a mouthful of bacon, French toast and maple syrup. 'Your father ...' he began. He waited until he had eaten what was in his mouth: then he started again: 'Your father has everything going against him, but I will admit that he's trying.'

'Trying what?'

'To see what's got to be done.'

'What ... what has got to be done?'

Danny took another mouthful of food: then a sip of coffee. 'I mean he's so caught up in the whole academic thing of discussing and discussing and never doing anything.'

'Of course,' said Louisa bitterly. 'He'd never do anything because he doesn't want anything changed. Talk doesn't cost him anything.'

'You could say the same for you,' said Danny.

'I guess you could,' said Louisa.

'I mean ... what do you want changed?'

'Myself ... at least, not myself. I want to get out of myself.'

'That's right,' said Danny. 'So you should.'

'I want to do something that's important and unselfish.' Louisa looked at Danny who was sipping his coffee.

'I *intend* to do something that's important and ... well, I guess you'd call it enlightened self-interest.'

'What?' asked Louisa.

'Fight.'

'Fight. Yes. But how and whom?'

'Take your pick, for Christ's sake. There are plenty of them. We just have to pick one at random and get the whole thing started.'

'The revolution?'

'Yes.'

'I'd be with you, Danny?'

Danny looked at her over his cup. 'Would you?'

'Yes.'

'I'm talking about the real thing, Louisa. Not just therapy for neurotic little rich girls.'

'No,' said Louisa, swallowing. 'No. I know'

Danny put his cup down and looked at his watch. 'As it happens,' he said, 'you've come at the right time.'

'Why?'

'Well, in half an hour a couple of others from the seminar are coming over to talk about what's to be done.'

'Does Dad know?'

'No. And he mustn't know.'

'I won't tell him anything.'

'I know.'

'Does *your* father know?'

'He has an idea. . . .'

'What does he say?'

'He's against it.'

'Why?'

'He has his reasons.'

'Louisa said nothing: she waited.

'He thinks it's dangerous,' said Danny.

'I guess it is.'

'Yes,' said Danny. 'What we have in mind is very dangerous. But it's important: and it's got to be done.'

10

The two others from the seminar who came to see Danny were Alan Gray and Julius Tate. The latter seemed acutely embarrassed to see Louisa; and both he and Alan looked askance at Danny when he proposed that she should join their discussion that morning. But neither of them could come up with any adequate reason why she should not and Danny told them that he had known Louisa for three years and was quite confident that they could trust her.

The four of them then went up to Danny's own room under the roof of the house and settled down either on his bed or on cushions on the floor. Danny himself sat on the chair at his desk.

'You start,' he said to Alan.

With a final uneasy glance at Louisa, the priest started to talk. 'The way I see things is this,' he said. 'We've reached a point where we know how revolutions are started and how they're won: and we all – at least all of us here – are agreed that a revolution is not only desirable but essential.'

'Agreed,' said Danny.

Julius nodded.

'Essential,' said Alan, 'not just for our own society, but as part of the struggle against imperialism abroad.'

'In Vietnam, you mean?' asked Louisa.

'In Vietnam,' said Alan, 'but also in South America, Africa ... all over the world American capital moves in to exploit the natural resources of under-developed countries – cut-price minerals, cheap labour and so on.'

'Now the three of us ... the four, rather ... so far as I see it, have got beyond the detached study of politics as a science to a definite political commitment: that is, an understanding of ourselves as part of the material way in which history proceeds.'

The three others nodded in agreement.

'As I said,' Alan went on, 'we know how revolutions are started and how they're won because we've seen Mao and Castro do it and we've read Mao, Che, Castro, Giap and Régis Debray on *how* it was done. All we have to do is to translate lessons learnt from their experience into tactics and strategy suited to our own particular conditions.'

The priest spoke softly, clearly, without hesitation: the three younger members of the cell listened to him with complete concentration.

'The rural guerrillas of Mao and Castro become, in this country, the urban guerrilla. The water in which this fish swims – the peasantry in rural societies – becomes the urban poor. The Sierra Maestra is replaced by the streets of Boston, Chicago, New York....'

'Do you think,' asked Julius, 'that an urban guerrilla can really be as invulnerable in the cities as Castro was in the Sierra?'

'I do,' said Alan, 'if he has the trust of the people. Look at the Mafia. Even that organization which is parasitic upon the people is invulnerable because the Italian-American poor know it – and in a sense trust it more than they do the government of the United States.'

'With some justification,' said Danny.

'Certainly,' said Alan. 'In the same way, the blacks will never turn over their own criminals to the white police.'

'The blacks,' said Julius, 'they're the worst done by in our society. Shouldn't they be brought into any revolution?'

Alan glanced at Danny. 'I don't know,' he said.

'I mean,' said Julius, 'shouldn't Sam be here?'

'I don't know,' said Alan. 'Do you think he should?'

'Well, I don't see why not.'

'The blacks are really taken up with race chauvinism at the moment,' said Danny. 'They won't accept cooperation, let alone leadership, from non-black groups.'

'And we have to recognize,' said Alan, 'that we live in a pre-dominantly non-black society.'

'Sure,' said Julius.

'Most blacks – Sam, certainly – see all class conflict in terms of race. . . .'

'Whereas the converse is true,' said Danny. 'As Mao says – all questions of race are fundamentally questions of class.'

'Sure,' said Julius, 'I accept that. And I guess anyone would have to accept it as a basis to a political revolution. . . .'

'Rather than just a slaves' revolt,' said Alan. 'I think that's true.'

Louisa readjusted her position on Danny's bed. 'How does it all get started, though?' she asked.

'That,' said Alan, clasping his hands together, 'is the sixty-four thousand dollar question – and that, really, is what we're here to discuss.'

'Obviously,' said Danny, 'a revolutionary act is produced by a revolutionary situation – cause and effect: but since we're human beings, we're conscious of our actions – so while, in a sense, the start of a revolution is like spontaneous combustion, in another sense it is not – because the molecules in this case are conscious of their own behaviour and can, therefore, fail to perform their rôle.'

'How?' asked Julius.

'Well, through laziness or cowardice. . . .'

'OK.'

'But assuming you get through all that, and understand social developments clearly enough to recognize your own leading rôle in them, then the actual direction of the first act. . . .'

'Act of revolution?' asked Louisa.

'Yes. Act of revolution. The actual consequence of the act is unimportant so long as its significance is understood. So long as the act is clearly one of *revolution*, its nature can be random.'

'I don't understand,' said Louisa.

'Look at it this way,' said Alan. 'You, or I, or Julius or Danny or all of us together, can't expect to achieve a revolution right away on our own: nor, on the other hand, can we wait until everyone in the country agrees that there ought to be a revolution. What we have to do is something – anything – to set the ball rolling.'

'I see,' said Louisa.

'The question is, what?' said Julius.

'It's got to be something extreme,' said Danny. 'It's no good parading around Harvard Square shouting "Let's have a revolution." '

'Agreed,' said Julius.

'In my opinion,' said Alan, 'it has to be an act of violence equal to that used by the administraton in Vietnam.'

'I think so too,' said Danny.

Louisa looked puzzled so Alan turned to explain to her what he meant. 'We've got to show that we're serious,' he said, 'that this is the real thing, not just another reformist balloon floating up into the air.'

'There has to be an element of retribution,' said Danny.

'You mean killing?' said Louisa.

'Yes,' said Alan. 'Killing those who kill.'

'Killing soldiers, do you mean?'

'They're pawns,' said Danny. 'I think we should go straight for the king.'

'You mean Johnson?' asked Louisa.

'Yes.'

They were all silent.

'You'd never get near him,' said Julius.

'Oswald got near enough to Kennedy,' said Danny.

'Yes, but they've tightened up. Johnson only moves in a bullet-proof automobile surrounded by a dozen security men.'

'I agree with Julius,' said Alan, 'to this extent: I think we must be successful in what we do. To fail would be worse than not to try at all.'

'Certainly,' said Danny.

'Johnson would be the logical target for a first blow of the

kind we contemplate, but just because of this it would diminish our chances of success to choose him.'

'Sure,' said Danny, shrugging his shoulders.

'What we need,' said Alan, 'is a man who typifies the class
enemy: not a jumped-up redneck like Wallace or a sabre-
rattling chief-of-staff, but one of the men in the real centre
of the establishment – a capitalist, not a dupe of capitalism,
an egg-head, not an imbecile, someone who has deliberately
and knowingly led America into its politics of imperialism
abroad and oppression at home.'

'You mean,' aked Louisa, 'someone like Laughlin?'

Alan stopped and thought. He hesitated and then said:
'Yes, someone like Laughlin.'

11

Julius and Louisa left the Glinkmans' house together.

'Can I drive you somewhere?' Louisa asked him.

'Yes . . . thanks,' he said, and got in the car beside her.

'Where to?'

'Oh, anywhere. . . .'

'Do you want to go to your apartment? Or where?'

'No, I guess I'd better go to the library.'

'Aren't you going to eat something?'

'Sure.'

'Let's get a sandwich, then.'

Louisa drove off towards Harvard Square. Neither of the
two spoke to the other for a while: then Louisa said: 'You
didn't seem too pleased to see me.'

'When?'

'At Danny's.'

Julius shrugged. 'Well . . .' he began.

'What?'

'Well, I don't like you being mixed up in all this.'

Louisa scowled. 'Not a game for girls?'

'No, said Julius, looking out at the street, 'it isn't.'

'Fuck you.'

'OK, OK,' he made a placating gesture with his hand. 'I
know. Don't tell me. Anything I can do, you can do better.'

'You don't have to be especially brawny,' said Louisa, 'to
pull a trigger.'

'No,' said Julius, 'but you've got to be cool, very cool.'

'Cool, calm and collected.'

'That's right.'

'And I'm not?'

'I don't know. Anyway,' he sighed, 'It's not that I don't think you could. I just don't think you should.'

'Why the hell not? I'm as sick of things as anyone else.'

'Yes, but there's no reason for you to want revolution . . . a Communist revolution. And to kill Laughlin. I mean, he's a friend of your family.'

'Maybe I'm trying to be unselfish for the first time in my life.'

'Maybe,' said Julius.

'I mean you don't have to be a fucking black or Mexican to want a revolution, do you?'

'No,' said Julius quickly.

'Well then?'

Julius sighed. 'OK,' he said. 'Let's forget it.' Then he added: 'Perhaps it's just that I don't want you to get hurt.'

Louisa's body bent as her anger subsided. The tone of her voice became suddenly gentle. 'You get hurt by more than bullets,' she said.

'I know,' said Julius.

'That's why we're going into this thing, isn't it?' she asked. 'To cure the pain we feel and see all around us?'

'I guess so,' said Julius.

'Isn't that why you're doing it?'

'I guess so,' said Julius.

He turned and smiled at her and touched her neck beneath her ear as she drove in the town's traffic.

12

Without bothering to invent an excuse for her husband or children, Lilian Rutledge left them on a Tuesday after lunch and drove up to the cabin in Vermont. Bill Laughlin had arranged to be there overnight on his way back to Washington from Montreal.

Both tired from travelling, they simply ate together and then went to sleep. It was only in the morning that they made love. Then Lilian lay beside her lover, leaning on her elbow, her body dead for a time to further sexual sensation. Bill smoked a cigarette, while she felt the weight of her right breast and then let it fall again to hang against her body. 'I'm getting old,' she said.

Bill Laughlin glanced at her. 'They're OK,' he said.

'I only notice my body when I'm with you,' said Lilian. 'I forget about it the rest of the time.'

'That's love.'

She did not answer, but looked across at his heavy, hairy body. He had put on his shorts: he always did, immediately afterwards.

'Do you think of yours?' she asked.

'I watch my weight.'

Lilian leaned across and dug her hands into the flesh above his hips.

'Hey, don't remind me,' he said. 'I'm getting fat.'

'The kids would think we were disgusting,' she said. 'Laura said she thought people over thirty shouldn't be allowed to make love.'

'She did?'

'Perhaps you should draft a bill in the Senate?'

They laughed together.

'How is it these days?' she asked.

'What?'

The Senate.'

'Much the same as usual. Fulbright's making trouble. . . .'

'Yes.' Lilian looked away from her lover and stared down at the sheets. 'There's sure to be trouble . . . as long as the war goes on.'

'It's a bugger,' said Laughlin, lying back on the pillow, 'when you're up for re-election. This damned peace lobby. . . .'

'I wish it would end,' said Lilian.

'Damn it, Lil,' said the half-naked right-wing Senator, 'it can only end when we win.'

Lilian shrugged. 'I hope it won't be too late.'

'Too late for what?' asked Laughlin, his tone irritated and petulant.

'Well, it just seems that everything's going wrong.'

'You can't blame what happened to Louisa on the Vietnam War, for God's sake. . . .'

'I don't know. . . .'

'Well, how? What's the logical connection?'

'There's no *logical* connection.'

Bill gave an exasperated sigh. 'You haven't even got a son,' he said.

'Bennie's at college, though,' said Lilian.

'Sure, but he'll have to go some time. I mean, my son can't dodge the draft. He wouldn't want to, anyway.'

'No, I'm sure he wouldn't.'

'Jeanie worries, though.'

'I imagine she does.'

Lilian looked sullen for a moment, because she did not like to have either spouse mentioned when they were in bed together: nor, she knew, did Bill, so she repaid him in kind, 'Harry worries too,' she said.

'What's he got to worry about?'

'About Louisa and Laura . . . and things in general.'

'Yes, well, we all worry about things in general.'

'He's become strange lately. He didn't even notice when I told him I was coming here.'

'I guess he's got used to the idea of you and me.'

'Perhaps.'

They were silent, each waiting to lose the unpleasant taste left by the image of the cheated spouse.

'Oh, heck,' said Bill, rolling over and kissing Lilian.

Her hand went to his fat side again, and then further down his body.

And then, after that second round, they both knew it would be optimistic to wait for a third so they got dressed. As Bill buttoned up his shirt, Lilian crossed to him and leaned her clasped hands and chin on his shoulder. 'Are you sure you still like me?' she asked.

'Of course I do.'

'Even after all those pretty secretaries?'

He smiled, knowing that she could not know for sure. 'Even after each and every one of them.'

'I need you,' she said. 'Very much. Every now and then. I guess that means I love you.'

'Me too,' he tightened his tie.

'When will we see each other again?'

He leant over and took a diary out of the inner pocket of his jacket which was slung over a chair. 'We'll be in Boston for that dinner in November. You'll be there too, won't you?'

'Sure,' she said. 'And you thought we might slip under the tablecloth after the dessert?'

He smiled. 'I thought,' he said, 'that I might come up the day before. We could meet for a drink at the hotel.'

'And go upstairs? '
'And go upstairs.'

13

When she got back to Cambridge, Lilian found that Henry really had become strange. She came into the house in the evening and he was having a drink, as usual, but instead of sulking as he usually did when she had been up to Vermont or down to New York on her own, he looked up at her with an expression of real affection. He mixed and poured her a drink: he even asked her how the drive had been, but, tactfully, did not enquire about the time spent in the country.

About half-way through her second cocktail, it suddenly occurred to Lilian that her husband was in love with another woman. It was the only explanation for that sublime manner and purposeful reading of a dull, political book. Lilian was imaginative; no sooner had the thought entered her head, than they were divorced – Henry happy with some tame little Cambridge woman, the girls contemptuous and away on their own and she, Lilian, left high and dry and alone. Would Bill leave Jeanie? No, not a chance. It would lose him votes. Anyway, she could never live with such an egotistical man as Bill Laughlin.

'Oh, God,' she thought (the third cocktail), 'what can I do?'

Then her mind turned to all the magazines she had read, and the advice they had given to women in a similar predicament.

'Let's eat out,' she said to Henry.

'Well, Mrs. Pratt got in some steak,' he replied, his eyes still on his book, 'and there are potatoes in the oven.'

'No, please,' she said. 'Let's go to a restaurant in Boston.'

Henry looked up and smiled. 'All right,' he said.

'I'll go and get ready.'

Lilian went up to her bedroom to make herself look alluring, as the articles had always suggested. She looked at her face in the mirror. 'Christ,' she thought, 'I really am getting old.'

She smoothed down her face, but the skin always leapt back to form the same creases and lines. 'I guess I deserve it,' she said to herself, still living in her mind as the divorced wife of Henry Rutledge.

Drunk though she was, she did make herself look pretty – for though there were lines in her face, they were elegant lines and tastefully shallow. Henry had turned off the oven, but he had not bothered to change out of the sweater and slacks he had been wearing when she came in.

In the car, Lilian became shy like a girl on her first date. Making up her face and adorning her body had been easy enough: making up a manner was more difficult.

'Have you seen the girls?' she asked.

'They're not in the house much,' he said 'But they seem to go around a lot together. I guess they can do for each other a lot more than we can do for them.'

'I don't think we ought to sign off just yet,' said Lilian.

'It's probably best if we do,' said Henry. 'I think parents have done their best or their worst by the time the kids are around sixteen.'

'It's a very impressionable age, sixteen,' said Lilian. 'They need a stable home.'

Henry glanced across at his wife: he thought of her just what she thought of him – that she was in an unfamiliar mood – but it did not seem to interest him as much.

They went to a restaurant in Boston where they had gone, on and off, twice a year or so, since they had first moved up to Massachusetts. It was French and expensive, and the waiters looked askance at Henry's clothes, but the manager recognized him and led him to a choice table. Moreover, Lilian made up for her husband's casual attire by gliding towards the table and sitting at it – the menu before her – with a graciously straight spine.

When their orders had been taken, Henry said to her, in an unemotional tone of voice: 'I like all this sort of thing less and less.'

'What?'

'Fancy restaurants.'

'I'm sorry,' said Lilian.

'Oh, no,' said Henry. 'I didn't mean just tonight. In fact, I'm glad you suggested it. I wanted to talk to you about something and somehow it's easier here . . . away from home.'

Lilian clenched her fists and started to talk quickly about the comparative qualities of restaurants in Boston and New York. Her conversation did not make much sense, since her mind was not on its content, but on keeping it up until she could get Henry out of there and back to their hearth and home. What a terrible mistake she had made in bringing him out – what bad advice those magazines gave to women.

After a time, however, she could no longer keep it up and, being brave and impulsive, she jumped over the edge. 'What did you want to say?' she asked, her voice breathless and an octave lower in tone than it had been on the subject of restaurants.

Henry leaned forward on the table. 'I want to sell the house,' he said.

Lilian scrutinized him. 'You want to sell the house?' she said.

'I want to move into something smaller.'

'Why?'

'I want to stop being rich.'

'You want to stop being rich?'

'Yes.'

'How?'

Henry smiled. 'By getting rid of my money.'

'I mean, why?'

'I don't like being rich.'

'What's wrong with it?'

'Do you like it?'

Lilian started to eat the lobster that had been put in front of her. 'Yes,' she said. 'Yes, I do.'

'I think it dehumanizes people,' said Henry.

'What do you mean by that?'

'It removes them from one important aspect of the human condition – material *need* and the striving for its fulfilment.'

'Thank God.'

'No. It's like putting lions in a zoo. They miss the point of life, since the point of life is the struggle to keep alive.'

'Lions, maybe.'

Henry started to eat his shrimps. 'And so they either just get bored and die, in their heads, or they thrash about for a substitute.'

'Lions?'

'Human beings.'

'What . . . ?' Lilian began, meaning to ask what substitutes were found, but she did not pursue it. 'Isn't it a little late?' she asked instead.

'I don't think so.'

'I mean, you said yourself, after they're sixteen. . . .'

'I'm not doing it for the kids. I'm doing it for myself.'

'For yourself?'

'For my self-respect.'

'Good heavens, Harry,' said Lilian, returning to her old manner now that the idea of divorce had gone out of her mind, 'I don't mind your having theories, but I wish to God you wouldn't experiment with them on me and the girls.'

'I thought you didn't mind the idea.'

'What? Of living in some slum in Roxbury?'

Henry smiled. 'I was thinking of Lexington or Belmont. Or we can even stay in Cambridge. I just want the sort of place an ordinary professor might have.'

'An ordinary professor might have a house on Brattle Street. '

'No, Lil, not our house, at any rate. Not unless he had a few millions outside his job.'

Lilian cracked a claw of the lobster and took a drink of white wine. Her eyes, camouflaged by the glass, looked across at her husband: but he knew this trick of hers and he met her look and laughed. She smiled too. 'You've certainly become very odd lately,' she said.

'Just taking stock,' he said. 'You get to thinking as you approach fifty.'

'The change of life,' she said. 'I know. It's going to hit me soon. The real thing, that is.'

'I'm sure you won't let it cramp your style.'

She blushed and looked at him again. She kept having to look at him to interpret what was behind what he said. His expression was remarkably clear of malice or jealousy now.

'I guess you want to fire Mrs. Pratt?' said Lilian.

'That's up to you.'

'My private income won't exactly stretch to luxuries.'

'There will still be my salary.'

'That's true.'

'I don't intend to take a vow of poverty,' said Henry. 'I just want to drop the swank.'

'What swank?'

'You know. The Porsche and the clothes and the trips to Vermont and the Virgin Islands.'

'Have those kids been getting at you?'

'Which kids?'

'Danny Glinkman and Julius Tate, and those others in your seminar.'

'It's partly that.'

'I don't know how you can let them influence you.'

'I'm inclined to agree with you, Lilian, but an idea is an idea, whoever holds it.'

14

The next day Henry noticed that the students in his seminar who normally contributed the most to their discussions had suddenly become silent and distracted: and that Alan Gray, who had so recently approached him at the end of a class, now left the room without a glance in his direction.

Since he wanted to hear more of the Jesuit's ideas, Henry sent him a note inviting him for a drink at the house in Brattle Street: and Alan sent a note in return to say that he would come, as indeed he did, at five-thirty on the following day.

Henry took him into his study and poured him a drink. The priest sat on the edge of one of the leather chairs, gripping his glass of Scotch.

'You've got quite a collection of books here,' he said.

'As a matter of fact,' said Henry, 'the collection is next door. These are just work books.'

'What are the others?'

'A few incunabula ... and some first editions. I used to collect them.'

'And pictures,' said Alan, glancing at the Braque. 'You've got a fine collection of those.'

Henry sat down with his own drink in his hand. 'Do you think it's wrong?' he asked.

'No,' said Alan, hesitantly and without conviction.

'I don't do it any more,' said Henry.

'Why not?'

'I just couldn't do it ... paying thousands of dollars for ... well, it seemed kind of selfish.'

'You have to do something with your money.'

'I preferred to give it to people who don't have enough.'

'The poor.'

'Yes.'

Alan laughed.

'I know,' said Henry. 'It was naïve. Mind you, I didn't subsidize play-groups in Roxbury to placate the suffering poor ... at least, that wasn't my conscious intention. It may have been the end result.'

'You'd have to be an anti-Marxist to *intend* to placate the poor,' said Alan. 'I'm sure even Rockefeller has the best of intentions.'

'Anyway,' said Henry, 'I understand now that it was naïve – to give to the poor: on the other hand, I don't want to keep my money. In fact, I want to get rid of it all.'

'Well,' said Alan, 'that's an admirable intention.'

'But I don't quite know how to unload it. I thought you might advise me.'

Alan laughed. 'This is what's called an *embarras de richesse*. I'm not so sure *I* know what you should do with it.'

'Obviously,' said Henry, 'it should go to the revolutionary movement, but there's no distinct party one can point to as the obvious recipient. There are the Panthers, of course. . . .'

'Black chauvinists,' muttered Alan.

'What?'

'They're out for themselves,' said Alan, 'for blacks. They're not really revolutionaries in our meaning of the word.'

'I agree. What about the SDS?'

'Yes,' said Alan. 'They might be the right group.'

'Who would you give it to?'

Alan hesitated. 'I think I'd wait a bit,' he said. 'In a year or so, things might be a lot clearer.'

Henry nodded. 'Perhaps. . . .'

'I think that at the moment it might just be wasted because the group you choose might not be the leading group in the movement.'

'That's true.'

'I'd wait.'

Henry nodded. He stood and fetched them both more to drink. 'When the rich man went to Christ,' he said, his back turned to Alan, 'he was told to give all he had to the poor.'

'That's right,' said Alan.

Henry turned, handed Alan his glass and sat down. 'Didn't that mean . . . placating the masses?'

'Christ,' said Alan, 'was concerned with men's souls. He was only interested in their souls and spiritual life. The rest – the material world – that was evil anyway and could be left to Caesar.'

'Has revolution nothing to do with men's souls?'

'I don't think so. Revolution is an objective, material necessity. Virtue is a subjective process of will.'

'But isn't it a subjective process of will which makes men into revolutionaries?'

'It shouldn't be. To understand an objective necessity needs only clarity of mind: it doesn't depend on your circumstances. But virtue consists in pleasing God – in repentance – and a prostitute may, by some good work, please God much more than Mao Tse-tung or Fidel Castro.'

'But since it all, said Henry, 'all of it . . . ends in death, shouldn't we be more preoccupied with the good than with the necessary?'

Alan looked around at the furniture in the room. 'It depends,' he said.

'On what?'

'On our vocation, I guess. Some of us are there to be saints, others to be revolutionaries.'

'Others to be bankers and generals?'

'No. We can all see the truth of a proposition because we have the faculty of reason. Bankers and generals are wrong, not evil: and even in error they may be saints whilst we, who are right, are not.'

'Are you sure you're not?'

'Yes.'

'Then why are you a priest?'

'Because I thought at one time that I was intended for . . . well . . . the spiritual.'

'What happened?'

'It all became less and less real.'

'The spiritual?'

'Yes.'

'And the material more real?'

'Yes.'

'But you still believe in the spiritual?'

'Yes . . . yes, of course . . . I still believe in it . . . in God. In Christ. Yes. I'm a priest. I say Mass. But it's less real, less and less real.' He looked at the glass in his hands and then drank down the whisky that remained in it.

'And the revolution,' asked Henry quietly, 'does that become more and more real?'

'Yes,' said Alan. 'For me . . . now . . . it's the only reality.'

15

Alan left at seven and at seven-thirty Henry sat down to supper with his wife and two daughters

'What did the priest want?' Lilian asked.

'I invited him over,' said Henry. 'He's an interesting man.'

'There's something creepy about him,' said Laura.

'Why do you think that?' asked Henry.

'I don't know. His being a priest, I guess.'

'Well, I think it's very good,' said Louisa, 'considering how reactionary the Catholic Church is, that some of its priests are radical.'

'He's certainly radical,' said Henry.

'I know he is,' said Louisa.

'Did you talk with him at the party?'

'No. Danny told me.'

'Well, I hope he isn't one of those violent radicals,' said Lilian.

'For Christ's sake, Mother,' said Louisa, 'what do you think he's for if he's a radical? Voting, perhaps?'

'No need to be ironic with me,' said Lilian.

'Alan certainly *believes* in violence,' said Henry, 'but I don't see him ever getting nearer to it than some bust-up with the police.'

'Of course he'll get nearer to it,' said Louisa. 'He's not just going to get his head smashed like a *liberal*.'

'Well,' said Henry, 'we'll see.'

'You think,' said Louisa, 'that just because *you* don't have the guts to do anything, no one does.'

'Here we go again,' said Lilian. 'The same old argument.'

'No,' said Louisa. 'It's not the same because now Dad admits that something fundamental ought to be done: he just doesn't know what.'

'Who told you that was what I thought?' asked Henry.

'Danny and . . . Julius.'

'Anyway,' said Lilian, 'it's not true, is it, Henry dear? You *do* know what to do.'

Henry blushed but said nothing.

'Don't you think you ought to tell your daughters? After all, they're interested parties.'

'What?' asked Louisa. 'What do you intend to do?'

'I haven't decided yet,' said Henry.

'Your father is thinking of giving away his money,' said Lilian.

The girls looked at their father. Then Laura asked: 'Are you, Dad?'

'Probably ... yes.'

'Well I think that's great. Really, I do.'

'Thanks,' said Henry, smiling at his younger daughter.

Louisa said nothing.

'What do you think?' Henry asked her.

She looked confused. 'Well,' she said, 'well ... I guess it's kind of ... well ... better than nothing.'

'Thanks,' said Henry again – ironically. 'As a matter of fact, he went on, 'as your friends Danny and Julius would no doubt explain to you, there are snags.'

'I'm glad to hear it,' said Lilian.

'What snags?' asked Louisa.

'For one thing,' said Henry, 'there's the problem of the beneficiary.'

'Can't you give it to the people in the ghettoes?' asked Laura.

'No,' said Henry, 'because by making things that little bit easier for them, you postpone the day of their rising in revolt against the whole system.'

'It should go towards a revolution,' said Louisa.

'Quite,' said Henry, 'but who is the revolution?'

'We are.'

'Who?'

'I mean, someone like Alan or Danny or Julius.'

'They're not the revolution,' said Henry.

'Yes they are.'

'They're a group of bright but immature kids ...'

'They are not.' Louisa's fingers gripped the handle of her coffee cup.

'... who get a kick out of conspiratorial conversations and dramatic fantasies of assassination....'

'Fantasies. We'll see.'

'The whole point is,' said Henry, 'that we won't.'

'You won't see,' shouted Louisa, rising to her feet, 'you certainly won't see. You're too darned smug to see. But it'll happen just the same. We don't need you.'

She kicked back her chair and left the room. Henry leaned across the table and poured himself some more coffee.

'You and Louisa,' said Lilian. 'Nothing changes.'

Henry shrugged: then looked perplexed. 'Are they up to something?' he asked Laura.

'I don't know,' she said.

16

Louisa went out of the front door of her parents' house and slammed it. Going to her Volkswagen, she sat without moving in the driver's seat, gripping the steering-wheel in fury. Then she started the motor and drove to see Julius.

He opened the door to his flat and once again looked embarrassed to see her but Louisa, still incensed, did not notice and walked straight past him into his ill-lit living room. She stopped short when she found that her smouldering eyes were staring straight into those of a tall, elderly man sitting in an armchair.

'Good evening,' he said in a tone of moderate amusement which meant, to Louisa, that he had noticed what kind of mood she was in.

'Hello,' she said, nodding towards the large head which was now lowered as the man lifted himself from the chair.

Julius came in behind Louisa.

'Won't you introduce us,' the man said to Julius, looking over Louisa's shoulder.

'Yes . . . er . . . Louisa, this is my uncle Bernard.'

'And you,' said the uncle, 'must be Miss Rutledge. Julius has told me about you.'

Louisa nodded again. 'I didn't mean to butt in,' she said.

'Not at all,' said Julius's uncle with a forced flourish of politeness. 'I have to be going, anyway.'

'Don't go, uncle,' said Julius.

'Well, in a minute I will,' said his uncle – Mr. Tate – sitting down again in the armchair.

Louisa looked round at Julius to see if he wanted her to stay but he had already turned to draw up a chair so Louisa sat down on the sofa and looked at the man.

'You're Professor Rutledge's daughter, aren't you?' he asked.

'Yes,' she said.

'An interesting man,' said Bernard Tate, 'such an interesting man.'

Louisa said nothing.

Julius shifted in his chair.

'I so often wish,' Tate continued, ignoring or unaware of his nephew's discomfiture, 'that my life might have been dedicated to the examination of ideas.'

'What do you do?' asked Louisa.

'Alas, a very dull job in Washington. But it pays a secure salary and there'll be a pension at the end of it, so I shouldn't complain.' He smiled – a smile as unnatural as his irony and his *bonhomie*. 'After all, he said, 'my father ... Julius's grandfather, was no more nor less than a steel-worker.' He laughed. 'Perhaps he worked in one of your grandfather's steel-works.'

'I don't think my grandfather had steel-works,' said Louisa.

'Didn't he?' asked Bernard. 'No, perhaps he didn't.'

'I guess he may have invested in steel, though,' said Louisa.

'Perhaps, yes,' said Tate. 'Perhaps he did. And now his granddaughter and the steel-worker's grandson meet on an equal footing in one of our great academic institutions. . . .' He looked around Julius' living room. 'That's the greatness of America,' he said.

Julius and Louisa said nothing.

'Nothing gives me greater pleasure,' said the uncle, 'than enabling Julius to be here.'

'Julius told me,' said Louisa, 'about how you pay for him.'

'He gives credit where credit is due. I'm glad to hear it.'

'And he told me about how you used to come down to see him on his birthday in Albuquerque'

'It was my pleasure'

'It was very good of you,' said Louisa.

The uncle shrugged his shoulders. 'After your father died,' he said, turning to Julius, 'I felt it a duty as well as a pleasure to see to your education. After all, I didn't want you brought up entirely under ... Latin influences.' He laughed.

Louisa watched him and decided that he must work for Health, Education and Welfare since he was half like a doctor, half like a school-teacher. Her eyes went up from his tight lips to his heavy lids which hid the expression of his eyes: then further up to his large, balding head.

'It's been a great pleasure to meet you, Louisa,' said the uncle getting up onto his feet which wore heavy black shoes.

'I hope I. . . .'

'No, no,' he said. 'I have to get back.'

Louisa glanced at Julius but his eyes were on his uncle.

'Would you see me to my car, Julius?' the older man asked his nephew.

'Sure,' said Julius. Then he turned and looked at Louisa – a neutral look. 'You can wait a minute, can't you?' he asked.

'Sure,' she said.

She sat down after they had left the flat and looked at her fingernails. She kept this up for five or six minutes – thinking – until Julius returned.

'I'm sorry to have been so long,' he said.

'No,' she said, '*I'm* sorry. I didn't mean to break up your evening with your uncle.'

'Don't worry,' said Julius. 'He's got to get up early in the morning. He would have gone back to his hotel anyway.'

'He's not like you at all,' said Louisa.

'I'm more like my mother.'

'I didn't just mean looks.'

'I know,' said Julius, 'he's different.' He sat down next to Louisa on the sofa and took hold of her hand. 'But let's not talk about him,' he said.

Louisa smiled. 'What do you want to talk about, then?'

'I don't know.' Julius looked at her hand, turning it to study the palm, then turning it back again. 'You bite your nails,' he said.

Louisa snatched her hand away and hid both of them under her legs. 'I know,' she said.

'Here, come on,' said Julius, trying to pull her right hand back into his.

'OK,' she said, allowing her hand to emerge, 'but don't say nasty things.'

'Who says it was nasty? You bite your nails. OK. But you've still got the . . . well, very nice hands.'

'Thanks.'

'We could talk about your hands, perhaps?'

'If you like.'

'Where they've been. . . .'

'With me, most of the time.'

'What they've done. . . .'

'Censored.'

'What they'd like to do. . . .'

'The left or the right?'

'Are they different?'

'The left never knows what the right hand's doing.' As she said this Louisa brought her left hand over to take Julius's hand which held her right: and her right hand, now freed, rose to pull her arm round his shoulder and settled in the thick hair behind his right ear.

'There was some coordination between the two hands on that,' said Julius, his face drawing nearer to Louisa's.

'I guess there was,' she whispered, 'a little.'

They kissed: and their hands and arms lost their separate identities and moved with the general movements of their bodies as they stretched against and around each other in this embrace.

Later the style of their kissing changed from the long, earnest encounters of the two sets of lips to short, humorous seals of affection on the ears, the nose, the eyes, the neck, the fingertips of the other.

When it was nearly midnight, Louisa said: 'Can I stay here the night?'

'Sure,' said Julius.

'I'll sleep here on the sofa.'

'You don't have to,' he said, smiling.

'No, I know, but I'd like to. You said, you remember, that there's got to be more, and now I think you're right: but I want to be certain that there is more ... much more ... as much as there can be.'

17

The next morning was the second occasion on which Julius had made breakfast for Louisa: and when it was ready he went into the living room and crouched by the sofa to wake her up.

'Come on,' he whispered, close to her nose. 'Breakfast.'

Her eyes opened. She blinked. 'Julius,' she said.

He went back into the kitchen and listened to her movements as she put on her clothes and then went to the bathroom.

'Shall I tell you something?' she said as she sat, finally, at the kitchen table.

'Go ahead,' said Julius.

'Today's the first day for ... for years that I've woken up happy.'

Julius blushed. 'It's that sofa,' he said. 'It's so uncomfortable that you're happy to wake up.'

'No,' said Louisa sharply, 'don't joke. It's true.'

'I think that's very good,' said Julius. 'Waking up happy.'

Louisa looked earnestly at her toast. 'I guess it means that I love you, only. . . .'

'Only what?'

'Well, when I think about it, I don't know if I do.'

'What a pity,' said Julius, smiling, 'we were almost there.'

'I wish you wouldn't make fun of me,' said Louisa.

'Go on,' said Julius.

'Well, I woke up with this feeling . . . well, that I was glad to wake up to a new day in this life . . . in this world. . . .'

'You don't usually?'

'No. No, usually I fight off waking up. There's nothing to wake up for. But this morning there was something. I thought at first it was you – but now I think it might be our plan . . . you know.'

'Yes. It could be that.'

'Do you mind me talking?'

'No.'

'Some people do mind. At breakfast.'

'I know. I don't.'

'Do you love me?'

'Do I love you?'

'Yes. I mean I know it's a lousy expression, but if someone asked you if you were in love with me. what would you answer?'

Julius took a mouthful of toast and through it said 'Yes'. He looked into his coffee and stirred it.

'Even if it's possible – in fact quite likely – that I don't really love you?'

'Since I met you,' he said, 'I loved you.'

'Since that party?'

'Yes.'

'After that first evening?'

'Yes.'

'You must love easily.'

'I don't,' said Julius. 'I've never loved anyone before.'

'And I always thought I'd never love anyone again.'

'Perhaps you won't.' Julius's expression had become almost angry.

'Don't,' said Louisa. 'Please don't. I'm sorry. I was being flippant and . . . and selfish.' She paused: then said, 'We know, really, don't we? We know how much we do and don't love each other.'

'I guess so,' said Julius.

'Just remember that the first time is the best and easiest because with love it's got to be the first time or it doesn't work. And sometimes if ... if you've thought it was love ... the first time ... before, then it's kind of hard to get back to feeling the kind of trust and hope that you need ... for love.'

18

Like a man who suddenly forms a complete picture of his clerk's embezzlement or his wife's infidelity, Henry came to realize that Alan, Danny, Julius, and quite probably Louisa, were mixed up in some political adventure of an extreme sort. Louisa's behaviour at supper had alerted him, but the recent and simultaneous indifference of his pupils to the academic discussions in the seminar was what quickly convinced him that his suspicions were correct.

The morning before the next session of the seminar he sat in his office at Harvard, twisting and pulling at his fingers and staring at the blotting pad on his desk. Next door his secretary typed out standard letters of acceptance or refusal to universities, societies and magazines which had invited him to conferences, *Festschriften* or symposia.

Henry's mind worked with less method than her typewriter. He found himself unable to concentrate on the problem – critical though it was – of his students' conspiracy. His eyes kept turning to the window and he would watch the effect of the wind on the few small things that it could move between the heavy buildings – the blades of grass, candy-wrappers and crumpled manifestoes.

How could he stop them? And was that what he should do? He recalled that at one session of the seminar he had conceded – he looked now along his shelf of books – conceded the hypothesis that a small group might initiate a revolution – 'a single spark start a prairie fire'. If he believed that, then how could he argue against their venture, whatever it might be? What convincing proof could he offer that they were not the few, singled out by history, to drag, kicking, the great capitalist power of America into the next, the final, stage of its social and political evolution?

Henry smiled to himself as he thought of his three students as the Lenins and Trotskys of the United States: and of

Louisa as Rosa Luxemburg, or La Pasionaria. And yet they
would say – he knew they would say – why not? Who was he,
an extinct liberal, to say that they were not? He would also,
at the time, have scoffed at Lenin in the reading room of the
British Museum; at Ho Chi Minh in the kitchens of Claridges;
at Che Guevara in the Medical School of Buenos Aires. Perhaps it was only a lack of imagination on his part that made
him so certain that Alan, Danny and Julius would never succeed.

He thought of the three students, each in turn, trying hard
to assess their qualities in relation to what they would like to
be. Danny, certainly, had the cerebral ability to form a theory
and stick to it; Alan had the fanaticism – the bitter, blinded
drive to an extreme act; and Julius, he thought, had the judgment. If any one of them had the qualities of all three – there
indeed might be a political leader: but as a triumvirate they
would only land up in jail.

His secretary brought in some letters for him to sign. He
did so, writing his name with a flourish which led the secretary – a woman in her late thirties – to blink uneasily: she
became almost alarmed when Henry turned to speak to her,
but all he said was, 'I wonder if you could get me some salami
on rye and coffee?'

She left the room and Henry looked down at the book in
his hand. It was Mannheim's *Ideology and Utopia*. He sighed,
stood up, and put it back on the shelf. His eye ran further
along, looking for another book, until it reached Saint Augustine's *Confessions*, where it stopped. With his forefinger he
pulled this volume from between two other books and sat
down with it at his desk.

19

The seminar met at three. Henry walked to the classroom
from his office, his mind returning from Saint Augustine to
the question of the conspiracy, still void of solutions – void
indeed of attitudes.

His suspicions – for they were still suspicions –
were strengthened by the position of Alan, Danny and Julius
in the class: they sat in the back row and their eyes had taken
on that glazed look which Henry associated with Communists, Mormons, Scientologists and others who felt certain of a

closed, exclusive truth. He readjusted his gaze – for refreshment – onto the eager, simple, decent faces of Kate and Mike and Debbie.

'Well,' he said, smiling at the front row, 'where did we get to last time?'

Kate looked down at her notes. 'We were discussing Hobbes,' she said.

'Hobbes,' said Henry. '*Leviathan.* The embodiment of the state with absolute power and absolute authority. It seems to us now something of a totalitarian theory of state: but you must remember that in those days most citizens were prepared to tolerate one major tyrant if he would protect them against many minor ones. The theories of Hobbes and, say, Machiavelli are based on the *a priori* assumption that civil order is a good thing. The rise to supreme power of the European monarchies in Europe – whether Henry VIII or Louis XIV – was founded on the need for order, whatever *post factum* justification it was given in terms of divine right. The growth of so-called democratic ideas came when it seemed that civil order could be improved by limiting the powers of these monarchies: and I think that in a hundred years it may be seen that certain societies in the present day adopted socialist systems of government because of the *disorder* of capitalism. . .'

Henry glanced at the three at the back of the classroom. Their eyes did not move.

'I use the word disorder,' he went on, 'in its widest sense. All that is clear from our present position in time is that there are certain contradictions in capitalism which lead to disorder: whether socialism resolves these contradictions remains to be seen. We've only had fifty years of Russian communism and twenty years of Chinese communism. I think one would need one hundred years at least before reaching any conclusions about these new political and economic systems.'

He paused Kate raised her hand. 'But surely, professor,' she said, 'we can't just wait a hundred years before doing anything about America.'

'No,' he said. 'We have to act to make decisions about our society all the time – but these decisions are based on unproven hypotheses. That's all I meant to say.'

'I really don't know how you can say that revolution is a movement towards order,' said Mike.

'I don't say that it always is. I said it should be. A revolutionary movement will attract support from the uncommitted if it is.'

Henry looked again at the back row: the six glazed eyes.

'A failed attempt, on the other hand, is worse than no attempt at all because it is only further disorder – a by-product of capitalism.'

'But you can't tell if you'll succeed,' said Sam, 'until you try.'

'You can't be certain,' said Henry, 'but can have a good idea if you analyze objectively the potential of any current situation. The chief danger in this, as in so much else, is self-deception.'

At the end of the class Henry called to Alan, Danny and Julius and asked them to stay behind. They looked awkwardly at each other but then came forward as the others filed out. Henry remained sitting at the table and he gestured to them to sit down at the front row.

'You don't make very good conspirators,' he said to them when they were alone. 'It's quite obvious what's going on.'

Julius looked out of the window: Danny blushed. Only Alan met Henry's eyes. 'We weren't trying to hide anything from you,' he said. 'It was understood, I think, that we were going to do something more radical then, well, giving our money away.'

'OK,' said Henry. 'But I'd like to know what you intend to do.'

'I think it would only make things difficult for you,' said Alan.

'I'm prepared to risk that,' said Henry.

'For God's sake, professor,' said Danny, 'you know we respect you and all that – but you're just not onto what we've got to do.'

'All the same,' said Henry, 'I'd like to know.'

The three were silent.

'You might try and stop us,' said Julius eventually.

'How?'

'By calling the FBI.'

'He wouldn't do that,' said Danny.

'No,' said Henry, 'I wouldn't do that.'

'Why do you want to know?' asked Alan.

'Well, I'm interested ... not just academically, either. As you say, giving my money away isn't going to change the world. I'd like to hear other ideas.'

Alan looked at Danny, then at Julius. They both shrugged so the priest turned to Henry again. 'Perhaps you'd let us think about it?'

'Of course,' said Henry. 'Come by my house this evening ... or tomorrow ... whenever you like, and let me know what you decide.'

Louisa was waiting for Julius outside the class-room. She glanced defiantly at her father: he smiled and went towards his office while she walked off in the opposite direction with the three others.

'Your dad seems to know what's going on,' said Danny.

'I didn't tell him,' said Louisa, her eyes on her feet.

'No,' said Alan. 'He must have deduced it.'

'How?' asked Julius.

'From what we said in class and then ... well, we haven't been joining in the seminar.'

'That was stupid,' said Danny.

'Luckily,' said Alan, 'it's only the professor, and I don't think he'll do anything about it.'

'But do we bring him in on it?' asked Danny.

'Bring him in?' said Louisa. 'Are you crazy?'

'He wants us to,' said Julius.

'He might warn Laughlin,' said Danny.

'No,' said Louisa, shaking her head, 'I doubt it. He doesn't like Laughlin. But he'd try to dissuade us.'

'That might not be such a bad idea,' said Alan.

'Do you think we shouldn't go through with it?' asked Danny.

'No,' said Alan, 'I think we should. But I think we should be sure of what we're doing, and your father, Louisa, might help us to be sure because he won't be able to dissuade us and if he can't, then no one can.'

20

Henry only returned to his office for a few minutes before walking home to Brattle Street. As he went into Harvard Square he saw Louisa and her new friends standing by the news-stand in the middle, absorbed in earnest conversation while travellers from the Transit came up from under the street and brushed past them.

Henry now crossed the street himself, dodging the slow-moving traffic, and went along the south side of Cambridge Common. He tried to imagine their conversation – the points that would be made for and against admitting him to their secret. His own feelings about the possible confrontation were remarkably even and undisturbed: he hardly seemed to care whether they told him or not. If they did not, he told himself, the danger would be that they would be arrested or even blown-up by some home-made bomb. That thought made him anxious – anxious for his daughter – though less so, perhaps, than the image of her alone and unhappy.

The anxiety that accompanied the other possibility – that they would tell him – was more subjective. If they planned, as he suspected, to assassinate the President or the Secretary of State, he would have to find words – to find logic, only logic would satisfy them – to express his own feelings that such an act would be ugly and futile.

Lenin, it occurred to him, must have written something against terrorism: but would they accept Lenin? He knew their answers before he had even posed his questions. Lenin only knew the situation as it was fifty years ago. Today it was standard practice for the revolutionaries to use terrorism: the Vietcong, after all. . . .

Kennedy, he might say: think of the revulsion felt by everybody at his assassination. And they would answer that it is quite right to feel revulsion for a death which has no political significance – but their assassination would have significance and all those against the system would see its justice.

Henry passed the house of a friend and colleague and thought of calling in to ask his advice but then did not. He felt he could predict what this man – a scientist – would say – that if he could not dissuade them, he should warn the President or call the police. But this Henry knew he would never do because he no longer felt that he had the right to denounce them; or that the police had the right to arrest them: for like them he sought a solution and if he held back from violence, perhaps it was only because he was afraid.

It was in this mood of self-doubt that he received the three students later that day. Louisa was with them and she came into his study behind them as if she were a stranger in the house.

Henry sat at his desk: Alan and Danny sat on the two armchairs. Julius and Louisa sat on the floor.

'Well?' Henry asked them, looking round at the group.

'We've decided,' said Alan, 'that you should be told.'

'Good,' said Henry.

'It's no compliment,' said Alan. 'We want to be sure and we think you'll help us to be sure.'

'Yes, I see,' said Henry. 'That isn't so complimentary.'

Louisa made a gesture of impatience with her hands and mouth but said nothing.

Alan looked at Danny: Danny nodded. He then looked at Julius but the Mexican's eyes were on the professor so Alan too turned to Henry and said: 'We intend to initiate a revolution in this country by a politically significant assassination.'

'I thought so,' said Henry. 'Who?'

Again Alan looked round at the others: Danny caught his eye again and this time he spoke. 'Senator Laughlin,' he said.

'Laughlin?'

'Yes,' said Alan.

'You can't be serious.'

'Certainly, we are. . . .'

'But there's nothing significant about Laughlin. He's a non-entity.'

Alan seemed confused and attempted to conceal it by adding a sneer to his tone of voice. 'He's not a nonentity when it comes to Vietnam,' he said.

'Of course he is,' said Henry. 'He just says what he thinks everyone else says, except he's slower than most to sense a change.'

'We know he's a friend of yours, professor,' said Danny.

'That's got nothing to do with it,' said Henry. 'If Laughlin was killed in a plane crash tomorrow, I wouldn't care a damn.'

Henry felt Louisa's eyes on him. 'Then why,' she said slowly, 'would you mind if we killed him?'

'I'd mind because of what would happen to you . . . all of you,' he said. 'You wouldn't get away with it.'

'We would,' said Danny, 'with Laughlin. That's why we chose him. You see, Louisa . . . I mean. . . .'

'I suggested Laughlin,' said Louisa, 'because I'd be able to find out from Bennie or Jean where he's going to be and at what time.'

'They'd remember that afterwards and they'd pull you in.'

'It's unlikely,' said Louisa sarcastically 'After all, I'm your daughter.'

Henry was about to say something else, but he stopped himself, shrugged his shoulders, and said nothing.

'You see,' said Julius ponderously, as if reciting lines from a play, 'Laughlin's well-known enough. Everyone knows what he stands for: but he's not so important that he's got a dozen Secret Service agents around him all the time.'

'We could bring it off,' said Alan. 'The three of us ... and Louisa.'

'And from there?' asked Henry. 'Where do you go from there?'

'After that it's a matter of recruitment and organization before we strike again on a wider front.'

'We have to start with something like this assassination,' said Danny, 'to establish that we're serious ... that we intend to fight to the end.'

'Yes,' said Henry, 'I understand that. But why kill someone? Why not rob a bank, like Stalin at Tiflis, or blow up IBM or something like that?'

'Just because you suggest it,' said Alan — his eyes staring at Henry. 'Because all those things are extreme but they're acceptable. They don't break the taboo of violence against people, which is the strongest weapon in the hands of the establishment — because they use violence against people with their police and National Guard. They use it all right and their only fear is that the people might direct it back at them. Because once the fighting starts, there's no knowing where it will end — and they know that.'

Henry shrugged. 'Perhaps you're right,' he said.

'We are, I know we are,' said Danny.

'And you, Julius?' asked Henry. 'Are you as confident as Danny?'

'Sure,' said Julius.

'And you, Louisa?' asked Henry, glancing at his daughter.

'Yes,' she said, 'we're right.'

'Very well,' said Henry, 'I concede. That's to say, I recognize that I won't be able to persuade you to change your minds. I hate the idea of violence and when it comes to assassination, I feel a real repugnance: but I suppose that if I'm honest with myself I must admit that these feelings may be the product of my class environment. Perhaps, also, of my age. If I were younger, perhaps I'd join you. I don't know, though, I don't know.'

21

When the three students left the house, Henry expected Louisa to leave with them but she was still sitting in his study when he returned from seeing them out. He sat down again at his desk.

'What do you really think?' Louisa asked him.

'What I said.'

'That we might be right?'

Henry shrugged. 'I seem to have reached a point where I'm not certain of anything.'

'You don't seem to mind,' said Louisa, getting up off the floor and sitting in a chair.

'Well,' said Henry, 'it's a kind of liberation.'

'To have no certainties?'

'Yes. To abandon all inherited and assumed beliefs and see both sides of every question with equal clarity.'

'Were all your beliefs inherited and assumed?'

'I think so. I might come back to some of them, but right at this moment I feel I've a clean slate.'

'You won't give up looking?'

'No. But I want to go slowly and I want to go to the centre.'

'What centre?'

'Of knowledge, or rather of wisdom. I no longer want to strike attitudes on the periphery. I want my convictions to come from a real understanding of what life is about.'

Louisa nodded and thought for a while: then she asked: 'Julius and the others, do you think their convictions come from a real understanding of what life is about?'

'You're in a better position to judge that than I am,' said Henry.

Louisa did not reply to this, but she looked at her father with an expression of great curiosity.

Later Henry and Louisa were called to supper: they went into the kitchen where Lilian and Laura were watching television. With her eyes still on the screen, Lilian made a gesture towards the food she had prepared. Then, a minute later, when the programme stopped for the commercials, she looked away from the television and asked either or both of them: 'Who's been visiting?'

'Three students from the seminar,' said Henry.

'Don't you see enough of them in class?'

'I said I'd lend them some books.'

There was a pause. Henry helped himself to the food on the stove. Lilian looked at Louisa. 'Have you joined the seminar?' she asked.

Louisa, confused, looked to her father.

'I thought she might if she'd like to,' said Henry. 'After all, she doesn't look much like getting a job.'

Lilian returned to face the screen. Henry and Louisa exchanged glances – glances of complicity.

22

Alan and Julius left Cambridge the next day to buy guns in Florida. Louisa, playing her part in the conspiracy, went shopping with her mother in Boston.

'What are you going to wear to the Democratic dinner next week?' she asked Lilian as they drove across the river.

'Anything will do for that,' said Lilian. 'I'm more concerned about the weekend.'

'The Ashtons?'

'Yes.'

'Are they grand?'

'A lot of jet-set people who make me feel frumpish.'

'Oh come on,' said Louisa. 'You look a million times better than most women your age.'

'Thanks,' said Lilian sourly.

'You do, really.'

'I don't know why I bother . . . at my age.'

'I guess it still matters, said Louisa. 'I mean, older men like older women, don't they?'

'Some young men like older women.'

'I guess they do.'

They drove on for a while in silence.

'You and Dad always did things together, didn't you?' Louisa asked her mother.

'When?'

'When you were young.'

'I guess we did.'

'Politics and things.'

'Yes.'

'I think that's important, don't you?'

Lilian, who was driving, shrugged her shoulders.

'And Bill. You knew him, then, didn't you?' Louisa asked.

'Yes.'

'Why did he become so right-wing?'

'It's like hardening of the arteries. It comes on with old age.'

'But you're not right-wing, and Dad isn't really.'

'I thought you thought he was.'

'He's changed. He's really opened his mind – wide open.'

Lilian made a face as if to say that she had not noticed it. 'You mean that spiel about giving away his money?' she asked.

'That's peanuts,' said Louisa.

'What else is he going to do?'

'I don't think he'll do anything. He's not really the active sort, is he? But his ideas are getting kind of . . . well, better.'

Lilian nodded. 'I'm glad to hear it.' She stopped the car at a red light.

'Is Bill coming up for this dinner?' asked Louisa, glancing at the Sheraton Hotel outside.

'Yes,' said Lilian.

'Where's he staying?'

'I'm not sure.'

'At the Sheraton?'

'I doubt it. He usually stays at the Fairfax.' Lilian bit her lower lip and felt herself blush which so irritated her that she let out the clutch of the Volkswagen too sharply as the light went green and the car lurched forward.

'Mother,' said Louisa, 'you've been happy with Dad, haven't you?'

'Sort of.'

'Only sort of?'

'No. We've been happy.'

'It shows that it can be done.'

'What?'

'Well . . . the whole business of marriage.'

Lilian turned the car into a multi-storey car park. She took the ticket and the striped bar lifted automatically to let them pass.

'It isn't easy,' she said, 'but I guess you know that.'

'Even for you and Dad? Wasn't it easy?'

'It's never easy.'

Louisa nodded.

'But it's worth it,' said Lilian, 'if you stick it out to the end.'

They drove up the spiralling concrete ramp. Louisa looked at her mother's face in the changing light – its features fixed in an odd expression of mixed melancholy and hope.

'You're not at the end yet,' said Louisa.

'No,' said Lilian, 'but we're nearly there. I think your father and I will have a very happy old age.'

Lilian parked the car: then the two of them got out and walked down to the shops.

23

Henry ran into Danny as he was entering the Widener Library and Danny was leaving it. They stopped as if to talk to each other but for a moment neither said anything: then Henry smiled and said, 'I'm glad you still have time for some work.'

Danny grinned and held up the book in his hand: Mao Tsetung – *On Guerilla Warfare*. 'Sure, professor,' he said. 'There's always time for work.'

Henry turned away from the library and walked down a few steps with Danny. 'I was wondering,' he said, 'does your father know about . . . about what we discussed yesterday?'

Danny's voice, like Henry's, sank to a conspiratorial tone. 'He has a general idea,' he said.

'Would you object if I talked with him about it?'

Danny hesitated – then shook his head. 'No,' he said.

'You see,' said Henry, 'I'd quite like a second opinion – especially from someone like your father.'

Danny nodded.

'Is he still a Communist?' asked Henry.

'He's not a Party member,' said Danny. 'He hasn't been for ten years.'

'But he still has the . . . convictions?'

Danny shrugged. 'I don't really know,' he said.

'Will he be home this morning?'

'He's almost always at home.'

'Yes, of course,' said Henry, remembering the blindness of Dr. Glinkman. 'How is he?'

'He gets kind of bitter sometimes,' said Danny.

'Yes,' said Henry. 'Yes, I dare say he does.'

24

Henry went back to his office and called Mrs. Glinkman. Having fixed up to go round there, he started to walk to their home: he walked because it was healthier and increasingly he appreciated good health – the sense of lightness of a slim figure and supple muscles.

It was not difficult to find the Glinkmans' house though

he had never been there before. He had met the couple at parties in the days when Dr. Glinkman went to such things. Henry had liked them and he admired the husband's work, but his strangeness – the mixture of Communism, blindness, Jewishness and poverty – had put Henry off the pursuit of any closer acquaintance.

As he entered the house and was shown into the study by Mrs. Glinkman, the sense of the alien returned to him – only now it was pleasant and exhilarating, like entering a cave or an Arab bazaar.

'Professor Rutledge?' said Dr. Glinkman, turning in his chair.

'Dr. Glinkman ... hello,' said Henry.

'It's good of you to come,' said Dr. Glinkman. 'Forgive me for not getting up.'

'Of course.'

'I'm not only blind and deaf, I'm lazy.' He laughed. He was hardly older than Henry but his demeanour was that of an old man.

'You seem quite cheerful,' said Henry.

'It comes and it goes,' said Dr. Glinkman – his face relaxing from a smile. He turned his black spectacles up towards the ceiling. 'Some days one thinks of one's sorrows, others of one's joys.'

'Indeed,' said Henry.

'I have lost the use of my eyes,' said Dr. Glinkman, 'but then I have a wife who is an angel and a son who is a very likeable devil.' He laughed again.

'It was about the likeable devil that I wanted to talk to you,' said Henry.

'Has he been playing hookey?' asked Dr. Glinkman.

'Not exactly,' said Henry. He leaned forward on the sofa where he now sat. 'I don't know how much you know – Danny said you knew something – but some of my students, Danny among them, have been abandoning political theory in favour of ... well ... political practice.'

Dr. Glinkman nodded. 'Yes,' he said.

'You know about that?'

'They have their discussions upstairs ... Danny tells me a little of what they say.'

'Do you know what they mean to do?'

'Something ... extreme.'

'They plan to assassinate Senator Laughlin '

Dr. Glinkman nodded again. 'Yes, I know,' he said

'It was my daughter's idea,' said Henry.

'Yes,' said Dr. Glinkman.

'Did Danny tell you that I'd been told?' Henry asked.

'Yes,' said Dr. Glinkman. 'I think he wanted to tell you.'

'Why?'

'Because he respects you.'

'That makes it . . .' Henry hesitated, 'more difficult.'

'Indeed.'

'I wanted to ask you . . . well, to find out what your attitude was.'

'And what is yours?' asked Dr. Glinkman.

'Well,' said Henry, 'I think they're wrong but I can't convince them . . . I can't really convince myself. I feel they're wrong but I can't see the error.'

'I'm afraid,' said Dr. Glinkman, 'that I'm in rather the same boat.'

'I thought,' said Henry, 'that since you are, or rather since you were a Communist, you might be in a better position to dissuade them.'

'Unfortunately,' said Dr. Glinkman, 'I'm unable to do so. I've tried, though, with Danny.'

'What arguments did you advance?' asked Henry. 'I find that their reasoning . . . their dialectic . . . is unanswerable if you accept certain premises, which I do. Especially the priest's. . . .'

'He has too much influence over them,' said Dr. Glinkman. 'And the Mexican – I don't understand him.'

'No,' said Henry. 'Nor do I. But tell me, what did you say to Danny?'

'I took off my glasses,' said Dr. Glinkman, 'like this.' He lifted both his hands to remove the black spectacles from his nose and he turned to face Henry, revealing to his guest the scarred sockets and lifeless, artificial eyes. ' "Look, Danny," I said to him. "That was the price I paid for the idealism of youth." You see,' Dr Glinkman went on, replacing his spectacles, 'I fought for the Spanish Republic and it cost me my sight.' He laughed and made a gesture towards his eyes. 'An old war wound. The siege of Madrid.'

'I didn't know,' said Henry quietly.

'And what was it for? Franco has survived Hitler and Mussolini: even Stalin. Now the United States makes treaties with him. And for me – thirty years of darkness. I said all this to

Danny. I'd rather have my sight now than all the Communist régimes in the world. What did they achieve, anyway? Five-year plans, great leaps forward: and lies, deportations, torture.... I don't know. Until the fifties I went along with it but then ... no, not Hungary. Nothing specific. I just felt, as I said, that it hadn't been worth it. I'd rather have my sight than Mr. Kosygin or Herr Ulbricht. That's all.'

'What did Danny say to that?' Henry asked.

'Unfortunately,' said Dr. Glinkman, 'he won't believe me. I've been a hero for him, you see. To have lost my eyes for the loyalist cause in Spain was the most glorious thing ... I used to think so. Miriam thought so .. and our friends, they were all Communists or fellow travellers. And Danny is the only one left, now, who still thinks so. And when I warn him, he dismisses me as a fussing parent.'

'I think we have a right to fuss.'

'Of course we have. They haven't a chance, those children. This country is overburdened with policemen who live and breathe conspiracies which don't even exist. They'll be only too pleased to find one which does ... and they will find it: because even if they do kill Laughlin, what then? If they form a wider group, as they think they will, four of every five recruits will be agents of the FBI.'

Dr. Glinkman spoke more quickly now: his caustic manner had left him. 'I tell you, these people feed off each other's fantasies. Those children believe in a capitalist conspiracy: the police believe in a communist conspiracy. But history is not made up of conspiracies. You know that as well as I do. It is made by great movements of social and economic forces which throw up individuals – Robespierre or Lenin or Fidel Castro – but they are not made by these individuals. This Ernesto Guevara – he had a clever idea: it gives a semblance of logic to the idealisms of youth, but it is nonsense, and because it is nonsense, it was inevitable that Guevara should die. But Danny and his friends – they have learnt nothing from Guevara's mistakes, and so they will make the same mistakes and either get killed or spend their youth in prison ... prison of some sort.'

This last remark was made with a further gesture by Dr. Glinkman to his eyes.

'But what,' asked Henry, 'would you tell them to do? They've tired of studying theories of society while their own society collapses around them.'

'Then they should go out and organize – agitate, if they like: and then, if a revolutionary situation should arise, which I doubt, but it may, then they will be there.'

'Yes,' said Henry. 'Yes, I'm sure you're right.'

'It will probably be a waste of their lives anyway,' said Dr. Glinkman, 'but at least when they're older and know better they will still be able to see paintings and nature and the smiles of young women. . . .'

25

When Henry returned home in the evening the house seemed to be empty. He took his briefcase into his study, and as he was re-crossing the hall to enter the living room, he saw Louisa at the top of the stairs.

'Hi,' she said. She smiled at him and came down the stairs. 'Do you like my new dress?' she asked.

The dress she was wearing was white and came down to her ankles. It was embroidered with bright thread at the hem and bodice.

'It's lovely,' said Henry. 'Where did you get it?'

'In Boston. It's Roumanian. Mother got one like it. She thinks she'll never dare wear it, though.'

Henry laughed and moved on into the living room.

'Shall I make you a drink?' Louisa asked.

Henry glanced at her. 'Don't feel you have to,' he said.

'No, I'd like to,' said Louisa, coming from the hall into the living room and starting to mix a cocktail 'Still the same?' she asked.

'Still the same,' he said, crossing to the fire and crouching to light it.

'Do you mind if I have one?'

'Not at all. Help yourself.' He stood up and watched the fire spread from the newspaper to the twigs. 'Where's your mother?'

Louisa crossed the room with two glasses filled with the mixture she had made. 'She went off to Boston again. She'll be back soon.'

Henry took his drink and sipped it. 'Perfect,' he said.

Louisa took a sip of hers: she screwed up her face.

'Don't you like it?' Henry asked.

'Sure,' She smiled. 'Perfect, though I say it myself.'

'I thought you didn't drink?'

'I'm drowning my sorrows.'

'You've got sorrows?' asked Henry, smiling. 'I thought you were never anything but perfectly happy.'

Louisa laughed – a breathless laugh of relief as well as amusement. 'Well,' she said, 'doctor,' she added, 'my boy-friend's out of town.'

'Julius?'

'Uh-huh.'

'Where's he gone?'

'I guess he and Alan are gun-running.'

Henry frowned. 'Buying guns? Are they really?'

'It's not so difficult,' said Louisa. 'In some states you can buy machine-guns and hand-grenades. . . .'

'I know.'

'They're just getting revolvers, though.' Her face became serious.

Henry sat down. 'I don't quite understand Julius,' he said.

Louisa also sat down, on an armchair facing her father. 'What don't you understand?'

'Why he's doing this.'

'He thinks it's right.'

'Yes, I know. But there are usually personal reasons why a man becomes a revolutionary . . . or at any rate, so revolutionary that he's prepared to kill in cold blood.'

'You think we're wrong, don't you?'

'I do,' said Henry, 'yes, I do. But if you've got to do it, you've got to do it. And I see Danny's reasons and Alan's and your. . . .' He looked at Louisa – his eyes still and sad for a moment. 'But I don't see the source of Julius's compulsion. . . .'

'Perhaps it's to do with being Mexican,' said Louisa. 'They are discriminated against.'

'Has he ever complained to you of that?'

'No.' She shook her head.

'He's too confident to let that sort of thing put him in a situation like this. He's confident – and yet he holds himself back. He lets Danny and Alan do the talking – and yet I'd say he has more judgment than either of them.'

'I know what you mean,' said Louisa. 'He's not as keen on this whole thing as Alan and Danny.'

'And you?'

Louisa looked down at her glass, now half-empty. 'I must

admit,' she said, 'I like it less and less. I mean, I was all steamed up about . . . about things when I suggested killing Bill: but now the idea of just shooting him. . . .'

'It's really going ahead, is it?'

Louisa shrugged. 'Yes, I guess so. I've even found out which hotel he's going to be staying at.'

'How?'

'Mother knew.'

Henry nodded. 'Which?'

'The Fairfax.'

'And will you kill him there?'

'*I* won't kill him,' said Louisa. 'I couldn't kill anyone. Alan's going to pull the trigger.'

'What will you do?'

'I'll wait in the lobby and when I see Bill come out of the elevator, I walk out onto the street. Then Danny and Alan drive up, shoot him and scram.'

'And Julius?'

'He's going to hang around in case of emergencies.'

Henry stood up and went to pour himself another glass of the cocktail. 'I wish I could persuade them to give it up,' he said.

'I don't think you can. I mean, they've really made up their minds. You could call the cops, of course. . . .' She looked up at her father.

'So could you,' he said.

She smiled. 'I'm sorry,' she said.

Henry rejoined her by the fire. 'That's really nice, that dress,' he said. 'I haven't seen you looking so elegant in years. And your hair's all brushed.'

Louisa smiled and threw back her hair but said nothing.

'You couldn't dissuade Julius, could you?' Henry asked her. 'Or at least get them to wait.'

Louisa thought to herself. 'It's difficult,' she said. 'You see, our relationship is kind of based on doing this thing together.'

Henry nodded.

'Do you get that?'

'Yes.'

'And I'm afraid that if there wasn't that, then there might be – well, you know – nothing.'

Once again Henry nodded. 'Yes, well, I wouldn't argue against that.'

'I guess there was something of that with you and Mother, wasn't there?'

'Yes,' said Henry.

'You didn't do much together, though, did you?'

'Well, we worked for Bill Laughlin,' Henry smiled at his daughter.

'He was different then,' she said – blushing a little.

'Times have changed more than he has. At least that's how it seems.' Henry sighed and was silent and he did not notice the intent, scrutinizing stare which his daughter directed at him while summoning up courage to ask something. Then she did.

'Dad,' she said, 'can I ask you something personal?'

'Ask me anything you like,' said Henry, throwing his arms apart, his glass held steadily in his right hand.

'Well,' said Louisa, 'did Mother, before she married you, did she . . . I mean, was she ever in love with Bill?'

Henry brought his hands together again and twisted the glass slowly backwards and forwards. 'She only met him through me,' he said.

'I see,' said Louisa. 'I'm sorry. I just noticed that whenever she speaks about him she puts on a kind of special voice.'

'Yes,' said Henry, his voice subdued. Then he drew in his breath and said in a louder, higher tone of voice: 'Perhaps you ought to know, in view of what you mean to do to Bill, that Lilian did love him but it was after we married, not before. . .

'No, did she . . .?' Louisa began.

'In fact,' said Henry with a slight shrug, 'perhaps she still loves him. She still sees him.'

'No?' said Louisa. 'Really? Sees him . . I mean . . .?'

'Precisely,' said Henry.

'But why don't you divorce her?' said Louisa.

Henry shrugged his shoulders again. 'There seemed to be no point. She didn't want to marry Bill: I don't want to marry anyone else. And there were you two girls.'

'I hope it wasn't just because of us,' said Louisa.

'No,' said Henry. 'Lilian . . . well, we're quite good friends . . . on and off.'

'That seems kind of like a compromise,' said Louisa.

'Yes,' said Henry. 'A compromise is just what it is.'

'But doesn't it hurt?' asked Louisa. 'To think of her and Bill?'

'Yes, but before, I hadn't been entirely faithful so I couldn't
. . . well, I didn't want to break up the family.'

'So you just kept on?'

'Yes.'

'Wow.' Louisa stood up. 'I need another drink,' she said.

'Help yourself,' said Henry.

'The things you find out,' said Louisa, crossing to the
bottles.

'I think it's probably best that you should know about it,'
said Henry. 'But bear in mind that I don't talk about it with
Lilian. Don't bring it up at dinner.'

'No, OK.' Louisa returned to the fire-place and sat on the
arm of her father's chair. 'Do you know what I think?' she
said.

'No?'

'Well, I think the revolution's got to be personal as well as
public: that you can't mean well for the human race if you
don't try your best with each individual member of it.'

Henry smiled and looked into the fire. 'Is that why you're
being so nice to me?' he asked.

'No,' said Louisa. She stood and crossed to sit in her own
armchair: then, with her eyes, like her father's, looking into
the fire she said: 'It's because for the first time in years I feel
that I understand you and that you understand me. In fact,
for the first time ever.'

26

Later Lilian returned and Henry left with her to dine with
friends in Lexington. He talked and laughed in the company
of these friends and would not let the conversation slip into
the morass of race or Vietnam. He was benign and friendly towards Lilian in the car as they drove back: while she was
guarded with him, fearing that he had hit upon another
scheme like that of giving his money away.

They went to bed and Henry went straight to sleep, but
unconsciously he must have been concerned because he
awoke in the middle of the night, his mind alert with an im-
precise panic. At first he thought it was the residue of an un-
remembered nightmare – but then there emerged from his
thoughts as the source of his anxiety the planned assassination
by his daughter and her friends.

He rose and went into the bathroom to drink some water and when he returned to bed he calmed himself with the thought that it would never come to that; that if he kept in touch with them, he would think of something to deflect them from their purpose.

He slept again but in the morning when he awoke the same anxiety was first to surface on his conscious mind. He moved and inadvertently with his knee touched the hot form of Lilian who was still asleep beside him. The impossibility of sharing his concern with her made it much harder to bear ... but as he thought of it, that impossibility suggested to him a way out.

This idea – a course of action which would pre-empt his students – grew rapidly in his mind as he washed and shaved. Then Lilian came into the bathroom behind him and made a face at him which meant nothing in particular but was affectionate and funny: and the idea suddenly seemed – not less suitable, but less attractive.

He went into the bedroom and started to dress and soon Lilian followed him and took her clothes from her cupboard and chest-of-drawers. As he buttoned up his shirt, Henry turned and watched her dress as she had dressed beside him many thousands of mornings before. Her face was drawn which had become usual in those past few years, but it was Lilian, as she sat to pull her stockings over her legs, who told him to cheer up. 'You look so gloomy,' she said.

'I'm not really,' he said.

'Well, you've no reason to be,' she said. 'just because one of your daughters tried to kill herself and another's probably on hard drugs. . . .'

Henry laughed and knotted his tie. 'What about you?' he asked.

'I'm an optimist,' she said.

He turned towards the mirror to adjust his tie.

'By the way,' said Lilian, 'since you're up here. Do you think a Roumanian peasant dress is too hippie for the Democratic dinner?'

'Are we going?' asked Henry.

'Aren't we?'

'I don't feel much of a Democrat these days.'

'Well, make up your mind. We're expected.'

'I guess we might as well go, then. And if your dress is anything like the one Lou was wearing, it'll be just right. We're expected for a drink with the Halevys tonight,' he added. 'You can try it out on them.'

Lilian hesitated in what she was doing. 'You never told me about that,' she said.

'No, I'm sorry. I forgot. There's nothing else on, is there?'

'I won't be able to come.'

'Why not?'

'There's something I've got to do.'

The stilted way in which Lilian said this, and the fact that she remained facing away from him, absorbed in her cosmetics, made Henry look across at her. 'What's that?' he asked.

'I promised I'd meet up with May Grant and some others to discuss bussing. It's not very important but I can't really change it now.'

She was nervous. She fidgeted with the bottles and jars on her dressing-table and Henry knew quite well that she was lying but it took him some time to work out why: but then, as he sat at breakfast, it came to him. The only occasions on which she lied to him like that were when she was going to meet Laughlin.

All at once the idea that he had had – which was of divorce – returned to him and grew to its former dimensions and surpassed them. As he sat drinking his second cup of filtered coffee he glanced across at Lilian who was reading the *Globe*. Either she did not notice his eyes or she did not want to meet them because she kept hers on the newspaper: thus Henry could study his wife's face and attempt to imagine how it could be if it was not there each morning. His feelings returned sadness as the answer to this question. The face was perplexing as well as familiar: it sounded off in him at different times sentiments of love and loathing but the combination of features remained for him what they had always been – the most complete image of living beauty he had seen. He could still watch her – and admire that face – quite detached from the passions it provoked in him, and feel, enveloping the passions and the beauty, a sense of complete identity with this other person. After twenty years she might still remain unknown, but he was content to remain as unknowing towards her as he might be towards himself.

In spite of this, the idea established itself: and when Louisa came down and had grunted good-morning and filled a bowl with cereal and milk, he turned to her and asked her if she would be seeing Julius that morning.

'I guess so,' she said. 'He was due back last night.'

'Then ask him if he and the others could look in at my office around noon.'

'OK.' She ate a few mouthfuls of cereal. 'What about me?'

'You too.'

She nodded. 'OK,' she said.

27

They all appeared – Alan, Danny, Julius and Louisa – at ten past twelve and were shown into Henry's office by his secretary, who then closed the door and left, as Henry had told her, to have her lunch.

Henry remained at his desk and the others sat either on the chairs that were placed against the wall or on the small sofa and armchair at the other end of the room.

'I'm gad you could make it,' said Henry. 'There's some urgency in what I want to say to you.'

The young men nodded and waited for him to go on.

'Now you intend,' said Henry, 'to kill Laughlin. I dare say you plan to get him tomorrow while he's here for the dinner. I'm against the idea; you know I'm against it, but up until now I haven't been able to think ... well, either of anything better or of any conclusive argument against it. Now, however, I've thought of both.'

Danny was about to say something but he turned towards Alan and noticed that he was leaning forward, his face intent on what Henry was going to say next.

'First the argument against it,' said Henry, 'against shooting Bill Laughlin in cold blood. It is this. It would backfire on you – the effect of such an assassination. It would horrify ninety-nine percent of potential militants: and it would bring the FBI down on you like a ton of bricks. As your father told you, Danny, four out of five recruits would be undercover agents.'

'We'd weed them out,' Danny began, but Alan gestured to him to be quiet.

'I think we know why you're against it.' the priest said – his voice especially controlled. 'What we don't know is your alternative.'

'Yes,' said Henry, looking for a moment confused. 'Well this has to do with Laughlin himself. He is, as you've pointed out, a kind of symbolic figure because he's more or less typical of those various Congresses and Administrations which took us into Vietnam and all that that implies I think, therefore, that it would be a good thing to ... well, discredit him. I think it would be better to discredit him than it would be to kill him: and I'm in a particular position ... a unique position, that is, to discredit him because he's having an affair with my wife.'

A wave of embarrassment passed through all those in the room except, perhaps, Alan, who said: 'Yes, I can see that that would discredit him if it were known ... with his constituency, anyway.'

'Exactly,' said Henry. He glanced at Louisa, who gave him a forced, brave smile. Julius, beside her, was looking out of the window.

'To be quite brief,' said Henry, 'because we don't have much time, I intend to divorce my wife and cite Laughlin as co-respondent. I intend to make as great a scandal of it as I can. I happen to know that she's going to meet him this evening at the Fairfax and I've already been onto a detective agency to collect the necessary evidence.'

'But Dad,' said Louisa, 'you don't *want* to divorce her, do you?'

'No,' said Henry. 'No, I don't. But I think I must, because it is a way to expose Laughlin and doing that would, I think, do something to destroy people's moral conceit about the war in Vietnam.'

'What's left of their conceit,' said Julius, glancing into the room but at no one in particular.

'Amongst Laughlin's supporters there's still a lot of conceit,' said Henry. 'And it's their confidence we have to destroy if we're going to end this war. I'm not saying that Laughlin is like Parnell – that we'll destroy the cause with the man. But this brings me to the other half of my offer which is that I'm prepared to support any political organization you set up – with my money and my reputation.'

The students were silent. They looked at each other and Louisa looked at them – not questioning but as if to judge the effect of what her father had said.

Julius shrugged his shoulders. 'Well,' he began: but though no one interrupted him, he did not continue and there was another silence.

Alan looked at Danny. 'What do you think?' he asked.

'Look, professor,' said Danny, 'we really do appreciate what you're trying to do – I mean, trying to kind of meet us half-way, but I really don't know if this sort of thing – a divorce, your money, you reputation . . .' He gave a slight shrug of his shoulders.

Then Alan spoke. 'I'm not sure you're right, Danny,' he said. 'I think that the professor may be right. That there would be more sense in destroying Laughlin politically like that rather than running the risk of making him into a martyr.'

Everyone in the room looked surprised to hear Alan say what he had just said. Henry even blushed as if there was irony intended, but the priest's features were straight and sincere. As if to reassure his listeners, he went on: 'I think we should think about it, anyway, and call off what we'd intended to do. What do you think, Julius?'

'I think it might be best.'

'Louisa?'

'So do I.'

'That leaves you, Danny.'

'Well,' said Danny, twisting his hands together, 'well, I don't . . . I mean we've put so much into it . . . theory and planning . . . but if you all think we should, then I guess I'll go along.'

Henry did not conceal his relief. His body relaxed as the breath which he had held in his lungs was released. 'I do think . . .' he began but he hesitated and said something else. 'We'll meet later in the week,' he said, 'and discuss how we can make best use of the scandal.'

'OK,' said Alan, rising to his feet.

'And then,' said Henry, 'we'll talk about wider strategy.'

'Yes,' said Alan.

He went to the door and Danny followed him. Julius glanced at Louisa.

'I think I'll wait and talk to Dad,' she said.

'OK,' he said.

'Will you be at your place later on?' she asked.

'I should think so.'

'Can I drop by?'

'Sure.' He smiled at her and nodded to Henry and left the office.

Louisa, alone with her father, sat down again and leant her chin on her clasped hands. Henry, still at his desk, looked across at her. 'Well?' he asked.

'Well . . . she replied. And then: 'Are you doing anything for lunch?'

'I was,' he said, 'but I can cancel it.' He picked up the telephone and rang the colleague he had intended to meet, his eyes always on his daughter. The engagement was cancelled and he stood and opened the door for her. 'Where shall we go?' he asked.

'Somewhere nice?'

'All right.'

They set off walking down Massachusetts Avenue, talking about nothing in particular, and eventually came to a Chinese restaurant. 'Will this do?' said Henry.

'It's fine.'

They entered and sat down and ordered their food, their conversation still general: but then, when the waiter had left them, Louisa leant forward and said: 'Can I talk to you?'

'Of course.'

'I mean, can I talk to you straight – as another person, not as your daughter?'

Henry smiled. 'If you can.'

'It's silly, I know, I *am* your daughter. But I've been looking at you objectively today – or trying to – as if you weren't my father.'

'And what do you see?'

'Well,' said Louisa: she hesitated for a moment, then seemed to come to a decision and went on – 'I see someone who's been weak and still is weak in a way because people don't change really. . . .' She paused and looked at her father as if to see how he was taking this and was encouraged to go on. 'I think that for a time you believed what you wanted to believe like your whole generation; and you went on until a lot of evidence came along which contradicted your beliefs, like Vietnam and the riots . . . do you follow me?'

'Yes,' said Henry. 'Go on.'

'And it was the same in your relationship with me and Mother. You just avoided unpleasant facts until, well, until I threw myself out of that window. Then you flipped and you decided you had to do something and you picked up the idea of political revolution partly because you believed it but also because it was there – in Alan and Danny and Julius.'

Henry nodded but said nothing.

Louisa had become agitated: she thrust back wisps of hair that fell over her face when she leant forward on the table. 'But when they suggested killing Bill,' she went on, 'you dithered because you couldn't really stomach it but you didn't want to give up the idea of revolution because it was the only thing you had left. So you thrashed around for something better and came up with this idea of divorcing Mother.'

'You certainly have been looking at me,' said Henry.

'And thinking,' said Louisa.

'Have you reached a conclusion?' asked Henry.

'Yes, sort of.'

'Aren't you going to tell me what it is?'

'Yes. It's this. I think you'd be wrong to divorce her and make a fuss because I don't think it would affect the political situation one way or the other, but it would affect us – you, me, Mother, and Laura – and it's crazy anyway because you love Mother and in her way she loves you.'

Henry nodded. 'You think, then, that I should do nothing?'

'I think you should do,' said Louisa, 'what you're cut out to do which is thinking and writing and analyzing ideas. Give the benefit of your knowledge and judgment and experience to people like Danny who need it.'

'But if I only believe what I want to believe. . . .'

'Not now,' said Louisa. 'Not any more.'

'I dare say you're right,' Henry said. The waiter brought the various dishes they had ordered and while they were being placed on the table the father and daughter said nothing. Then, when he had gone again, Henry said: 'I don't know why you go to a psychiatrist.'

'I don't any more,' said Louisa. 'I'm cured.'

'Are you sure?'

'As of today, yes. I'm sure.'

'I'm glad,' said Henry.

Louisa started to eat with great appetite.

'What'll we tell Danny and the others?' Henry asked.

'Don't worry,' said Louisa. 'I'll tell Julius, and Danny will come round if we can get him away from Alan. Incidentally, I thought it was very odd that he accepted what you said . . . just like that.'

'Alan?'

'Yes.'

'I know.'

'There's something creepy about him.'

'I think he's embittered and disappointed.'

'In what?'

'In God, I guess.'

'I think it's funny ever to expect anything from God.'

'Perhaps one should.'

'If you believe in him.'

'Yes.'

Louisa stopped eating for a moment and looked at her father. 'Do you?' she asked.

'Yes,' he said, 'I think I do.'

She shrugged her shoulders and continued to eat.

28

After lunch Henry and Louisa walked home, where he retired to his study and she to her bedroom. Louisa did not stay there long – just long enough to brush her hair and check in the mirror that her clothes were straight. She then left again and walked to Massachusetts Avenue where she found a cab which took her to Julius' apartment.

It was between three-thirty and four when she got there and he opened the door to let her in. He smiled when he saw her and when the door was closed took one of her hands into his.

'I'm glad you came,' he said.

'Thanks,' she said, smiling back at him. She moved into the room and then sat on the sofa. Julius sat on an armchair.

'What did you think of Dad?' Louisa asked.

'Well,' said Julius, his eyes immediately leaving hers and looking out of the window, 'I guess it takes a certain amount of courage to divorce your wife when you don't want to: but I'd *want* to if I was him.'

Louisa smiled. 'You wouldn't stand for your wife sleeping with a senator?'

'Not with anyone,' said Julius. 'It'd be the worse for her if she did.'

'You'd kill her?'

'I might.' His eyes met hers. 'So you'd better watch out.'

'I'm not your wife.'

'No, but you're going to be.'

'Am I?'

'Yes.'

She smiled and shrugged. 'If that's the way it's going to be. . .

'It is.' Julius stood up and crossed the room to sit next to her.

'And I've no choice?'

'No.' He took hold of her in his arms.

'Then there's nothing more to be said.'

'No,' said Julius – and nothing more was said. They kissed and later moved into the bedroom and made love – silently and quickly as if for each of them it was the first time.

29

Henry spent the afternoon alone in his study in Brattle Street. First he had telephoned the detective agency to cancel the contract he had made with them: then he sat at his desk and looked through the notes he had made over the past few years – inconclusive scribbling towards a new book which had never been written because he had never had anything to say.

Now he pushed them aside and took a pile of clean paper out of a drawer. His desk seemed cluttered so he put the old notes into the waste-paper basket, tearing them in half in shaves of twenty pages before he did so. Then he faced the blank paper.

After ten minutes or so he picked up his pen and wrote 'A Sudden Effort to a Higher Purpose'. He then rose and went to his book shelves and took down one volume of Tocqueville's *Democracy in America*. He stood, looking through it, until he came to the chapter entitled – 'Why Great Revolutions Will Become More Rare'. He started to read this as he returned to his desk and, seated again, copied out under the title he had already written – 'I dread, and I confess it, lest men should at last so entirely give way to a cowardly love of present enjoyment as to lose sight of the interests of their future selves and those of their descendants, and prefer to glide along the easy current of life rather than to make, when it is necessary, a strong, a sudden effort to a higher purpose.'

After writing this Henry laid aside this piece of paper and took up another on which he wrote 'Notes for article on revolution' which he underlined. Beneath that he started to jot down various phrases:

Revolution as social renewal

The relationship between chiliastic ideology and social renewal

Cycles of social renewal

Analogies: caterpillar, chrysalis, moth

Marks of social degeneration: failure of paternal authority

The ethical value of social renewal: is it good to be revolutionary?

Is social good ever in contradiction to good as the will of God?

Here he hesitated and then, on yet another piece of paper, he wrote: 'Notes for an article on good and evil.' This too was underlined and beneath it he wrote down what he had written last on the other piece of paper: 'Is social good ever in contradiction to good as the will of God?' After this he wrote other phrases:

Conflicts between the two: exposure of babies (Sparta?), contraception (India)

Methods of knowing the will of God: objective – revelation, tradition: subjective – humility, self-knowledge, repentance, self-sacrifice, love. . . .

Behind him the door opened. He turned and saw Lilian.

'Hello,' she said, 'am I disturbing you?'

'Not really,' he said.

'Which means that I am.'

'It can wait.'

'I'm off in a minute, anyway.' She picked a hair off the front of her dress.

Henry glanced at his watch: it was already five. 'Will you be back for supper?' he asked.

Lilian hesitated before she spoke. 'I'll try to be,' she said, 'but don't wait.'

'No. OK.'

Lilian smiled, then made a movement towards the door as if to leave, but for some reason she seemed unwilling to do so just then, and so turned and came further into the room to sit down on one of the armchairs. 'What are you writing?' she asked.

'An article.'

'The same one?'

'No. I've abandoned that.'

'What's this one?'

'It was going to be on revolution,' said Henry, glancing down at his notes, 'but now it may be on something else . . . well, on religion.'

'Religion? But you're not religious.'

'I know.'

'Then why the article?'

'It's not so much on religion, as on religious ethics and their difference from social ethics.'

'Is there a big difference?'

'I think there is, yes. In fact they're often contradictory.'

'I should have thought,' said Lilian, 'that social and religious laws usually coincide: thou shalt not kill, thou shalt not steal. . . .'

'In some instances they do, yes.'

'Where don't they?'

'Society likes heroes,' said Henry, 'whereas Christ blessed the meek.'

'Yes,' she said, 'that's true.'

'All one has to decide is whether to please God or men.'

Lilian looked own at the carpet. 'Which did you choose?' she asked.

'I'm one of the many,' said Henry, 'who can't make up their minds and so end up neither good nor heroic.'

'No one expects you to be heroic,' said Lilian, blushing.

'Nor good,' said Henry.

'I hadn't thought about that,' said Lilian.

'Nor had I,' said Henry, 'until now.'

'What's set you off on all this?' Lilian asked.

'Lou, I guess.'

'What's she been saying?'

'She pronounced herself cured.'

'I'm glad to hear it.'

'And she demonstrated her fitness by giving me some advice.'

Lilian laughed. 'She may be cured but she certainly hasn't changed.'

'No,' said Henry, 'but it wasn't bad advice.'

'What did she say?'

'She told me that I wasn't a man of action; that I should stick to books.'

'Were you planning to leave them?'

'In a way.'

'I agree with Lou. Stick to books.'

'Yes, I will.'

They looked at each other in silence. Then Henry said: 'You'd better go.'

Lilian stood up. 'I guess I'd better.' She looked around at the seat of the chair as if she might have dropped something, then she faced Henry again but still hesitated.

'Harry,' she said eventually, 'I ... well, if you're going to be here, then I will make it back for supper.'

'OK,' he said, 'then I'll wait for you.'

'Yes,' she said, 'good, and ... well, I'll see you then.' She tried to smile but apparently could not – not because she did not want to but because some emotion more powerful than benevolence made itself evident in her expression: but by then she had turned towards the door so that this anguish was hidden from her husband.

30

After they had made love, Louisa and Julius lay quietly beside one another and for a time Louisa slept. When she awoke, ten or twenty minutes later, she looked across at Julius's long, brown body and saw that his shoulders were shaking, and that his face was hidden in the pillow. He was crying.

Louisa leant over and put her hand on his neck. 'What is it?' she asked.

The back of his head jerked to and fro. His features remained in the pillow: he continued to sob.

Louisa moved further over, lifting her body onto his. The languor and familiarity of her movements showed that she felt no real anixety at her lover's tears. 'Tell me,' she said.

He turned his head and looked at her through red, wet eyes. 'Oh God,' he said.

'I love you,' she said, kissing his cheek, 'and you love me.'

'How can you know?' he asked.

'But you do, don't you?'

'I do, yes, but you can't know ... and you can't love me.'

'Why not?'

'Because you don't know me.'

'I know all I need to know.'

'No,' he said, still sobbing, 'no, you don't.'

'Tell me, then,' she said, continuing to kiss his face – softly and methodically.

'Then you won't love me,' he said – the tone of unhappiness in his voice unchanged by her kisses.

'Yes I will,' she said.

Julius sighed and stopped crying. He thought to himself while Louisa's lips lay on his cheeks and her hand stroked his ear. 'My uncle,' he said at last.

214

'Yes?'

'Do you remember him?'

'Yes.'

'You remember he said he worked in Washington?'

She hesitated. 'Yes,' she said.

'He works for the FBI.' Julius waited: then he added – 'He's an assistant director.'

'So?'

'He arranged for me to come to Harvard.'

'I know. You told me.'

'Not just to study. He sent me to . . . supply information.'

Ah.' Louisa lifted her face from his.

Julius fixed his eyes on hers, waiting to see their expression change. Louisa looked for a moment into mid-air; then she returned to kissing his cheek and temple. 'And did you?' she asked.

'Yes.'

'About Alan and Danny?'

'Yes. And your father. And you.'

'So the FBI knew all about it all the time?'

'Yes.'

'Then it's just as well it's not going to happen.'

Julius buried his face again and said, 'But it is.'

Louisa lifted her head and adjusted her body because her left breast was being squashed against his shoulder. 'How do you mean?' she said.

He faced her again. 'Alan – agreeing with your father about the divorce. That was a put-on. He thought it was ridiculous. He said no one would care a damn about your mother screwing with Laughlin. He said a scandal was a worn-out cliché of bourgeois politics.'

'But why did he agree?' asked Louisa, sitting up at last. 'He didn't have to pretend like that.'

'He thinks your father's out to stop them and if they hadn't agreed, he'd have warned Laughlin.'

'I see,' said Louisa. 'So they're going ahead?'

'Yes. Tonight.'

'Tonight?'

'Yes. The professor told us, you see, that your ma was going to see Laughlin tonight.'

'Yes of course. But the FBI know all about it?'

'Yes.'

'So they'll be arrested.'

'Yes. In the lobby.' Julius turned his head away.

'Do you want them to be arrested?' Louisa asked.

'I don't know,' said Julius. His voice was quiet, now, and sad. 'I don't know any more what I want or what I believe. It was all right until I met you and the professor. I saw my uncle every now and then and told him what I'd seen and heard. I didn't think about it. But now, I don't know. . . .'

'I'd hate to see them arrested,' said Louisa. 'I mean, Danny's a friend. . . .'

'I know,' said Julius. 'I guess he's my friend too.'

Louisa moved her body and put her feet on the floor. 'We'd better warn him,' she said.

'We can't,' said Julius.

'Why not?'

'It's aiding and abetting a felony and . . . and my uncle. . . .'

Louisa remained sitting upright on the bed, thinking to herself. Then she stood up. 'Come on,' she said, 'we'll ask Dad.'

Julius shook his head. 'He'll despise me,' he said.

'No, he won't.' Louisa, uninhibited by her nakedness, was searching for her clothes on the floor. 'We're none of us in a position to despise anyone,' she said, 'except ourselves.' She found her underclothes and started to put them on. 'And we mustn't do that,' she said.

Julius climbed off the bed and following her example started to retrieve his clothes.

31

In the cab on the way to Brattle Street, Louisa asked Julius: 'But what did you think, all that time, pretending . . .?'

'Until you came along,' he said, 'I didn't care. I just took it for granted. I thought it was the right thing to do. My uncle, you see, he kind of persuaded me.'

'I didn't like him,' said Louisa.

'No,' said Julius, 'I guess he's not very nice – but he was the only one . . . outside Albuquerque.'

'And you didn't believe a word of what you said . . . about revolution?'

'Not at first,' said Julius, 'but now I think I do.'

'I don't want to marry a cop,' said Louisa.

They reached Brattle Street and paid off the cab. 'I just hope Dad's at home,' said Louisa.

They entered the house and she burst into the study. Henry

sat at his desk but he turned and looked at his daughter over his spectacles when she came in. 'Hello,' he said.

'Dad,' said Louisa, 'something awful's going to happen.' All at once, in her father's presence, she became less calm.

'Well, tell me,' said Henry.

Julius followed Louisa into the room and they both sat down. 'The first thing is,' said Julius, calmer now and more assured, 'that the assassination is going ahead.'

'It is?'

'Alan didn't really accept what you said. He only pretended.'

'I see,' said Henry. He pressed his lips together.

'The second thing is that it's going to happen tonight.'

'At the hotel?'

'Yes.'

'Of course . . . they knew about Lilian.'

'And the third thing,' said Julius. 'The FBI know all about it.'

'How?'

'I told them.'

Henry looked across at Julius. 'Yes,' he said. There had to be something like that. You were holding yourself back.'

'My uncle,' said Julius. 'He's an assistant director.'

'I see.' Henry raised himself in his chair. 'Well,' he said, 'I guess they'll be arrested. And then they'll come for Lou and me.'

'They won't arrest you,' said Julius, 'because they know that you're against it.'

'And Lou?'

Julius looked confused. 'They think that she's against it too.'

'Don't you think we should warn them?' said Louisa.

Henry looked at his watch. 'It may be too late,' he said.

'If they found out we'd warned them. . . .' Louisa began.

'They needn't find out if we could catch them in time,' said Julius. 'They're going to arrest them in the hotel. They need the evidence.'

'If it were only Alan,' said Henry, 'I think I'd leave it. But I'd like to get Danny out of a mess if I could.'

'Yes,' said Louisa. 'Think of Dr. Glinkman.'

'Aren't they expecting you to join them?' Henry asked Julius.

'Yes,' said Julius. 'In the lobby at six.'

Henry looked at his watch again. 'That's in twenty minutes.'

'Yes,' said Julius.

Henry hesitated: he glanced at the paper on his desk and then said, 'Perhaps we'd better get down there and see if we can stop them.'

'My uncle will be there.'

'We can try and prevent them from entering the hotel.'

32

They drove quickly into Boston and parked the car in a side-street behind the Fairfax Hotel. Henry reached into his pockets for a dime for the meter: then he, Louisa and Julius stood for a moment beside the car discussing what they should do.

'They'll probably be in the lobby by now,' said Louisa.

'So will my uncle,' said Julius.

'We ought to try and get them out,' said Henry. He thought for a moment. 'I'd better go in,' he said.

The two others nodded.

'You may be recognized,' said Julius.

'We'll have to risk that,' said Henry. 'You wait here and I'll go and see if they've arrived.'

He crossed the street and walked a few steps towards the back entrance to the hotel but then heard Julius shout: 'They're here.' Henry turned and saw Alan and Danny climb out of a Chevrolet which had drawn up behind him. He turned and stood in their path.

'Look who's here,' said Alan as he recognized Henry. 'The professor.'

'You must wait,' said Henry as Julius and Louisa came up behind Danny and the Jesuit.

Alan turned to face Julius. 'You punk,' he said.

'The FBI is in there waiting for you,' said Julius.

'That's crap,' said Alan.

'You must believe us,' said Henry, placing his hand on Alan's shoulder.

'Please . . . Danny,' said Louisa.

'But how do they know?' asked Danny – his head jutting out from his shoulders in his confusion.

'I told them,' said Julius.

'You?' said Danny.

'We'll explain later,' said Henry. 'The important thing now is for us all to get out of here.'

'You're transparent,' said Alan, shaking Henry's hand off

his shoulder and thrusting his own hands into his coat pockets. 'The FBI is no more in there than we are.'

'They are,' said Henry.

Alan now tried to step forward and push his way past Henry but Henry stepped across to prevent him. 'You must wait,' he said.

'I always knew you'd try to stop us,' said Alan, 'and this is your last throw.'

'Please,' said Julius, 'please believe us.'

'Get out of my way,' said Alan, staring wide-eyed and unblinking at Henry.

'No,' said Henry. 'I can't let you go in.'

'Get out of my way,' Alan repeated, taking a revolver from his pocket.

'Christ . . . no, Alan,' said Danny.

'No,' said Henry.

Alan fired his gun. The street was empty so the sound was loud. Henry stepped back and Julius leapt on Alan from behind, his right hand going round his body to grasp the fingers which held the revolver. Alan jerked the gun towards his stomach in an attempt to retain it and it fired again.

'Get him out of here,' said Julius to Danny, because by this time Henry only stood upright because he was held by Louisa. Danny came forward to help her and together they dragged Henry, stumbling, across to his car and pushed him into the back seat. Louisa got in beside him.

'Are you all right?' she asked her father.

'I don't know,' he said slowly.

From his face Louisa could judge that he was in great pain.

She turned and looked back at Julius as Danny climbed into the driver's seat. Julius was standing astride the inert body of the Jesuit.

'The keys,' said Danny.

Louisa leant over her father's body and felt for the car keys in his pockets. She found them and handed them to Danny. As he started the car and drove off she glanced round again at Julius who was half-obscured now by some men who had come out of the hotel.

'We'd better take him to a hospital,' said Danny.

Louisa looked at Henry to see what he would say but it was clear that he had not heard what Danny had said. His expression was of someone concentrating hard on a particular problem.

'Yes,' she said. 'Mass General. Quickly.'

Danny glanced around – then swung the car into the left lane and sounded the horn like a siren. This too Henry did not seem to notice.

'Poor Dad,' said Louisa, placing her arms around his shoulders to stop his body slipping off the seat. She was hardly strong enough, however, and his knees began to lift slowly towards his chest. No sound came from his lips, nor did the expression of concentration leave his face.

When they reached the hospital, Danny ran in to fetch help: at once orderlies appeared and opened the doors of the car. Louisa, when she was out of the car, saw her father laid sideways on a stretcher which was then wheeled through swinging doors. Danny came back to her side but then a man stepped forward and asked him to move the vehicle.

While he did this, Louisa went into the hospital and a woman at the desk began to take down her father's name and address and then her name and address. Louisa gave a few answers without thinking and then asked: 'Is he all right?'

'I don't know,' said the woman. 'What happened?'

'He was shot.'

The woman said nothing except 'Do you know his date of birth?'

'18th March, 1920,' said Louisa, her eyes on a man in a white coat who was walking towards her. 'Is he all right?' she asked this man when he reached the desk.

'Are you a relative?' he asked.

'I'm his daughter.'

The man looked confused. He glanced at the woman at the desk and then returned to Louisa. 'I'm afraid he's dead,' he said. 'He died just now.' He glanced at the half-filled form in front of the woman. 'Are you Miss Rutledge?' he asked Louisa.

'Yes,' she said.

'I'm very sorry,' he said. 'There was nothing we could do. The bullet must have severed an artery or gone close to his heart.'

Louisa nodded.

'Do the police know?' he asked.

'I think so,' she said. Then she asked if she could see her father.

'Of course,' said the doctor.

She followed him through another set of doors and was shown into a brightly-lit, white-walled room. There, half-covered by a white cloth, was the body of her father. She approached it and looked at the face. They eyes were closed, the muscles still. A swab of cotton wool had ben placed between the lips.

Hesitantly she lifted her hand and placed it on his cheek: then she brought it down to her side again. 'Poor Dad,' she said.

33

Lilian lay naked and in tears on Laughlin's bed while he rose in his shorts and poured himself a Bourbon and ice. 'Come on Lil,' he said. 'You can't expect to get there every time.'

This remark stopped her tears. She sat up. 'It's not that,' she said.

'What is it, then?'

'It doesn't matter.'

'Then cheer up, for God's sake. I've gone to a hell of a lot of trouble to get this evening clear, so let's enjoy it.'

'I've got to go back,' Lilian said, quickly and without looking at Laughlin.

'Oh come on,' he said. 'You're not as crude as that. A quick fuck and then back to the family.'

She looked at him now with apparent loathing: but seeing him seemed to remind her that Bill Laughlin, after all, was the man he had always been – that age and political frustration had not changed him that much. The same look, however, remained in her eyes: not hatred, now, but the reflection of her own remorse.

She stood up. 'If you like,' she said. 'A quick fuck and back to the family.'

'But why?' asked Bill. 'I booked a table.'

'I'm sorry,' she said. 'I should have told you before.'

'I don't understand,' said Bill, shaking his head.

'I hadn't meant to ... well, that,' she said, glancing at the bed. 'I came to say good-bye.' She got up off the bed and began to dress.

'I still don't understand,' said Laughlin, his hands holding his socks.

'I don't want to see you again,' said Lilian.

'You can't mean it.'

'I don't say what I don't mean,' said Lilian. She spoke sharply and dressed with greater rapidity.

'Then why did you? That.' He too looked at the bed.

'I don't know. I just did. But it was the last time.'

Laughlin sighed and shrugged his shoulders and sat to put on his socks. 'I guess I'll miss you,' he said.

'We'll meet at the dinner tomorrow,' said Lilian caustically.

'Sure.'

They said nothing more as the finished dressing. When Lilian had straightened her clothes and combed her hair she made towards the door.

'Wait,' said Laughlin, 'and I'll come down with you.'

'No,' said Lilian. 'No, I'll go alone.'

She left him standing in the centre of his hotel room, neither kissing him nor shaking his hand nor saying good-bye. She closed the door behind her and walked away quickly as if afraid it would open again: and once safe behind the automatic doors of the lift, and descending, she drew all the air she could into her lungs and held it there until she reached the ground floor.

There was some commotion in the lobby. She hurried towards the front of the hotel and stood there for a few minutes while a cab was called for her.

'A guy just got shot,' said the cab-driver as they drove away. 'Right there behind the hotel.'

'Why?' asked Lilian. 'What happened?'

The driver shrugged his shoulders. 'The guy that did it got shot himself so maybe we'll never know.'

'It's getting as bad as New York,' said Lilian.

'Lady,' said the driver, 'nowhere's safe in this country. . . .'

He went on talking but Lilian gave no more answers: her eyes looked out of the window across the Charles River to Cambridge. When they reached Brattle Street she half ran up the path to the house but found no one at home but Laura.

'Isn't Harry back?' she asked, watching her younger daughter eat a triple-decker sandwich.

Laura shrugged. 'I don't know,' she said. 'I only just came in.'

Lilian left the kitchen and went into the living room where she poured herself a weak bourbon and ginger. She then lit the fire and straightened some cushions and sat down. She did not read or play a record: she waited.

Louisa came home three-quarters of an hour later. She came straight into the living room and looked at her mother with the same stricken expression that had been on her face in the hospital.

'Mother,' she said, 'Dad's dead.' Whereupon she started to cry and came to her mother and threw herself in her arms.

Lilian looked up at Danny who had followed Louisa into the room.

'He was shot,' said Danny. 'By the priest . . . Alan.'

'Why?' asked Lilian.

'I don't know,' said Danny. 'He was crazy.'

Lilian's glance went down to her daughter and neither with eyes nor with words did she ask any further questions. Her arms held Louisa: and then, when the girl's weeping had reached a calmer rhythm, she left her and went to find Laura.

'Will you come with me?' she said to her daughter who was still sitting in the kitchen watching television. 'Something's happened to Harry.'

With Laura she returned to the living room. 'Where is he?' she asked Danny.

'Mass General.'

'I'd better go down there.'

'Would you like me to come with you?' Danny asked.

'No,' said Lilian. 'You stay with Louisa. Laura will come with me.'

When Lilian got back to this same living-room later that evening, Julius had joined Danny and Louisa. Both the girls were now tearless like their mother: Louisa's eyes were dry but blotched and red, whilst Laura's and Lilian's tears had not yet come.

Lilian sat with them for a while but showed no reaction when Julius told her that Alan Gray was also dead – killed by the second bullet from his own gun. Soon after she went into the kitchen to make hamburgers and coffee because none of them had eaten.

It was only much later that night, when the two boys had left and the two girls had gone to bed, that Lilian went into her husband's study to tidy up his papers. As she gathered them together she glanced at the last words on the last piece of paper: 'A family will always be the basic unit of society. Neither political revolution nor changes in the status of women will alter this. Our attitudes towards the community at large are learnt in the intimacy of the family, and happiness within the family is the source of optimism and accord in the citizens it provides. Since this happiness must come from the parents, the success and permanency of love between husband and wife becomes all-important for a nation of millions. This love itself may have to combat the corrupt values of a degenerate society: but in every man and woman there is an impulse to idealism in love. Thus society can renew itself with each union. . . .'

Then at last she started to cry.

34

The morning after the death of Henry Rutledge, Danny Glinkman was arrested by the police: but he was released later that day when it became clear that no firm evidence could be found against him. Julius, the only witness to the conspiracy, refused to confirm his previous account of it – maintaining now that only the dead Jesuit had planned to kill the Senator. It became generally accepted thereafter that the priest had been mad and the professor a victim of his lunacy. The small group who knew the truth kept it to themselves, discussing it only when they were alone together in the kitchen or living room of the Rutledges' house in Brattle Street.

Towards the middle of December Louisa was married to Julius. His mother came from Albuquerque for the ceremony and remained with the Rutledges over Christmas. It was decided that in the New Year Julius and Louisa would find an apartment in Cambridge and Lilian talked of selling the house.

In the meantime Danny came by almost every afternoon to talk with Louisa, Laura and Julius – sometimes about the professor's death for which he felt himself largely to blame; and sometimes about the political ideas which had produced the events leading to the tragedy. For what had occurred had not diminished the desire of any of them to do something about America. No one mentioned assassination but Danny still held that violence against property might be justified in the furtherance of revolution. Julius, on the other hand, thought it premature to abandon the democratic institutions of their country and Louisa talked of example and persuasion. Laura usually came out on Danny's side: Lilian listened to their discussions but would not be drawn into the argument.

Then, in January of 1968, a Senator from Minnesota – Eugene McCarthy – declared that he would stand against the incumbent President in the New Hampshire primary on the issue of the war in Vietnam: and like so many other young Americans at that time, Julius, Louisa, Laura and Danny made up their minds to go North to help him and give the system one final chance.